Behind Closed Doors:
Stories from the Kamloops Indian Residential School

Secwepemc Cultural Education Society
Kamloops, British Columbia
Canada

National Library of Canada Cataloquing in Publication Data
Jack, Agness, 1950
Behind Closed Doors

ISBN 0-919441-97-1

1. Kamloops Indian Residential School. 2. Indians of North America--British Columbia--Kamloops--Residential School. 3. Shuswap Indians--Education. 4. Shuswap Indians--Interviews I. Title.
E96.6.K34J32 2001   371.829'979   C2001-910305-0

Conceptual Design/Photo Arrangements and Chief Editor by Agness Jack
Cover Artwork by David Seymour
Cover Photo by SCES Photo Archives
Cover and Text Design by Judy Manuel-Wilson
Typeset by Jenna John

Co-Published with Theytus Books Ltd., Penticton, B.C.
Printed and Bound in Canada by AGMV Marquis Imprimeur Inc., Montreal, Quebec Canada

Secwepemc Cultural Education Society acknowledges the support of the Aboriginal Healing Foundation in the publication of this book.

Secwepemc Cultural Education Society
Suite #202-355 Yellowhead Highway
Kamloops, British Columbia
V2H 1H1
Canada

The publisher acknowledges the support of The Canada Council for the Arts, The Department of Canadian Heritage and The British Columbia Arts Council.

Dedication

This book is a true testament of the events that took place at the Kamloops Indian Residential School. It was 'behind the closed doors' that the storytellers, as children, experienced mental, spiritual, emotional and physical abuse and trauma. The stories that follow speak of that 'trauma'.

There are many survivors out there and many more have lost their lives as a direct or indirect result of this school. While attending residential school, the children felt a hunger, not only for food but also for love and comfort from their mothers and fathers, grandparents, aunts and uncles and even from their brothers and sisters.

This book is dedicated to those numerous individuals who have lost their lives either while attending the Kamloops Indian Residential School, or during the years following, up to the present.

As we read these stories we can only begin to understand the loneliness and despair those individuals lived with every day of their lives. With the sharing of these stories, we sincerely hope that their spirits will find peace.

STORYTELLERS

[top row , l-r] **Cedric Duncan,**

Ron Ignace & Margaret Abel

(middle) Lorraine Billy

[bottom row, l-r]

Jennifer Camille, Dorothy Joseph & Diane Sandy

[top row, l-r] **Eddy Jules, Mona Jules & William Brewer**

(middle-right) Christina Casimir

[bottom row, l-r] **Terry Deneault, Ralph Sandy & Robert Simon**

Introduction

Behind Closed Doors: Stories from the Kamloops Indian Residential School is about healing. Thirty-two individuals who attended the Kamloops school came forward to tell their stories as part of their personal healing journeys. They agreed to share their stories in the form of a book so their families and communities could learn and understand what happened behind the closed doors of the Kamloops Indian Residential School (KIRS), and so all Canadians could know the truth about residential schools so that history is never repeated.

KIRS was operated from 1893 to 1977 as part of the Federal Government's residential school system. Government policy was to "civilize and evangelize" Indian people – to assimilate them. Residential schools were generally operated in partnership with religious organizations that played an integral role in the implementation of this policy. The goal of these joint government/church institutions was to remove children from the "harmful" influence of their "uncivilized" parents and Indian traditions.

Initially attendance at these schools was voluntary, but when parents refused to send their children legislation was passed to enforce attendance. By the 1920s, parents were forced to send their children to residential schools. Children as young as six or seven years old were rounded up and taken away, often in cattle trucks, to residential schools. Parents had no say. When children got to the schools, they were isolated from their families and forbidden to speak their language or practice any part of their culture. The children who attended residential schools experienced every form of abuse – physical, sexual, emotional and spiritual. The residential school experience has had a profound impact on First Nations people and their communities.

Behind Closed Doors was developed by the Secwepemc Cultural Education Society, under the direction of an advisory group made up of residential school survivors, health care professionals, and community members. The project was funded by the Aboriginal Healing Foundation which was formed by the Government of Canada to address the healing needs of individuals, families and communities arising from the legacy of sexual and physical abuse at residential schools. The government also offered a Statement of Reconciliation, which acknowledged its role in the development and administration of residential schools, and made the following apology;

"Particularly to those individuals who experienced the tragedy of sexual and physical abuse at residential schools, and who have carried this burden believing that in some way they must be responsible, we wish to emphasize that what you experienced was not your fault and should never have happened. To those of you who suffered this tragedy at residential schools, we are deeply sorry."

This project encouraged and supported individuals who experienced or witnessed physical and/or sexual abuse in the Kamloops Indian Residential School to start or continue their healing journeys by providing a safe, culturally appropriate environment and process in which they could tell their stories. Involvement in the project was voluntary, and storytellers decided how, when and where their interviews took place. A counselor and/or a traditional helper was available to support participants as they recalled often personal and painful memories.

The stories told here represent a wide range of experiences – some are good, but many more are not. The stories are told in the storyteller's own words, edited for brevity, and are told with honesty and humor. Many of the stories tell of oppression, abuse and cruelty, but they are told without malice. All storytellers came forward to share their stories, not to find blame, but so that there would be a better future for their children, and their children's children.

This book provides a record of the residential school experience from the perspective of the people who attended the school. It also provides a legacy attesting to the resiliency, courage and strength of First Nations people.

Lori Pilon
Special Projects Manager
Secwepemc Cultural Education Society
February 2001

Preface

by Wayne Christian

We are living in an important time for Indigenous People throughout the world and specifically for First Nations people in Canada. It is clear that the movement to asserting control and jurisdiction over traditional lands and resources are on the minds of all First Nations, the leadership and the community members. The recent court decision recognizing Aboriginal Title and Rights coupled with the historic modern day treaty signed by the Nisga'a signal a movement toward some level of self-determination. The Federal Government's official statement on the residential schools and the $350 million Healing Fund also indicates there is recognition of the Federal Government's role in the destruction of First Nation families. The seed for control by First Nations families and communities over all aspects of our lives is a direct result of being oppressed and controlled for many generations by government systems and structures.

The voices of our ancestors whisper in the winds of change if we listen. I was asked to write an article on the effects of the residential school and what we need to do to begin the healing process. At first I struggled with what to say since I did not attend residential school. I am a child of a survivor of residential school. I know the affects of residential school from my own personal experience. I experienced foster homes and the same issues these storytellers talk about. As a child I was involved in the era 60s Scoop when alcoholism was rampant in our communities and provincial authorities begun another cycle of removing children from their families.

The history of the residential school system is well documented with the first schools opening in the early 1800s and the last one closing in the 1980s. These schools were the foundation of the Federal Government's assimilation policy. I believe the Federal Government practiced a policy of cultural genocide where there was a systematic removal of children from their families, communities, language, traditional spiritual beliefs and practices, cultural values and rituals.

It is hard to imagine that the laws of Canada dictated that children as young as four years old were to be taken from their mothers and fathers to live in a hostile environment where there would be no contact with their primary caregivers. Upon arrival the de-humanizing process would begin immediately with the shaving of heads and the de-lousing. Children were physically punished for speaking their own language. These genocidal practices carried on year after year for almost 150 years. In the process, families were destroyed, language nearly became extinct, cultural, spiritual beliefs and rituals were eliminated. It is within this 150 years of systematic oppression that the cycle of abuse began within First Nations families across Canada.

The sexual, physical, psychological and spiritual abuse perpetrated by the people in power over the children who attended these institutions have left a deep imprint on their minds and spirits. The stories told by the people in this book tell of the feelings of terror, helplessness, shame, guilt, abandonment, loneliness, starvation and hopelessness. These warriors have survived and are now giving voice to the thousands of children who died feeling that they did something wrong because their parents abandoned them to this horrible place called residential school.

These storytellers give voice to the thousands who turned to alcoholism in order to deaden the emotional pain of their abuses and died a slow or violent death because of their addiction. These storytellers as is in our tradition will help the next generation to understand the pain and the suffering of the generations who attended residential schools. These storytellers give a voice to the thousands of Elders who lost their role as the teachers of the language, culture and traditions. These storytellers give voice to the parents who suffered tremendous guilt because they could not protect their children from harm. These storytellers give a voice to the thousands who were not allowed to be children and to hold on to their innocence. These storytellers give hope to the thousands of children who are now in the care of provincial institutions throughout Canada by making sense out of why their parents did not know how to be parents.

We are on the threshold of a new beginning where we are in control our own destinies. We must be careful and listen to the voices that have been silenced by fear and isolation. We must be careful not to repeat the patterns or create the oppressive system of the residential schools. We must build an understanding of what happened to those generations that came before us. As survivors we must experience the feelings in a safe and therapeutic environment, we must develop a thriving attitude and not a victim mentality. We must begin to experience life with all the natural stresses and joys. When we say that, the children are our future, and the future is now.

CONTENTS

In this early photo one can see the handmade clothing and bob haircuts the girls were given. Look closely at the children's expression, many of them do not look happy to be at Kamloops Indian Residential School.

Girls were taught sewing in the early years and they made most of the childrens' clothing. Additional clothing was made and sold locally.

Coping

"I was throwing a fit and screaming and I was hanging on the bottom of my mother's pants and I didn't want to leave with anyone. I didn't want them to send me to school."

Ron Ignace

The life I had before I went to residential school was a very simple life, but one that was a good life. I remember before I went to residential school the community I grew up in life was filled with a lot of Elders, both men and women. In the summertime we did fishing down the river. It was a communal activity, the whole family, grannies, grampas, aunts, uncles, all of us, would go down to the river and fish. At night time we would build a fire by the river. The salmon would be attracted by the fire and would come up closer to the edge of the water and we would be able to catch the salmon that way. The salmon would be taken home and old Julienne, my granny and aunts they would cut it up and dry it. They would salt a lot of salmon. And we ate a lot too, boiling up salmon eggs and salmon head soups and all of that. It was just great fun. Although it was work – it was fun.

I remember working in the gardens. We would all go down there. My granny, grampas, great-grandmothers and great-grandfathers would be out there plowing and harrowing and clearing the fields and preparing it for the gardens. We had apple orchards as well, and different types of fruit trees. The whole family would be out there, planting and weeding, and we'd be playing around and throwing clumps of dirt at each other and having fun, but yet being productive. And the beauty of that was all of this type of activity back then was conducted in Shuswap. Everybody spoke Shuswap. The Elders had high moral values.

In haying season, people had horses and cattle back then, some people had ten acres of land, some had forty acres, or larger acreage. They would start haying, going from one field to the other, helping each other doing the haying, you know. We would start from one end of the valley and go right down to the other end. In the springtime everybody would go out and clean the irrigation ditch because there were no irrigation pumps like today. It was flood irrigation and people would take turns on taking water from the ditch. So you had to be well organized. People went up the mountains and chased the horses down and helped each other brand and cut their horses and their cattle and move them up onto the next range. There were range riders helping each other. Everything was like one big cooperative, you know.

That's why today I can still speak the language because I worked in our language. Back then it was a living language. There would be times when my grandfather and I would go. He would put me on the back of his saddle on his horse and we would take off. For the whole day I would be gone. He would forget that I would be riding back there, you know, in Shuswap you would call that *ckemqenups*, riding in the back. And sometimes he would be galloping the horse all over the mountain, and my hands would be red and purple just trying to hang on to the saddle strings just so I didn't fall off.

I remember the house that we lived in. Today I don't know how in the hell we lived in that kind of house. I remember we had one long rectangular kitchen. We had a huge table, it had to handle fifteen. We had up to that many people living in our house.

The house had one huge living room and there was one, I guess what today you would call a queen-sized bed in one corner and a double bed on one side of the wall and a double bed on the other side of the wall. There was another little room where my grandfather and grandmother slept that had a double bed in there and a little closet and that's about all you could fit in. The upstairs was one big open room and you could see through the roof. In the wintertime when the winds blew we'd have to put canvasses and big coats at the bottom of the door so the snow wouldn't blow in and drift into the house. We had pillows where windowpanes used to be, but hell, you know, we never suffered, we never got cold. It wasn't something that we thought there was anything wrong with. We had a big wood heater made out of an oil barrel to heat up that part of the house and a wood stove that we cooked on. That was our central heating, you know.

When you had a bath you had an old round tin tub you heated on the stove. You filled it up and bathed in that, you know. You had an outdoor toilet, you had to run about a hundred yard dash in the wintertime. I can't see people doing that today.

Wintertime brings out memories, especially in the full moon in February. Those were some great times for us, because that's when quite a few of the old people would go sleigh riding with us. We would build our own bob sleighs and sleigh ride all night long. If it wasn't bad enough we'd go out there and spill water and make it icy and we had fun.

In summertime, you know, my hotrod was a one-horse buggy and we would go hotrodding around the Reserve, there was a big back eddy down in our creek and I would go galloping down there on my horse and buggy and then go into this big deep eddy and float around in there. I would be sitting in the buggy and the horse would be swimming.

In summertime we ran around all over the mountains. We'd go fishing up and down the creek. We'd come back really proud that we would have maybe twenty or thirty trout, you know. Four or five of us kids would be gone all day long. You don't see kids doing that nowadays. They just sit in front of a video machine, play station, nintendos, TVs, you know. They're not happy unless they have some kind of toys. We had to make up our own toys. I remember playing cowboys and Indians, and if we got shot we'd fall off our horse at full gallop. Stuff like that.

But those were good times and, you know, the Elders were there and if you broke a window, the owner of the house would whip you, your granny would whip you, your uncles would whip you, everybody would whip you. By the time they were finished, you'd swear you would never break another window. Today, you threaten to raise your hand up at a kid they throw you in jail. So they get away with murder today. Back then you couldn't, but, you know they loved you. And that didn't happen all of the time, you didn't get that kind of a beating all of the time because you get one or two of them and you learn fast.

When a funeral would happen, people from all over, different reserves, would come in and you would share. The Elders telling stories all night long, you know. Hunting stories, work stories, stories about the deceased person, you know, even though it was a tragic moment there was time for sharing those kind of good stories to try to help each other along the way. The family that had a deceased member wouldn't have to do any work. Everybody else would tell them to sit aside and they would do it all for them. Help them out, give them food, do the dishes, the cooking, you know, everything. When we went to bury them, the family of the deceased would be asked to stand back, they wouldn't be allowed to touch the shovel, or do any kind of work. They would just tell everybody what they would want and what they needed and how they wanted it done. Today, you go to a graveyard you see the families left alone, having to do the digging and all of that themselves. It's sad, you know, that kind of cooperation is not there today.

I was in a state of shock or in awe about the school when I was first brought there. Then when my relatives decided it was time for them to leave and the priest or brothers come and grabbed me by the hand and started leading me down the hall, it dawned on me that something was happening. I gave out a type of scream that I had never ever given out in my life. I learned that there is a name for that kind of scream. It's called a primal scream. That is a cry that a person gives, a cry of distress from the centre of the soul. I was watching a movie and apparently slaves gave that kind of cry too when they were captured and put into slavery. After that I heard that cry a few times when I happened to be in the hallway and other children were being dropped off at the residential school.

Being put into the dormitories wasn't a very pleasant experience for me. I had aunts and uncles in the residential school that looked out for me as best as they could, they slipped me the odd cake or the odd orange. I remember just getting up and praying and going to class and praying, you know, every day, you were praying and praying and praying. I just had a few friends, you know, it was a pretty lonely place there.

People got pretty cliquey in there. If you weren't in one of those cliques, then you were an outsider and you got picked on. They took your apples, your oranges, your candies, stuff like that and you had to fight for your life there. I also remember us playing cowboys and Indians down by the lake and if you got caught they tied you up and threw you into a big pile of tumbleweeds that were pretty thorny. There was a lot of fighting with each other, fighting with different people from different areas, fighting with other kids all of the time.

I was in and out of residential school. I went and then I got really sick. I got scabies all over my body when I first went into residential school. I don't know, it might have been rickets. My great-grandmother heard about it and she came and took me home. And she doctored me up so when I got healed I went back to the day school at Skeetchestn for awhile.

I wound up back in residential school for a year or two and then my parents took me out early because they had to go down and work in the strawberry fields in the summer before the school year was out. They took me out of the residential school and off we went to the States.

My parents weren't too strict about me going back to school so I was late going into school. My dad and my mom made good money down there. But for some reason or another alcohol got the best of them. I gave them an ultimatum. I said, "You know you guys quit drinking in a couple of weeks or I'm going home. I need fifty dollars to catch the bus and I'm going home." I must have been about twelve, I don't know how old I was. They gave me fifty dollars. They didn't want to give up their drinking. I caught the bus and came home and that was the last time I ever lived with my mom and dad.

I came here (Kamloops) and bummed around the Reserve. I lived with the Gottfriedson's for awhile, they took me in, and then from there I went up to Skeetchestn, and Katie Humphrey took me in. Then I was around the Reserve there and helped look after my grandmother.

The welfare workers started coming around the reserves and taking away kids. They heard about my grandmother, nobody caring for her, which wasn't true, I was caring for her. She was starting to get up and walk around and making her own food, then laying down, and getting stronger. And I was happy that was happening and then they took her away, as she was going out the door she said, "I'll be home not too long from now but it won't be the same way I'm going." Sure enough, she came back, she passed away in the old age home. I think she passed away from a broken heart there, and I was sad because she was really key in my life.

Then they came out to get me and take me back to the residential school in the 60's. I remember picking up a .22 and running along the ditch and running up the mountains and hiding up there. But the priest came along and caught me and turned me in, and so I got taken back to residential school. I really tried hard to learn in residential school. I studied hard, but the harder I tried, the less I learned. I remember even going to the priest and saying, "Look father, you know I really want to learn but my grades are getting worse, and worse, and worse. I don't know what I want to do you know." I said, "I'll even become a priest if you help me learn better or something." I was ready to sell my soul to the priesthood just to learn something to get my grades up.

I started getting into trouble – fighting with a lot of the kids here, kids fighting each other, it was pretty rough that way. I was by myself from Skeetchestn so I had no gang to live with and so people would set me up for a lot of different things. I'd always got threatened to get expelled from school. I remember sitting up all night because some kid had stolen some other kids shoes or something and I got blamed for it and I was going to be expelled for being a thief. I was told to pack my things and sit on my bed and they would come back and let me know when I was going to go and I would sit there until two or three o'clock in the morning and then the priest would say unpack and go to bed.

The other hard thing in residential school too is that I became a bedwetter. And the thing they did with bedwetters is that you had to wash your own sheets and pack it down to the girls' side. That was devastating because during the day you are standing around outside trying to look like a champ in front of all the girls, smiling at them, and you're walking down the girls' side, being a bedwetter. It was not too good for the morale; it was very, very tough.

You know, we would sneak away sometimes, I had some friends from the Reserve and we would sneak away, climb over the mountains and go bum some coffee and melt snow up in the mountains and boil up a cup of coffee and have some coffee up there. We enjoyed that, just to get away.

One time before I ran away we had a field trip and the priest took us to Riverside Park. We didn't have any money and they had these machines they had little cranes in there that picked up fifty cent pieces, and nickels and dimes, you know. I was trying my luck, and I got frustrated and I looked around, and I said, "Hey nobody's guarding this thing," and crawled under and I got a big handful of money and filled up my pockets. I went running around and gave money to all the other kids. We all went on rides and rides all that day.

Somebody else tried to steal something, he was from Lytton, Spences Bridge. He wasn't a very big guy but he was in the boxing club. I never got into that. That's another thing too, that a lot of guys went into the boxing club and they were the ones who beat you up a lot because they had experience in boxing. He did something and he got caught. In order to get off he told them what I had done. So he got off and the police came and picked me up and threw me in jail about five o'clock or so, early in the afternoon.

My first time in jail, I sat there, being interrogated by the police and all I had was about five cents left out of all the money I had taken because a lot of it I gave away to the other kids and a lot of it I spent. I remember telling the police, "What are you going to do throw me in jail for five lousy cents." And they were saying well they could throw you in jail for stealing a penny. I said, "Ohhh!". It scared the hell out of me, I'll tell you that. They left me in there and said, "We're going to talk to the priest and see what we're going to do about you." So it wasn't until about around one to two o'clock in the morning one of the priests came over and brought me back.

Hawkeye, he was always going around and threatening the guys, "I'm Hawkeye you can't get away from me." A lot of guys would try to run away. Swim across the river climb over the mountains, go down the road, a lot of different ways. And old Hawkeye was out there and he had a good track record of catching you, hey.

Brother Murphy was there too. I remember getting whipped by him for doing something or getting blamed for something. The way I remember getting whipped up there was at nighttime just before everybody lined up to go to bed and get your cod liver oil poured down your throat and then they called the names of the guys up there who were going to get a strapping. And then I got called up. You bent over and they put a wet towel on your bare ass and they got a strap out and you got hit. Yeah, you try not to cry and give them the pleasure of letting them know that they're hurting you but that was tough to do.

On my sixteenth birthday I was allowed to go to town. That must must have been 1964. I turned sixteen on May 4th. My dad was around and he came to visit me and I told him, "Dad I don't like this place. I want to quit school." And he said, "Well it's up to you son. You make up your mind and you've done that in the past, you've made up your own mind and so, whatever you think is right for you." So I went to town.

Oh years after this, when I was in Vancouver, I figured I would go back to school. I went down to the Indian Affairs office, and son-of-a-gun, within fifteen minutes this guy signed me up. I give him credit for that. Signing me up, looking for guinea pigs. Always a guinea pig. See if the Indians could make it in college, hey. I just happened to be at the right place at the right time.

I wrote back for my transcripts and you know you put on there what you hoped to be someday. I said I'd like to become a teacher, that's what I put on there. And they wrote back, I remember I had a twenty-five percent or twenty eight percent average on my math and my other marks were like thirty-five-percent average. And they had comments on there. They said something like you're aiming too high and you're not going to make it. What the hell, you're going to get disillusioned because you're aiming too high. You should look at trying to become something else. I remember they even put on there that you should look at becoming a sign painter or a caboose man. Lucky I didn't become a caboose man, hey, they're all extinct now. I wished I had kept that letter. But then I'm glad I got that letter because it totally pissed me off. I beared down and I wound up getting a Master's Degree at the University of British Columbia. That's how mad I was. I said I'm going to show you guys. But in a nutshell that's kind of my life story.

Andrew Amos

I was born at Esperanza, in August, 1941 to George and Christine Amos. We lived at Queens Cove Reserve and Cee Pee Cee and Nootka canneries on the West Coast of Vancouver Island, all very remote at the time. My father was a fisherman and my mother stayed at home with us. I attended Christie Indian Residential School in 1948 from Grade One to the completion of Grade Eight in 1956, and Grade Nine in the fall of 1956 to my graduation in 1960 at the Kamloops Indian Residential School. I had no choice but to go to Kamloops because we were Roman Catholic and Kamloops was the only place to go at that time and after a while it was to Mission City.

I remember going on a steamer, the Princess Maquinna from Nootka Cannery to Christie School, we were not allowed to mix with the general public, we stayed down on the cargo deck. I got to Kamloops by train, my mother put me on the train. I would travel all by myself on a train. I was lost, you felt lost. When in Kamloops, I didn't know how to get to the residential school, I forgot to mention this, that I was a little later than the rest of them that went up there. And I didn't know how to get to the residential school.

My first day in Kamloops Residential School away from home was quite a lonely experience, yeah. So far from home. I'd never been past Port Alberni. was a culture shock going into a strange place. There were about fifteen or twenty of us from the West Coast area that went from Grade Nine to Grade Twelve. Maybe about twenty out of 350 some odd students.

The feeling I had on arriving at the residential school was of displacement in the strange surrounding. I was homesick in this doom and gloom situation. On my first day I had a black eye from a boy that was two years older, he grabbed me by the hair and kneed me in the face, for no reason. Kamloops was more of a culture shock with students from all over British Columbia. With a huge cross section of students, we had many disputes. This in itself was a challenge, but to be so far from home was another. I had never been out of my own area. Iwas fifteen.

When I first went to school I could speak English and my Native tongue. But, many of my friends could not speak English and we were absolutely not allowed to speak our own language in Christie. Kamloops was the same, besides we all spoke different dialects.

We had to make major adjustments. We learned to cope with the resident bullies who would always pick on us and take our extras, such as apples, oranges, even slices of bread, and fend for ourselves we did! As in street smart, we became residential school smart. We were very much alone. We could not go to anyone for our grievances and myself, I believe it was here I created this inner

25

toughness that I have carried all my life. Many of us carry this toughness even to this day. All feelings shut down.

In our daily activities we did the same more or less as everybody else. You had your churches, your prayer time, we did a lot of praying then. We would pray when we just got up in the morning, and before meals and bedtime. Everything was regimented pretty much more or less, hey. But we just had to be more or less regimented particularly if we were functional in a day.

We would start early in the morning milking cows and cleaning gutters. I think we started about 5:30 in the morning. I think we were the last bunch that did that. I think it was 1957 that we didn't have to get up so early in the morning. After that we started about 7:30. When we first got up everybody that came in did milking cows and stuff.

Hygiene was pretty good, it was up to yourself more or less, in high school. We never had much to do with the younger kids. You were in Grade Twelve you had your own homeroom. You more or less were on your own. Our sleeping room was on the second floor... there was the boy's side and the girl's side, so we were on the second floor on the boy's side. We had our own homeroom down in the basement. They were large. There was about forty high school students in there. We were told when to keep quiet, when to talk. Many of us never learned to express our feelings. Today, I am very good at clamming up, not dealing with situations at hand.

I didn't see too much physical punishment at the school, we were on detentions. Sometimes we would run away to town just for pie and ice cream and when we were caught, we were punished for a month. We couldn't go to town again. We used to... maybe nobody knows, but we used to run into town and go for pie and ice cream and run back before bedtime. That was a part of our training but we weren't allowed to go into town for pie and ice cream! We used to do that all the time 'till I got caught, then I was punished; for a month and I couldn't go to town.

There was a reward system. It was in sports that we were rewarded. If you wanted to go through the reward system you had to travel through BC where you actually won. I expressed myself through sports where the rewards were through special privileges and meals. The opportunity to travel to sporting events was always exciting and to see the many different places, such as Vancouver, Vernon, Lumby, Mission City or just across town. These were privileges many of the school children never did see or realize.

The treatment was good as long as you excelled in sports. We had to compete for boxing or basketball. The four years that I was there I was quite competitive, you know, in the sports. So we were sort of treated special and I was accepted in Kamloops. In boxing we were treated somewhat special. We would go to our instructor's home in North Kamloops. This was also special to be able to leave the residential school surroundings. I was the 135 pound BC champ in 1958 and runner up at 139 pounds for the BC Championships in Vancouver where I had the pleasure of meeting Jay Silverheels – better known as Tonto. Two of our boys turned professional, one in England and the other in Los Angeles. I myself had entertained a pro-career in boxing. Kamloops Indian Residential School had a very excellent basketball team. We beat the BC champions of the day, the Kamloops Red Devils from the public high school. We could not compete in the BC Basketball Championships because we were under the Federal Government. It was through competitive sports, and the girls with their dancing and travel, that we were able to cope and survive the daily routine of life at the residential school. I did grow to love Kamloops, but my passion for the sea was foremost and I became a commercial fisherman.

Today I still fish, I have my commercial fishing licenses and my own boat, but I work for the Nuu-chah-nulth Economic Development Board in Port Alberni as a Fishery Adjustment Co-ordinator. I work with retired fishermen and our existing fishermen in our fight for survival and hopefully to maintain our connection to the sea and the resources.

To summarize the impact residential school had on my life, I have problems showing my inner feelings towards my family, showing my feelings for people who are in pain or in sorrow over a loss. If I feel joy or if I feel sadness I find it very difficult to express my emotions, especially to my immediate family. I believe I should not show any emotions whatsoever. I know something is wrong and I have many regrets because of this.

I never could sit down with my mother or my father and just talk. We were just too far removed. We never really shared our feelings and concerns because we never bonded when I was young. And with my own family, many issues are unresolved and will stay that way unless I decide or we decide to find help. This dysfunction has carried over to them. At times this leaves me very bitter with life. With my grandchildren I feel displaced when we should be bonding and spending quality time together. We all have serious hangups. For this, I am mad at the world because this has affected my grandchildren.

E.L.

I started school when I was eight or nine until I was thirteen. Our mom started sewing, sewing us underclothes. The worst part, when we reached school, was they took away our clothing. The clothes were the closest thing to us, from Mom, and we had to take all that off. That was very hard. We had numbers given to us as they gave us our uniforms. They took our clothes Mom gave us to wear and we never saw them again till we were ready to go home. The shoes we had to wear until we left. I used to get sores on the back of my foot because my shoes got too small, sores that never seemed to heal. That I'll never forget. That was painful.

My parents were so poor that they couldn't come and see us. They had to go by train or bus if they came to see us. I wished though, that I'd see them in the crowd. I had an aunt who lived nearby, my dad's sister. I saw her once in the parlour. I was wishing she'd come over or call me or something. But she didn't. I just peeked at her and I just took off. We used to always peek in the parlour to see if our mom or dad were in there. Even though I knew they wouldn't be, I was just hoping. Oh, I would have been so happy at the beginning but the leaving would be so hard, too hard. The happiest part of the whole year was when we were ready to go home, yes. I used to be so full of happiness.

I had to clean everything or get punished if I didn't. I never knew that some people didn't care how their house is when people visit them. Mine has just got to be clean. I used to think the white race was perfect, until I got married and my husband had some friends and some of them were as poor as we are.

Oh, I was going to tell you about my friend. My friend, she's from Chase, she's a counselor. I saw her at the treatment centre one day and she said, "Oh I used to envy you girls when you used to go to Kamloops School." Like she saw us getting on the truck and thought it was so great, now she's got a different story. She's heard so many bad things. Oh I told her she was lucky that she never went to school there. Her mom never did send her. I had some hurt feelings about my mom and dad thinking they gave me away, but the president of the treatment centre said, "No, they were threatened – that's how come you had to go." And after that I never blamed my family. My poor parents, how they must have hurt too.

My husband says, "One of the things that comes out strong in her, is she is not able to cry with people."

Oh yes, and I hardly go out and associate with people and I thought it was just me. But I guess we're so used to being locked up for so many years and it doesn't bother me if I stay at home all the time. I guess some of my sisters are that way, too. They're the same, you never see them going out. I go to meetings and things but not very much. Wow, you go in there and you hear so many things and it's hurtful. That's the way meetings are.

I remember the times at recreation, the senior girls would come and the nuns made them throw apples on the floor and then we'd all scramble for them. And there'd be so many of us that never got any. Other girls would have a lot but they wouldn't share with us. Same with the fudge, great big pans of them. Oh I used to just die to have one but you couldn't because you had to pay a dollar for one. I never did have any money, even now I just see fudge and I just about die for it and I can't take it, because I am a diabetic. I just have to accept it, I guess. I cheat once in a while.

I went to day school at the Reserve, then we were supposed to go back for Grade Eight to Kamloops and I begged my dad. I asked my mom first, she didn't know what to say. I think I was fourteen and she said, "Either go to work or go back to school." I told her, "I'll do anything." I didn't want to go back, so I found a job as housekeeper. I wasn't ever going to go back again, no, no, no, but, I heard it got easier after. I was telling my husband, probably people kind of found out we were humans. Some of the people from around here, smarter people started going over there. And I think they started taking it easy. It's just my thinking, they got a swimming pool and they could go out. They could do things that we couldn't do. We did without everything, we never got nothing. We just had to do with what we had there and we didn't have anything.

We used to see movies. They used to show us westerns where Indians always got beat. And we used to always go for the cowboys, not the Indians. We used to get so scared these Indians were going to kill these cowboys. Imagine that we were sort of ashamed of being Indians. We were ashamed, I guess because they showed us how to be. I don't know how, but they did. I didn't think I was an Indian for goodness sakes.

We spent Christmas in Kamloops School. Oh my first Christmas I'll never forget. At home, Mom used to get us to hang our stockings up on Christmas Eve and it would be just full of candies and nuts. But at the Kamloops School I snuck and I found my stocking and hung it up and there wasn't anything the next day. Oh that night though, the lights came on through the dormitory, nuns singing carols. We thought they were angels coming in. We really didn't know what was going on, just all puzzled. But no Santa came, he didn't find us. Some of the girls went home. We used to wish we could go home. We just got oranges or candies for Christmas.

So many blanks. I guess that is what you mean by closed doors, hey? Goodness, wished I could remember. But, I guess it's best the doors stay closed. I didn't think there wasn't anything the matter with me but I guess it sure affected me. They took away my belongings, they took away everything from me. Everything that's important to me, mother, father, culture. But not my spirit, no way. They stripped us of everything. Gave us brown uniforms and a number. And they put what they wanted in us, made us ashamed of who we are. Even right to this day, it still affects me. Like I really want to get into Indian things and I just can't because of them telling us it was of the devil. Every time I try, something blocks me. I can't, because I'm afraid. Like to go to the Sweatlodge. I had a chance to go because I was working at the treatment centre. I'd say I'd go but deep inside, I'm not going to go. The same with *Yuwippi* Ceremonies. I want to go so badly.

Everything was of the devil. Stick games were of the devil and even used to scare me when I used to watch them. And it still affects me, right to today. I want to get into our culture and I just can't, there's just a big block in there. So I put my Catholic and my tradition together and just pray to that one God. Maybe that's the way it should be with everybody and maybe there won't be so much fighting and wars and everything. Yeah, that is so true.

I coped by trying to be a clown, yeah, nothing hurts me. I used to act crazy, silly. So that I wouldn't be hurt, right to this day I won't let anybody see me feeling hurt, except in the treatment centre where I cried all week. Sometimes I wish I could cry like some people but I can't even for my mom. There's always people around and I always had to cut it out. I had to control myself. So I find a lot of things to do. Summer time is good because I can get outside and really work.

I used to steal candies, we used to have those long bloomers, hey. I stuffed them in there. Oh, that was fun but not to get caught. I never got caught, but that one girl got caught. I don't know what happened to her I never looked back, just ran. I don't remember eating the candies or if I gave it to other kids, or what. Maybe I threw it away, I don't know. And once I stole a camera from a senior. I did'nt know what I was going to do with that camera. I went down into the locker room. It was dark and I stole it. Oh it felt so good to have something but I don't remember what kind of camera it was, but it was really nice. Anyway, they found out and the sisters got us all together and they told us whoever stole it is going to get punished by God. God saw them do that and they're going to get punished. I got so scared, I returned it that night. I never stole after that. The seniors were allowed to bring a few personal things from their home.

We used to drink when we were younger, the first years of our marriage. We just quit, I'm glad we did. I am sure lucky, but you can easily be driven into it. Probably would have been dead like all of my friends have been. I counted nine girls that I used to be friends with in school and they all died of alcoholism.

We never knew the boys, we weren't allowed to talk to boys or nothing. That year I left, I was supposed to go back to school again. They were going to put boys and girls together and I was too scared to go back. We were so far away from boys. You know, boys on that side and girls on this side, we weren't to look at them or anything. They put us all together in church but all on different sides. That was the only time we ever saw the boys. But then I used to look for my brother all the time when the boys used to come in. We had no contact with them. They were different dining rooms. We just saw them from a distance, never close. I remember this one boy I used to feel so bad for him. He used to always wet his bed and they used to put that sheet over him and they'd make him stand in the middle there where we'd all go to church. He'd be in the middle of everything, with the sheet over his head. That was pitiful. We sure didn't find it funny. It is cruel. I see that boy all grown up and he has a wife and kids. He's still alive though, but I don't think he drinks. Maybe he did when he was younger, I don't know, I lost track of him. But, we sure knew him because everybody knew who was under that sheet. I don't know how, maybe someone told us, because his head was covered. I don't think any of the girls laughed or anything. We had nobody to tell our feelings to in there, that's for sure.

You have to cope with it to live in that place. When I left school, when my younger sister went in, they were allowed to smoke and go to dances and things we were never even allowed to do. I remember that one winter they went skating, but we were still juniors. Just seniors were on skates. I don't know where the sleighs came from, but they were sleigh riding too. That was the first time I ever saw sleighs or skating, but we were just juniors and we just hung around on the outside.

I don't even know what my brother went through, he never talked about school. Most of my sisters just don't talk about going to that school. I have nine sisters and two brothers, eight of my sisters went to that school and one brother. Oh, I used to like having an older sister there but she quit school. I thought she'd help me when the other girls picked on me. But I never used to get in contact with her either. She was a senior and I was a junior.

There was the juniors, the intermediates and the seniors. We never did mingle or even talk to one another, you'd get in trouble. So I guess it really didn't matter when she quit. It was sad though because I'd never see her again, only when I got home.

I visited the school about seven years ago. Goodness, it looks so small inside, but when I first started there it seemed so big. I even went to the bedroom. I don't even know how we all fit in there. It sure gives me sad feelings, just sad. It seemed I lost my childhood or something there. I was thinking about it, I was wishing for my childhood back or something. But, I wouldn't want to go back again, no way. There's parts where you pretend nothing hurts you, everything doesn't matter there. That was a hard, hard time. My mom hardly ever talks about her time there. She went to school in that building that burnt down. The only thing she ever talked about, she said they had a queen. We all had queens, I think. You know a girl that takes over a bunch of girls and beats you up and everything if you cross them or anything. Oh, we didn't dare cross them, but my mom's queen was worse. Mom was telling me they'd join hands with another girl I guess and carry her around. Mine wasn't that bad, but we were scared of her and whatever candies and things we got, we had to share it with her. If she didn't like you she'd get the other girls to do things to you. Like this one poor girl, I don't know what happened to her. They didn't like her and they put water on her bed all the time, like she was wetting her bed. But she didn't wet her bed and we didn't dare say anything or we'd get it.

That girl with a wet bed, she was severely punished. I didn't know what they done with them the minute they walked out the door, we didn't hear anything. All we knew was that we pity them because they would get a licking or whatever. Never heard what they did. We used to be kind of scared of that one brother who used to work down in the furnace. We used to can tomatoes down there and do laundry on the side and there was a door to the furnace room. We used to be scared to enter that door because they said the brother was in there. I remember one or two girls going in there, too, but we were so scared. I don't know if there was any force or anything. There's one thing I'm glad about, I never got abused, you know. But, my husband was saying I did get abused. I can't even deal with people.

We didn't know nothing about sex or anything like that and whatever was going on in that room was scary, I don't know what it was. We all ran by every time we saw that door, I guess he scared us. We wouldn't dare enter there. It seemed like a dungeon. I know there used to be a brother, oh I forgot his name, he was a tall one anyway. Never saw priests either, hardly ever saw them. I worked upstairs in their rooms but I didn't see them. I just fixed beds and cleaned, then just leave and that was about it. Today, maybe I go to extremes in cleaning, I don't know, maybe I do. My other sisters aren't like the way I am, even the ones that went to Kamloops School. That's how come I had to make everything perfect. I remember the times in school where you had to make your bed. The nuns got the seniors to show us how to make our beds. If you didn't make it right it got stripped off and you have to do it over and over until you got it just perfect. Then we folded up our night gowns and kneel down and pray.

I don't even know what kind of prayers we said. We had to go on our knees. You know, when we say the whole long prayer and another person can come and say "thank you Creator for this day," which has more meaning than a long drawn out prayer. I don't know how else to pray. I remember the Easters. We had to be silent for three days. You were not allowed to talk out loud, just whisper, because God is supposed to be in that box.

I think it was very harsh. I think it affects me right up to today, I didn't realize it did. Probably my withdrawing too. It's probably got a lot to do with that. If I have to I go and be in a crowd, I'd just tell my husband sometimes, "nope, I'm not going to go." If I'm forced to then I will go. I'm too easily hurt and if anybody says something wrong or puts me down or something I take it too much to heart and I kind of resent that person. It's best to not say anything and just keep away, so I won't let people hurt me. But I don't know if that's got anything to do with it.

My sisters, right up to today, wouldn't talk about their days at school. The ones that went in before I did. If you ask them they'll say, "Oh it was okay." I never heard about any of them being abused but I heard my nephew was. He was telling my sister that he got abused by brothers, I think, or priests. I was surprised. He went in around the 60's, I think, because my nephew is only around thirty something, near fourty. He must have been really hurt. He went to the treatment centre and it was the first time I ever heard about it. But I didn't think that it happened at that time, that it only happened way before, like in our time. I don't remember the abuse.

My husband says, "The school has been there a long time and it took a long time for anything to come out? There was a code of secrecy that stayed there for decades."

No one wanted to talk about it. It seemed like something is controlling us. If we ever talked against it, that they'd get us, whatever that is. We were always being punished for talking too loud. We used to be scared of the nuns. When we played around, one of the girls would say that there's a nun coming, but they'd say it in Indian - *stl'ek*. We'd all run and I'd just sit down and be quiet. We used to be afraid.

My sister said that she used to get strapped if she talked in her language. She talked the language but we didn't understand Indian. My mother taught us all English and only spoke English, because she was sending us to school. So what Indian I know I learned it from going home on holidays, I just picked up on it. I told Mom years later, she thought it was so funny because I knew what she was talking about in Indian. I did ask my older sister if we spoke and how did we learn our language. That was the way we learned it, just by listening.

I wrote down most of what I was thinking about. Imagine going to school all that time and all I got is this little crumpled piece of paper.

You didn't dare cry either, but I'd watch Moma and Poppa until they were out of sight, just turn, just go on from there. Yes, that was so hurtful, especially getting to the school you didn't know anything. Who hurt the most? Our parents or us? When we got there we didn't know what was going on. We just stood around puzzled. We used to have to cut our hair almost bald. I remember the girls used to have purple all over their head. It used to be some kind of liquid. I don't even know the name of it but it sure stunk. We used to have to put it all over our head. They cut our hair off almost bald. I should start talking to my sisters. Then maybe we'll put things together, we'll remember things.

They used to write a letter on the black board for us to copy, no adding anything else or they wouldn't send it. I remember it well, it said "Dear Mother and Father, How are you? I am fine. Your daughter, name." If some girls got a letter, they read it before giving it to them.

I used to like working in the nuns and priests dining room because I could eat their scraps. It used to be so good, you know their scraps. I was always hungry we never seemed to get enough. I even used to eat leaves on trees, it sure wasn't good though but it was something to eat. The food they gave us sometimes was sour, but I ate it anyway, because I was always hungry.

I want to say many thanks to the people who have opened the doors of my dark past. I give thanks for the light in my life. It helps to make the rest of my journey lighter, thank you everyone. Thank you everyone from the Behind Closed Doors Project and the staff of the treatment centre where I work for getting me started. Thank you, from a survivor of the Kamloops Indian Residential School.

I just figured why I don't like Fall time. It reminds me of when we started school. Spring is happiness, that's when we were going home. Trains were sad because they reminded me of home and also it took my parents away, the sound of the train whistle. Christmas is always sad because we didn't have our mother and father with us. We couldn't go home because there was no money. Easter, just another day, happy in ways because we'd be going home soon. These things still affect me to this day. I often wonder why these things saddened me, just the other day I figured out why. So I thought I'd write it down.

Girls attending an outing to the Kamloops Museum to learn about the history of Canada. There was nothing of First Nations language, culture or history taught to the children at the residential school.

The purpose of the residential schools was to do away with First Nations' language and culture and to assimilate the children into the white society.

Dance troupe from the residential school who did public performances. Only girls were allowed to participate in the troupes.

34

Margaret Abel

My father and mother had separated two years before. I was living with my mother, Mary Ann Bennett and, I guess it would be my stepfather, Dick. We all lived up in Juliet, which is not far from Merritt. It is along the new highway now called the Coquihalla. There was only my brother Adam and me. My sister and her husband were there and they used to work there and then I had a niece, Annie. When we got older, we were able to start school there. My niece was a little bit younger and, of course, they put her in the school because they had to have, I think it was, seven kids to start the school up.

I don't know how long that lasted because we used to have fun there in Juliet. We used to go pick wild strawberries and I remember me and my younger brother used to go down and get water down the creek and dip up pails. I remember I used to just swing them as we were taking them home. And it was a little ways. We just had a shack but we were quite happy. I remember my stepdad was working in a sawmill and all of a sudden I noticed there was a fire, there were flames coming up. I guess the shed had caught on fire and first thing it started going all through the mountains.

I guess there was a big fire because I remember my mom wetting down blankets and she was trying to protect us, protecting the house, from sparks and stuff. Next I remember that we were on the train and getting out of there. Everybody moved, and that's when we moved back to Kamloops. That is where our Aunt Rosalie Mitchell lived. My mother and stepdad left to go back to Juliet where Dick worked in the bush, so we stayed with Aunt Rosalie. After the summer was gone, a huge truck pulled up with a bunch of school girls standing up in the back. I was put on the truck. I guess I was afraid, I don't know. You know you're put on the truck and you don't know what's going on and I don't know where my mother and dad are and everything was just sort of blank. They did not take my brother. He was a year younger than me. I believe I was about six years old then. I was born March 11th, 1922. This was either 1928 or 1929. I do not think I was scared as I had a couple of cousins on the truck, May Jules and her sister Eileen. They looked after me.

I was given a uniform, shoes and so on, and also a hair cut. Lots of times the girls had to be deloused, there was so much lice going about. We had to stand in line and listen to what orders the sister gave. We all had our beds in a row up on the top floor. There was always a sister close by to watch over us.

I guess it was all in the learning experience. We all seemed to get along well. No one was to talk in their language, we all had to speak English. We made pretty good friends and then, of course, the girls, they couldn't talk their own language. Sometimes when we were out for recreation I'd ask some of the girls how do you say this word in Indian, you know, in Shuswap. We used to have some fun there. But you weren't supposed to talk the language at all. I didn't know how to speak my language; I didn't know anything about it until after I got out of school. Then I started learning about different things and what my background was.

The sisters were French. You could hear them speak in their own language, French. Early in the morning we had to get up, wash up, get dressed, and all line up to file to the church for morning mass. After church we lined up to go in for our breakfast, which was a bowl of gruel and milk. I'm not sure if we had a slice of bread or toast. In the summer time I remember getting corn and tomatoes, you know, fresh from the garden, and those were kind of nice. I remember having ham and we'd have potatoes and once in a while we'd get baked potatoes and I don't remember any desserts of any kind. I guess if we were hungry, we just stayed hungry. We never had any snacks in between. I guess that was a good way of keeping slim, I suppose.

I remember one morning in the bathroom, I must have had a gut ache first thing. I heard the door being locked. We had only certain times for the bathroom. I remember I and another girl were left. We helped each other climb out of the window and went to have our breakfast. Father rang the bell and wanted to know where we were. Father had called the Sister Superior. Then this girl and I both got the heavy straps on our legs. I don't know how many straps we got, ten or so, on the legs then we went to sit down. We looked at each other with tears and started to grin and laugh. Father rang the bell and we were quiet.

We all were in one huge dining room, two long rows of the girls and two long rows of the boys. On the other side of the girls, two round tables up in the front held the priests and brothers. I guess once in a while there was flirtation going on which wasn't allowed.

We all had our jobs marked out for us which were changed about once a month: cleaning the hallways, the church, recreation hall, which took up half the morning. Then it was lunch time. After lunch it was time for school, we all went to our classes. We had our own school and the boys had their own school. They kept us separate all the time.

Well, my school work, it wasn't too bad. I know we had to have catechism when we first went into school and they asked you questions about the bible. One time I was at the board and I was stuck on a question and then I was copying from another girl. I guess I was caught watching another girl and sister gave it to me on the knuckles with a ruler.

I guess maybe it seemed like it was kind of long (being in church), but I don't know. You just didn't pay any attention to it, that's the way you were brought up. Going to church everytime, yep. Now-a-days I guess they don't bother with the Catholic church. They don't have hats now. We just all sang together. How we learned the songs I don't know. I know the midnight masses at Christmas time. I used to love those and Easter mass was really wonderful.

One time I was assigned to the scullery drying dishes. I and another girl decided to change jobs; she had the job of dumping out the garbage or something.

Well the sister in charge saw this and I got smacked all the way to one room back to another. I guess it was fun in a way, a good way of learning also. It didn't feel so good then.

We had our outing down to the lake, that's about where the Pow Wow is held now. That lake we used to swim in and did it have a bunch of polywogs! Suckers used to come out of the water and they'd suck on your skin, ugh!

We also had our photos taken, which was nice, with all the boys and girls together, sisters and priests too. Yeah, we had several pictures taken then with the mountainside, that was quite nice. I don't know how old I was – ten or eleven, but I was quite skinny. The kids have to laugh when they look at me and I say, "Oh can you find mother there?"

We had sewing lessons also. To this day I still sew. While in school I learned to make aprons, also boys' shorts. I liked sewing, they had the old machines there.

I also remember some girls had run away from school. They were caught and we were all down in the recreation hall. Benches were lined up, with the girls laying on them with faces down and with just panties on. I believe it was Father Kennedy who strapped the girls one after the other.

There was some children that wet the bed. I know they had to go outside and hold the sheets up because they had wet the bed. They were in front of the other girls showing what they had done. It wasn't private, you knew who the bedwetters were.

The nuns would swat you if you did something wrong. There were some nice sisters and they were pretty good. It was all nuns that watched over us all the time.

I guess some of the girls were feeling homesick and isolated, as one went to school in September and had to stay until the end of June to go home for two months holiday.

I was assigned to cleaning the toilets. Another time I worked in the sisters' dining room serving them their meals. Another time I had to do one of the father's room, do up his bed, straighten it up and dust.

I went to school there and it seemed to be just natural that I went to school and it seemed to be okay. As time went on, it seemed like the girls were a little more carefree. They were able to go into town and different things and they were able to get out of their uniforms as time went along. So, things changed there quite a bit.

I wasn't really lonely because I had my cousins there and they were always looking after me and you just got along. I remember, we used to go out for a walk, down by the lake there where the Pow Wow is now. Oh, we went in for swims too. I don't remember any sports. We never had any sports there, but I guess everybody was busy in the morning and the afternoon. I don't know what the weekends were like, I can't remember.

We were never allowed to go to town and it was not very often that people had their mother or dad coming along. But I guess a lot of them were living far off. My sister came once in a while. I remember my sister and her husband coming over there one time; I guess they had a few drinks when they came.

When I was in school, I remember my dad coming over. He had a horse and one time I was able to go from the school to where he was in Kamloops and he'd give me a ride on the horse, cloppity, clop, clop. I remember him putting his big gloves on my hands and that was all in fun. I got to know my dad off and on, but he passed away when I was ten years old. He got pneumonia and was in the hospital, so my sister came and got me and I was going to visit my dad there. It wasn't long before he passed away then.

I don't remember any parties, but I know they used to have concerts. I was in a couple of the concerts which was really nice. I remember after one of the concerts I met my one brother, Eddy. He was sent down to school in Vancouver. That's the first time I met him; I think he was about nineteen when he was released from school. Someone took me down to meet my brother and they said, "This is your brother Eddy," and that's the first time I knew I had a brother Eddy. I just knew of my sister, my brother, Adam, and then course my younger sister, Elsie. I had another sister, Laudie, and another brother, Wilfred. They were sent down to school in Vancouver, too. My sister Laudie, she was sent to the monastery. She was eleven or twelve when she went.

My sister, I guess she was a little stubborn at the beginning, and they swatted her around the ears. We didn't know anything about it but after she came home (she was twenty-five years old by the time I met her), when she came out of school she was deaf. So I had to learn sign language.

I was the only one that went to the residential school, and the rest, I don't remember what happened to them. I know there was twins and my older sister said that they had died. I guess my Aunt Rosie brought up most of the family though. Anyhow, we all got together and then I find out that I had a family and it turned out okay.

Sometime towards the end, I was reluctant to go. Me and my niece we used to eat this, lime candy. We used to eat a lot of this lime candy, trying to get sick to keep me from going back to school, but it didn't work. I had different things happen to me. It's just sort of like, all forgotten or something. I don't know, it just seems like a dream.

I was entered into school in 1929, went as far as 1936. I ended up in Grade Six, was promoted to Grade Seven, but I decided not to go back. I was fourteen years old. I had decided I wanted to work. I started working in the fields. I'd walk about three miles. I and my niece we took a job working in the tomato fields. And then we'd walk all the way home and have supper and get ready, take in a show or something. We worked nine to ten hours a day, and ended up with seven dollars and fifty cents a week. That was good money in those days.

We go back to the school there and we take in the Pow Wows. It seems kind of strange but it's always nice to go back. It seems to be changed, you know. It seems smaller, somehow.

The Kamloops Indian Residential School boy's brass band marched in local parades and at times competed with other residential school bands.

Junior boys by the pool. For some of the boys 'swimming' time was an unpleasant experience. A couple of our storytellers talk about being thrown in the pool and not knowing how to swim. It seems one of the brothers enjoyed doing this to some of the boys.

William Brewer

About life before I went to school – my mother died when I was ten years old and it was just around then my dad started drinking. I was on my own most of the time, and I used to go and work for a lot of gardens. When I was ten, eleven and twelve, I used to work for the Chinese for one dollar a day, ten cents an hour. In those days the dollar was quite a bit of money. So I made about five bucks a week. I could get a pair of shoes for a dollar-and-a-half. In those days when you went to town and if you had fifty cents, you could have a pretty good day in town. Like you could get a hamburger steak dinner and you could go to the show for ten cents and a pop for a nickel.

Everybody at home spoke Okanagan. I had a little problem when I went to school, because sometimes I would make a mistake, I would start talking my language and then I'd catch myself. But they'd beat you up when you spoke your language. Most of them kids that were coming to that school, they could hardly speak English in them days. They got to learn by themselves like I learned pretty good when I was still here. My sisters all taught me how to speak English. And they taught me how to say the Our Father and the Hail Mary and all that, you know. Then when I went to school, I remember the priest or the teachers told me I must have went to school before. And I told them no, I didn't go to school. I could write my name and everything and he was trying to think I was just lying to him. I told him my sisters taught me what I had learned. I was twelve years old when I went to school. I remember, I wanted to go to school, because I used to want to be with a bunch of kids.

I remember going to residential school. When we first landed there, they took us to the dining room and they gave us a couple slices of bread and some jam and some milk. We were waiting for the main course and that was it. So they put us to bed. The next day at breakfast they give us that cracked wheat or some damn thing. Some kind of a porridge, hey, and couple slices of bread and tea, I think. But, like at home we always get bacon and eggs and all that stuff. That's the thing I didn't really like when I was going to school. You know, you can't feed 400 kids with bacon and eggs or anything like that. You got to cook big potfulls, I guess, in order to feed them. I was a kid, but a lot of kids didn't realize that. They figured, oh jeez, they're feeding us like pigs and stuff like that. But, you got used to it, I guess.

But I didn't mind it while I was going there. You went to school half a day and you went to work either mornings or night. We took shifts, half of the kids went to work and half went to school. So in the afternoon you went to work and then the other bunch went to school. So that was a really self-supporting school. They had pigs and chickens, and dairy cattle. In the gardens they grew potatoes and carrots and all that stuff. They grew corn for the cows, and so you got to work all that and you got to learn about it.

First thing in the morning we'd get up and we'd go and milk the cows. We came in and then we went to church, then the barn boys would go for breakfast. The guys that went to work would line up. Then the farm guy named McKenzie would select different groups to go and work on different things. Like you'd go over and weed the garden or work with the chickens, because they had a lot of chickens or you'd work in the pigpen. Well I didn't have any favourite jobs.

One time, I got to work with a carpenter. He was building a house for the guy that was taking care of the farm, he got married, so they built him a house. So I was working there everyday, and I would work with this carpenter and he was showing me what to do. It helped me because I built this house myself.

When I was around fourteen, I started in a band, you know a brass band. We used to go and practice every day instead of going to work. I used to practice the trumpet. That was pretty good, but I never took it on to keep going with it. I just did it while I was in there. We would go march through town every once in a while and we played mostly around the school. I think it was Father Kennedy who was the principal and he was getting quite old. There must have been around twenty boys in the band. We had capes and sort of a wedged hat and dress pants. We used to march through the dormitories around Christmas at midnight and wake the girls up. And we used to have a little lunch after midnight, then go back to bed. After we woke the girls up we go to mass, then we go back to bed. That's on Christmas day. We never left there, even when your kin died. They never let you go. Because my grandfather died in 1938, I was in there one year, I didn't get to go to his funeral. We did come home during the summer holidays for two months. After I was old enough, I used to go and work for these farmers stoking the grain and stuff like that.

In 1942, I didn't want to go back. When I was fourteen, I was there two years and I was promoted to Grade Five. That day I was finished and when I got back here, my dad asked me if I could read and I said, "Yeah, I could read a bit", and can you write and I said, "Yeah." So he said, "Well you stay home and I am going to teach you how to work." So I only knew the work he did. In September after kids went back to school, I was driving a bunch of horses in for the guys to ride, for a Sunday ride.

Most people used horses in those days to go anyplace they wanted. So I was riding a colt and I went out and I got the horses, and the damn thing spooked and took off and went right through a bunch of horses and the colt fell and all the horses, they didn't know what happened. I don't know whether the colt fell on my leg or what the heck, but I broke my right leg. I went to the hospital and I had it fixed and so I couldn't work any more, so they sent me back to school.

That was a good thing because I learned a little more. The first teacher I had was Mr. McGuire, he was a Grade One to Four teacher. And then from five to six or seven it was Mr. Leslie, he was a good teacher. I didn't do very good on math. When you were sixteen they let you go to make room for somebody else. Father O'Grady was the principal and he tried to get me to keep going. He even came here and tried to get me to go back. But, I was back in my own range, I guess you'd call it, and I didn't want to go back there. I didn't like school, so I didn't go back. He tried two different times to get me to go back and I didn't go. I guess I should have went back when they wanted me to stay in school. I'm not the kind of guy that wants to sit in the office or go to work in places like that. I'm the kind of guy that wants to be in the outdoors all the time. So I did mostly logging when I got out of the school. I was logging most of my life.

The priests, brothers, and sisters in the school were pretty strict. You know a lot of kids ran away from there and then when they got back, they got a strap. I know I remember my buddies ran away. Frank, Phillip and Andy ran away and they got them back. They got a good strap and then, by golly, they took off again. They never brought them back again. One of the parents, I guess, protected them. But I knew if I ran away, my dad would have taken me right back, I never ran away.

One time I saw my relative, Millie Steele, way down the aisle. The hallway went right straight through to the girls' side. I started running over there to talk to her. One of the staff caught me and took me back and he gave me hell. We were not supposed to go there, that was out of bounds. So the only time you saw the girls was when you went for meals, because they had no partition there. Then you could just wave at them. You practically know where all your relatives were. The priest and the staff had their table right in front, and they had all that good stuff to eat. I thought that was terrible. We could see what they had. I thought that was cruel for them to do that. When Father O'Grady got there, he put a partition in between the girls and the boys. They took the staff away, so they ate in a different place, so we couldn't see them. That wasn't too bad I thought. Father O'Grady made a lot of improvements, like they built that auditorium. When Father Kennedy was principal there, he didn't do much because he was getting pretty old. Father O'Grady built a new technical school and new classrooms. I was gone when they finished the classrooms.

They had an orchard at the school. In the Fall we used to go over into North Kamloops and we used to pick a bunch of apples for the school. They'd go there in the truck and they'd get a bunch of kids and they'd pick a lot of apples. They would put them in the root cellar. So sometimes we would go and swipe some apples from there. They were good. When you were hungry, anything's good.

We went to mass every morning through the week. On Sundays we went to High Mass and around 4 o'clock we went to benediction. It was always different guys being alter boys every day to serve mass. I remember I went to mass with Jody. He was from Penticton, but his mother was from here. We were serving mass together one morning. When we got there, the priest wasn't there. I looked down and we saw a bunch of hosts and Jody was just a eating the hosts. I don't know if he was hungry, but he didn't really care about going to church and everything like that. He went because he had to go. When he got out of school, he never did go back to church.

At noon we had different teams to go play softball or hardball. You take turns at whatever you played ball or soccer. We used to get to play, I used to like the hardball but I didn't like that softball, I figured that was a girl's game. I didn't like basketball, I figured that was for girls too. One year I remember they had quite a bit of skating there, because it stayed cold most of the winter, but hardly any snow. We skated there and they had the pond down below by the river. They put a ditch through, so the water would come into the pond. We swam there in the summer. It got pretty warm, not really that hot but most of the time the wind was blowing and that whole valley was just dark with sand storm, because all that industrial area was just all open and it was very sandy.

Kamloops has changed quite a bit since I was in the school. When I first went, the city was just a small town. North Kamloops was mostly orchards and farms.

About once a month we had movies. We used to have it in the dining room when the partition was all out. We used to watch the movies with the girls. They used to be on one side and the boys on the other side. I think later just the boys watched a movie, and the girls had a different date to watch it.

When I went to the school and I first woke up in the morning, I thought it was the end of the world. I was homesick and hated all the rules you had to go by. Some of the kids say, when you're in there you're doing time. My younger brother went to school. I think he was about six years old when he went. I still had a chance to keep going, but I didn't. Things might be different now if I went. Well you know you'd have a trade you go into. When I got into my late teens I was horse logging. I drove horses all the time, but I could have got a trade if I kept going to school.

There was always some bullies at the school, but they pretty well had them controlled. If there was one who was going to be a bully, well they'd get a guy a little bigger than him and put him in a ring. They didn't train you but every once in a while they had boxing gloves they put on you. You fought it out and they didn't stop it or time it either. We were getting our frustrations out, I guess. I was in the ring once or twice, might be more. I remember I got in with a guy that knew how to box and I didn't. We had it out and I kept going down. They put him with another guy, so then he started going down, he got punched out. When we were back home, I had a pair of boxing gloves and I used to go over to the barn and spar with my buddies. Some of my half sisters were good scrappers, too.

When you were at the school towards the end of the year, you sort of get used of it, you didn't mind being there. Towards the end I was thinking maybe I should have stayed there, and worked in the school and kept on going to school, but I didn't. I got back home here and I got jobs, logging and stuff like that. Then we started going around to rodeos. I was happy with what I was doing when I got out of school, and when I got married I kept working in the logging jobs. I loaded logs on a truck for about twenty years.

I don't do much these days, I go to the arena, feed the horses and I do a little bit of running in the mornings. Then I have a shower and go for breakfast. I always get up around 5:30. I have eight horses of my own. Through the winter a lot of people board their horses and ride in the arena. That's the reason I built the arena. I figure if it wasn't for my eyes, I would still be out there, you know, roping with the guys. I used to rope quite a bit, in the rodeos but my eyes went and I never tried it again.

Janie Marchand

There was no bus or anything at that time so, my dad took us to Kamloops to go to school. He drove us into Kamloops and we went to school for one month because he wanted us to get used to it before we stayed in for a year. I can't think of what year I went to school and how old I was, but I know I stopped school when I was fourteen because I had to look after my mother.

When I first went there it was sort of lonely, but there were a lot of kids there. We went to school all through the year and the sisters were all very good. Only that first month I was there, there was a sister that was very, very mean, she licked you over every little thing. But, Father took her out and brought a different nun there. Sister Inese and the other one is Sister Mary Mallakey, they're from Ireland. Sister Inese, was a very nice person. She treated the kids really good. The other one was mean, you couldn't do anything, she'll whack you. Oh, she always had a little stick.

Well the first time we got there I didn't know anything about what you had to do there. This girl that had been there before was told that her and I were to go and grade the apples, but I didn't know how and we didn't do it fast enough, so a sister gave us the strap. I thought that was unbelievable that she gave me the strap because I was so new there. I didn't know what was going on. So they changed her, they put a different nun in there.

The third year we went in a truck. They brought a truck from the school and picked up all the kids. It was a great big truck with a rack and the seats around, and they took on kids from Penticton and Westbank. I went to the Indian school when the old school building was there. I didn't mind the old school because we used to go out for a walk if we had time. They used to take us out for a walk.

The nuns and priests, had work for us set up every day. We could go do some sewing or if there was two of us, we used to go down to the laundry room. I used to work in the kitchen, that's where my sister worked the most.

One time, this was really funny, me and another girl were working in the dairy. They always got us to do the dairy work, make the butter and clean up the place. So one day we churned this great big barrel of cream, churned it and churned it and churned it and it never turned into butter. Then we had to go to school. When we came back down to the dairy, we were going to churn the cream. The sisters said they churned it into butter and told us to be careful. The boys came in through the other door and turned the crank. The lid wasn't on tight and it flew off. The butter went straight all over the ceiling, all over the floor. Boy they sure had to get in there and clean it. Oh, lots of butter. Must have been about fifty pounds.

When we finished doing the butter we put them in pounds. In those little wooden things. We put them all in those containers and the guys took them to the cold storage room. It was all ice in there, all cold. They have two sections, they put the milk in one section to keep it good, and put butter and stuff that could spoil in another room. I didn't mind that job, we used to have lots of fun in the kitchen.

They had radios but they didn't have any movies or anything at the school. We walked into town to see movies. We went to the show and that's where we first saw a show about Jesus, when Jesus was born. They didn't have sound on, there was no sound.

Some kids say they didn't get enough to eat, but, I did. Sometimes I gave some of my stuff to the other kids because you had to clean up everything that you had on your plate. If I couldn't eat it, I gave it to one of the other kids because some of the kids didn't get enough.

The boys did the milking. They milked cows, they separated the milk. They looked after the gardens and there was one guy, I think his name was Brother Joseph, he used to be the gardener, and if he needed help he got the boys to help him.

We worked half a day. We learned how to sew, I used to make dresses and make underclothes, you know slips and vests and stuff like that for winter. In the summer, we used thinner material, we made dresses and aprons. You know, they had aprons that covered them all except the sleeves, and we made all the stuff like the slips, the dresses, the aprons, everything. When my kids were small I used to make six dresses in one day. I learned how to sew, I learned how to crochet, and I learned how to darn. I could darn socks really good, and I could sew quite a lot of stuff by hand and by machine.

One time I got into trouble with this girl. Her and I got into a fight. So Father John came over into the playroom that evening and he had two pairs of boxing gloves, and he made us wear the boxing gloves and fight it out. Oh I licked her again. Father John was laughing. We fought because she was pushing my other friend around. She never bothered me ever again. Father told her, "Next time you fight you get those boxing gloves on." Those girls were just a hollering for me.

Then one day Eva Williams from Penticton, started to fight with this woman from Cache Creek. This woman was not supposed to do that, because she was working in school, she wasn't going to school. So they got in trouble and Father John really bawled the heck out of them and told them next time they fought they were going to have to fight it out with gloves. So they never fought anymore. But one evening Catherine Alex had a fight with this woman from Cache Creek and boy they were just a fighting. Sister Mary Delores went over there and she thought she was going to stop them. That woman took her and swung her around and she stood up and ran and got Father John. So Catherine got punished by Father John. And Father told the lady from Cache Creek, "Next time you fight Theresa, you don't work here anymore, you know these are all school children, they're not like you."

I don't know if it would have been different if I didn't go there. We wouldn't have went to school, because there was no busses them days and the only school was over at Six Mile. My dad was always working so he couldn't take us back and forth.

My dad wanted us to go to school, he didn't want us to be like he was. I often thought about him, he was a pretty smart guy you know. He could figure out how many tons there were in the hay and the wheat, how many bushels there were. He used to grow grain and he used to grow hay, and he had a few head of cattle. We talked our language but when we got in the school we couldn't. They told us we couldn't talk our language. We used to hide and talk with those Penticton Indians. You see they talk our language. But we used to never let the nuns and priests hear us talk Indian.

Mary Anderson

I remember my parents drove us up to the corner of Highway 97 on Westside Road and a truck came to pick us up. It wasn't just us, there were other children from the Reserve. It was a pick up point and we were taken away in a big truck. It was a flatbed truck with rails around it, like the kind you carry cattle in. It was a big truck and they had already picked up other children so I don't know where their starting point was. They continued to pick up more children along the way, through Tappen and Salmon Arm and through various points like Enderby, Chase and Squilax. I don't remember exactly where, but they picked up others and took us all to Kamloops. It was a long trip.

The year was 1948 and I was six years old. We rode all bunched up sitting on wooden benches. It was a long, tedious, and tiring journey for a six-year-old. I remember one time it rained and we were wet. There were no rest stops. I don't remember my brother Percy being there, but I do recall whispering, "That's my brother over there." It was strange not being able to talk to him.

I didn't know we were going to be gone for ten months and I felt like I was abandoned; it felt like my mother and father left us and we would never see them again. When we arrived, I was disoriented and tired. There were all these strange people and they all were wearing black. That seemed strange. I had no idea at all what to expect. We were taken to the recreation centre and then had a bite to eat. That night they showed us our bed, and the things that were assigned to us for our use.

There was the odd kid that cried at night. I do remember the nun had a little room off to the side and she'd holler to be quiet. No one ever really seemed to listen or no one ever seemed to get any comfort. No one got any comfort of any kind.

I had my hair cut off the first day of school. I don't know why they cut my hair, but they did. I think they cut everybody's hair. You couldn't curl your hair, I remember some of the girls used to get those cocoa tins and they'd cut strips and they'd roll their hair in it to curl it. The nuns would take them and dunk their head under the cold water tap to straighten their hair.

Another thing, I never had a hot bath there once that I remember. It was always cold. Maybe because I was further down the line getting my bath or something.

Maybe some of the rooms had showers but what I remember was the old fashioned tub, that tall one and the older girls were supposed to help us with our bath. There I was sitting in this tub of cold water almost up to my neck, then she'd dump all this water on my head and it was down right freezing. Then we got out of there, got dressed and went into the rec room. They combed our hair with those lice combs and put coal oil into our hair. This happened every Saturday. They did everybody. I don't know if or how they cleaned the combs but God if anybody had lice and they run it through your hair you'd get it too. It was a good way to spread it. It was terrible, always dripping this coal oil on you.

My sister and I were separated and assigned different rooms. Naturally, they started us going to church right away. Everybody was in the same boat as we were. I remember my first trip to church, I'm sitting, I'm kneeling, it was in the evening. I was kneeling and when you're young like that you're used to going to bed early. I'm kneeling there and I fell asleep. The next thing I knew I was picked up by the ear and drug into the middle of the aisle of the church and I had to stand there for the rest of the service. Another time I remember, I don't know what little thing I did, but they sure didn't like it. I ended up with a chop to the side of my ear. You know this nun came over there and gave me this chop to the side of my ear for something, and I don't know what it was for.

Ten months is a long time to be separated from your folks. They came to visit us at Easter. I can't remember if we came home for Christmas or not, but Gerry said that we didn't. I don't remember a thing about spending Christmas at the school. It seemed like we were always praying.

I remember corn flakes for Easter and I think there was an egg or two or a jellybean for a treat. I don't remember any Christmas dinner. I don't know what we had for bread and butter because our niece Rose would take her bread and keep rolling the butter into her bread until she couldn't see it before she could eat it. It was bad, I remember I couldn't keep anything down. The butter was rancid, everything was horrible. We got this white fish soup, and to this day I cannot eat fish. The meat was fat, tough and gristly. I had to swallow the whole thing, fat and all. The milk was always sour or made into burnt hot chocolate. To this day I don't drink milk. I use it in cooking but I will not drink it. I think this has a lot to do with the spoiled, sour, and burnt milk from boarding school.

We never got sugar. There was this friend that lived up the road a ways and her mother used to send her about a five or ten pound bag of sugar. One day she was going to give me a little treat, so she scooped into her bag and gave me a handful of sugar to lick. She liked her sugar, so her mother would send her a bag of sugar.

Snack time was really something. I used to really wonder when it was snack time and you had to fight for your food. You'd be standing there and all of a sudden they'd be throwing crabapples out there and everybody was trying to catch these crabapples and if you didn't, you were just plain out of luck; if it wasn't crabapples, it was other apples. They'd be throwing them out there and everyone was just a scrambling away, just about trampling each other to get themselves a little bite to eat. That was our snack, if you got it. I had a hole in my coat and I thought I was putting these apples in my coat pocket and I guess they were all falling out. That was real disappointing because I went to sit down somewhere to have a bite and I didn't have one, after all that I thought I managed to get. That was not a very good day.

I remember our parents sending us a dollar each. The nuns would take it and they would enter it in a book. They'd call out your name if you had money and you'd go up and they had these penny candies or whatever they had there. You got to spend how much you wanted. You got yourself a few little treats, I think it was every Sunday they did that. You'd spend up until your money was gone and then you were out of luck.

It was funny, they didn't seem to punish people for some things and some things they did. I remember we were all in the rec room and I was standing looking out the window. There was this girl, I don't know why in the heck they even let her keep this kerchief she had. She was running around choking people. She passed me out, she thought it was a great joke. It was a wonder she didn't kill someone. She came from behind me, wrapped this kerchief around my neck and pulled until I blacked out and hit the floor. The next thing I hear is, "Oh she's starting to move, she's going to be okay." As far as I know they never did a darn thing to that girl.

I remember the concerts. A lot of the time they would kick us out. Oh, you'd just freeze your hands and stuff. I remember being kicked out on a Saturday after getting my hair washed and oiled and my hair was still wet, my hair froze on the ends you know. But they kicked you out and I'd see some young girls out there without a coat on because they didn't get their coats. They were kicked out anyway. It was not very good. It's a wonder some didn't get pneumonia, especially getting kicked outside with wet hair.

I remember those nuns, I guess there was a war breaking out because they were saying that the Japanese or Chinese were going to come over and torture us. That they would stick things under our fingernails, they'd do this and they'd do that to us. When you're tiny and you're hearing all this, I was thinking where could I hide, where could I hide, could I hide in my locker? Maybe they'd find me. I just didn't know what I was going to do. But oh, they had us all in the rec room telling us all these scary things that could happen. What were we supposed to do? I figured we were all going to die, because of all the stuff they were telling us at the time. Oh, it sure frightened me. I didn't know where I could possibly hide where they would not find me and do all those things to me.

Geraldine Schroeder

We all went to the residential school together, me, my brother Percy and my sister Mary. We went in 1948 and came out in 1950. I don't think we really realized what we were really getting ourselves into once we were loaded in the truck. All of a sudden we came to this big recreation area. I didn't know I was going to be left there for ten months. The nuns and brothers were all dressed in black. Nobody explained nothing. At night they showed us the bed, and everything on top of the bed. Mary was put in another room and I hardly recall seeing her. It seemed really strange because when I saw my brother, even though I never had anything to say to this little girl beside me, I whispered, "There's my brother over there." It seemed strange not being able to talk to him, never seeing him or just seeing him from a distance, he was eleven months older than me. I knew he was there, it was just like there was a border and I was on one side. They kept us separated.

I remember my sister, Mary, getting her braids cut off the first day of school. Couldn't wear makeup, otherwise you'd get a bar of soap. On Saturday we would wash our hair and put coal oil on our head. It would even be down my neck. No wonder I took up hair dressing.

I was confused. All of a sudden, just like night and day, there was nobody to talk to. Once I was talking to somebody down at the church, somebody grabbed me and pulled me right to the back. I got hauled out into the hallway and a nun gave me the strap. I moved my hand and she grabbed my wrist and gave me the strap. I still don't know what that was about.

There was too much religion. I still feel today that I'm not that good a reader. I felt I was illiterate. I didn't feel like I learned.

I didn't ever tell my parents what was going on. My mom went to the same school as us, so we're second generation. She doesn't talk about it. She won't talk. I don't think my parents had a choice in sending us to residential school. The government had a lot to do with it. My dad was on the Indian Inquiry Committee. He traveled all over Canada. He worked at getting the day school built beside our house. But even then we never got much from there either. One big room, Grades One to Six, how could the teacher teach in that situation?

We were at the residential school during Christmas. At Easter time our folks came and took us out. I don't remember much. We had High Mass and something special. The Bishop came at Christmas and at Easter. At Easter we wore red and white, white blouse and a red skirt. The only time we got corn flakes was at Easter, along with three jelly beans. That was supposed to be a treat.

I was sick from the time I got there to the time I left. I didn't care for the food at all. If the milk wasn't sour, it was burnt. They'd make hot chocolate and I guess they tried to boil a big pot of milk and burnt it. So it was burnt chocolate and sour milk. And this mush that we had to eat sometimes had big lumps in it and we were supposed to eat that. If we didn't eat it we had to sit there until we did. The butter was rancid and everything was horrible. I had to adapt to losing a lot of my teeth because of the beans. They would have young kids clean the beans and there was little rocks in them. You know how you're eating and all of a sudden you'd bite down on a rock and it would crack a tooth.

I ended up losing a lot of my teeth. By the time I was eighteen I ended up having to pull what few teeth I had left. They pulled me off the bench one day and I happened to be sitting where someone else was supposed to be sitting to get their teeth fixed, so I ended up getting hauled off to the dentist. They pulled my teeth and filled them and all kinds of stuff. I thought I would be careful not to sit there again. That was one visit I did not count on.

The food sure left a lot to be desired. Sometimes there were one-dimensional meals, like a soup bowl full of mushy crabapples. That was it or some big old lumpy hunk of gristly thing, called "meat" and something dunked in your bowl. I've become anorexic. Even after I got married I still couldn't eat food and keep it down.

Snack time happened once in a blue moon. It was a treat if you got it. They threw it out to you. You had to catch it and everyone fought for it. You were supposed to catch it, I can still see the crowd.

You could buy treats until your money was gone. Then you were out of luck. So I stole it, I stole cookies from one of the lockers next to me. I saw this big parcel come in, so I went and helped myself and nobody was around so I climbed up there and got them. I got caught in the act. I wasn't punished, I just had to take the darn cookies back.

Every morning you had to open your mouth and they would come along with this big can of castor oil (possibly cod liver oil). They would shove it in your mouth. I went and spit it out but got another dose of it. I think it was only in the winter months.

Everybody followed one another, when you went to church or you went to breakfast, dinner, supper or you hauled yourself up to the dormitory, always following the line ups.

We had fire practice at two o'clock in the morning, all the bells went off. Come out just the way you were, out of bed in your nightgown. Bells whistling in that whole building, girls were on one side and boys were on the other. The nuns were scaring us. They told us the Japanese or Chinese were going to get us, the bomb was going to get us. We were so scared, huddled in a corner and these nuns were telling us this. No one paid attention if you cried, it was, "She's just a cry baby."

What did I do to cope? What could you do? You just did what you were supposed to doWhat I think would be important to tell people about my experience in residential school is to stay away from it, never to see it again, in the year 2000, I hope we never have to see this again!

Anonymous

Before I went to the residential school, I lived at home with my mother on the Deadman's Creek Indian Reserve. It's not that I lacked anything at home when I came to the residence, it was by choice. I wasn't forced to come, I chose to come because there was too much drinking at home and I just wanted to be away from it because I enjoyed school.

My brothers were already at the residential school and I wanted to be close to them, so I asked my mom if I could go. The year 1972/73 is when I first went. My first day there I was really nervous. I was scared because I wasn't going to know anybody other than my brother. But my brother wouldn't be in the same part of the building with me. My Uncle Harvey, my Auntie Elsie and my Mom brought me.

I got to know a few of the girls right off because I was fair. I had light hair and a lot of the other students had dark hair, darker complexion and they looked down on me. There are a few other girls like Ida John and Carmen Gottfriedson, who were fair and we got picked on, so we ended up being friends. One thing, though, we wouldn't let them push us around because we knew we were Native. We had just as much right to be there as they did.

I ended up being friends with most of them towards the end, because I just wouldn't fall into their little trap. Go ahead call me names. It doesn't bother me. I'll just ignore you and that's the way I was. I got pushed into a fight once and I'm a person that doesn't like to fight but I'll fight if I have to. And after that little incident, all of us girls got along because they realized that I wasn't going to take it anymore.

We got paid for kitchen work and for working with the junior boys. We used to switch on and off, I would work maybe a month with the junior boys and the next month go to kitchen and just switch off with Shirley. If we needed two workers, the two of us worked with the junior boys and two in the kitchen.

Working with the junior boys with Irene Deneault was awesome. You had your bed wetters, but we weren't there to heckle the kids or anything, you know. Because, obviously, they're new, they're scared, just like anybody else. I'm a person that always liked working with little kids. I'd go there and do my job, strip all their beds and if it was a nice day out we would throw their mattresses out on the stairwells to dry out and air out. And then help them get their clothes together to dress. We'd take all their laundry to the laundry room.

We had church seven days a week. Father Noonan told us something one morning at mass. He said that, "I'm having a lot of complaints about students that don't want to partake in mass everyday. If you can bring me in a note from your parent stating you don't have to come to mass daily and Sundays, you only come when you choose to, it will happen." That weekend I and Eddy went home. We were the first two kids back with notes. No more church for us! The odd Sunday I would go, you know, because I had a choice.

The first year, I know Father Noonan was still there as principal. Nathan Matthew was being trained to take over and the whole thing was changing, like the whole era of the bad into the good I guess. The way I looked at it, the food changed big time, what you wore changed big time. That choice was yours, you could either wear jeans or you could wear dresses. My first year when we had to wear dresses, it didn't matter. I always threw a pair of pants in my gym bag and took it to school anyways.

The first day I came in jeans, t-shirt, sneakers and just a light jacket because it was nice out. I get there and within the first few weeks they kind of let you go and then all of a sudden, boom. That's when everything changed and they want you to wear these dresses. There was a lot of us that got bussed out to the same public school and there was no way I was going to wear the same dress as my best buddy even if they were different colours. So it's like if I got to wear that, no problem. I threw a t-shirt and a pair of pants into my gym bag and took it to school. Everyday I carried that and not once did any one of the supervisors ever check our bags. There were a few that would wear the outfits because they didn't really have other clothes to wear.

The year my younger sister had come was the year I wasn't there, so it was really hard on her. The year that I came back, she wasn't allowed to visit me. I was now in the annex building and she was a Senior B and the supervisor seemed to always pick on her. If I and her were caught talking anywhere, Colleen got grounded. She wasn't allowed to come to the annex to see me. If I come over to see her, we could only meet in front of the main building. I was not allowed to go down to the Senior B room to look for her.

I don't understand why there should have been a difference. We were all the same, just different age groups and each supervisor did their own kind of disciplining and I didn't agree with a lot of it. I mean when Irene Deneault was in working with the junior boys, those were probably the happiest times you saw for the little guys. But when you'd have Mr. Johnny Jack there, their whole attitude, everything changed. I was just a kid then and I could see that, their bed wetting routine would change. It would be increased when they would have Mr. Jack, and when it was Mrs. Deneault it would decrease. Even their whole personality changed. You know, like maybe, just happy, and bubbly, and then the following week it's a whole different child you know, quiet.

With the change in the administration, things were changing. From porridge, it went to where we received bacon, eggs, hashbrowns, toast. Sometimes you'd have your choice of bacon, ham, or sausages. You'd have your hashbrowns or pancakes but they always had a selection out there. I always remembered the big milk jugs. They were the big silver things, they kept them full and the milk was always good. The meals, like you got a variety. You know, you got mashed potatoes with a vegetable and a meat. It may have been porkchops, beef or straight hamburger, but it was always something different. Once the whole menu started changing, everybody was prompt at getting to the dinner table.

That first year, you learned how to sit at a table. That's one thing for sure. Mrs. Leslie, she was great about it, like she'd come by and say, "Your elbows." Whereas Ann would come by, and you'd get a smuck on the elbow with a butter knife or spoon, fork. Whatever she had in her hand. Johnny was the same, he'd hit your elbow out from under you, I've seen him do that with the boys.

I wouldn't know if the Native supervisors attended the residential school. I'd be curious to know whether or not they had because, maybe the way they treated us has a lot to do on how they've been treated. Their upbringing and how they were treated does affect lives of others. Just like my upbringing would affect the lives of others. The way I was brought up, affects how my children are brought up.

One year we had the Kamloops Chiefs come over and we all buddied up with each hockey player. The hockey players just said, "Okay you're my buddy, you're my buddy," sort of thing. Each one of us had beaded headbands on the loom. I did a headband and a medallion. The hockey team went to play one of their games. They had invited us all over, all the Senior A and B girls and boys and the supervisors, to watch the game. All the ones that beaded them something, went down to the ice to present it to them. Every one of them wore it for their game.

We started planning for a year end trip. We planned fund raising events. We did car washes. There was a Robo station in town we used to work with. When we would put up car washes, we might do three in a month. The first two, all the profits went to us, and the other month went to them. It was just totally awesome, because from the first one, to the very last car wash we did, we'd built our clientele. We had our regulars, it was really good, because people would make you feel good. They would come along and say, "Oh you did such a nice job last time, I had to come again," and you know, they were more generous. We also did bottle drives, bake sales and we did a slave sale.

We went across Canada for our year-end trip. Our goal was to raise somewhere between four and five thousand dollars. The students earned their own spending money. We took a bus from Kamloops to Calgary. From Calgary we got on a plane and our first stop, I believe, was Toronto. We stayed over there I think seven hours, from there we went to Montreal, Quebec. From the Montreal Airport we got bussed to La Touque, Quebec and we stayed at a residential school. We were there for five days. They were lucky because they all knew their own language, so they could speak English plus their own language.

There were a lot of them that knew three languages. I'd say multi-talented because I understand some of mine but I don't know it. At La Touque the kids' food there, the only thing that was good was the milk. I lost weight when we stayed there because I refused to eat it. Our supervisor spoiled us, he used to take us out or they'd buy us lunch stuff and we'd get together and just make sandwiches. After that when we got back to the Indian School, we sure didn't complain about the food.

We went from Quebec into Ottawa. In Ottawa we went to two different museums there and we also went to the Parliament Buildings. We spent the whole day there and we even had lunch with Len Marchand. We even sat in their big Council room where they have their big meetings. We sat there with little headphones on so that we could hear everybody way down below talking. We went to the Tulip Festival in Ottawa, just a half a block from the Parliament Buildings.

I played snare drum in the band. I think it's because I caught on to how to roll the sticks and do the drum rolls that the teacher was requesting instead of just the plain old drum beat. The next time I went back my interest was the glockenspiel. It's like a xylophone, but you hold it. It stands up right and so I learned how to play that and we'd go on different band trips. One of the trips we took was to Port Alberni. I remember that one because we traveled to Port Alberni, down to Campbell River and we went right down to the ocean. There was a bunch of different residential school bands that got together. It was more or less where all different bands got together and they would go in these different parades and stuff.

I remember being in that winter festival one in Vernon. The girls had dark skirts, red blazers, we had white blouses, white gloves and we had nylons on and white boots. These white boots weren't winter boots. They were just fancy band type boots and then you had white hats. And you paraded from one end of Vernon to the other on one of their main streets and just froze. It was very cold out and they didn't have time to whip up pants for all the girls. Because all the girls didn't have pants, we didn't want to have our drum group looking off beat. We all chose to wear the dresses and freeze our asses off together. It was a group decision I guess. Even Mr. Gonne just wore his dress pants and his white shirt and his red blazer and conducted with his white gloves. He was a totally awesome guy as a teacher he had patience. When he'd line up these trips, he always got us such a cool bus driver. This bus driver we had, we knew him as Bunny and that's what his name was, he was the kind of bus driver who would say, "You're going on a trip, you're not just going to listen to your walkman or read a book, we're going to have a sing along, we're going to tell jokes, we're going to have fun."

There was bands from the different residential schools. There would have been, Lytton, Mission, I guess Port Alberni, Campbell River. They had a band in there but it wasn't Native, like, there was a mixture. It wasn't just all Native. After we'd all gotten together the first night and everybody was having their band play off there. One of the songs that all the bands chose to do together and to get in on was "Amazing Grace." It was really cool because we even had the bagpipes, from another school. I think it was probably Williams Lake (St. Joseph's Mission). It was just so beautiful. I love the bag pipes anyways. There was times that the kids at the spur of the moment decided, let's see if we could get the bus and go to this high school dance or something. Sometimes the dance might be at Valleyview Junior High. We used to talk about it, "okay." Couple of us would run and we always seemed to go talk to Brother Heysel, because he was the one that would arrange for either the bus or the van. And if it were the van, he'd make two trips over and two trips back. Like there were some of the supervisors who went out of their way to help you.

I loved my sports, I loved getting into different activities. I didn't like to be just there and do nothing. I filled my weekends there too, because I'd rather stay there rather than to come home, because there was the drinking and that, going on at home. So I just stayed at the Indian school. It was by choice.

There was that prejudice in the school. I got along with everybody. You know we gotta live together. I've got white in me so I can't hate them. It wasn't my choice, but I still can't dislike somebody because of the color of their skin. It just blew me away. I remember being in a princess pageant when I was at the residential school. I ended up being first runner up or something. I was next to the girl that won and one of the speeches I gave was on prejudice. It was happening in school then. You know, I just told them that people are judging people and not getting to know them. You're taking a look at their clothes and saying they're not well dressed. Get to know them first.

The residential school had a great impact on my life. A lot of the choices I made had nothing to do with the school. I didn't finish my education so I don't blame them. I think if they had of stayed open and by choice, I would have remained there and finished my education. I left the school, and I ended up being pregnant. I had my first child when I was seventeen, so I was really young.

We all ended up being pregnant young. That's one thing I try to help the younger kids understand. I use myself as an example, "You don't want to end up like me, home, stuck with the children." I say, "Go out and enjoy your teenage years, you know, have fun."

I think the Indian school had a good impact on me. I just wish they'd have stayed open. I think it would have helped a lot of the Native kids that are being troubled, like being put out into foster homes. And a lot of our supervisors were being more culturally aware. With the nuns I could understand with my Mom's era that they lost a lot. I think if they'd kept the residential schools open, we'd maybe have been able to help start reviving our culture, through our language, our different activities. Whether it's a game, or a learning process of tanning hides, or preparing food or something. I think it could have really helped in the long run.

I think I've benefited big time from the Indian school, because, through working in the kitchen, I got to learn how to cook and clean and be able to have everything sterilized, they had their dishwasher, so everything's sterilized. Those big steam cleaners. And working in the laundry room, you're learning how to load the washer and the dryers, plus you're using their ironing boards because they had the big press machines. Being taught your manners at the table. Well even right down to fixing your bed properly, everything had to be done just right.

When you hear of all the different ones that have gone out and actually went through the healing from being there, that really makes me feel good to know that, the ones that hurt have dealt with it. I got a girlfriend that's been hurt and really hasn't dealt with it. Right to this day, I and her talk and I say to her, "Go get some help. Not just for yourself or for your kids but for your grandchildren."

This photo was taken in the earlier years of the red brick building. It is also one of the rare informal group photographs of both boys and girls mixed together. It could have been taken during play time as the children are not all dressed alike and they seemed quite happy.

Boys getting ready for bed. They were usually 30 to 50 boys in each dormatory. They showered in large groups which meant no privacy.

Resistance

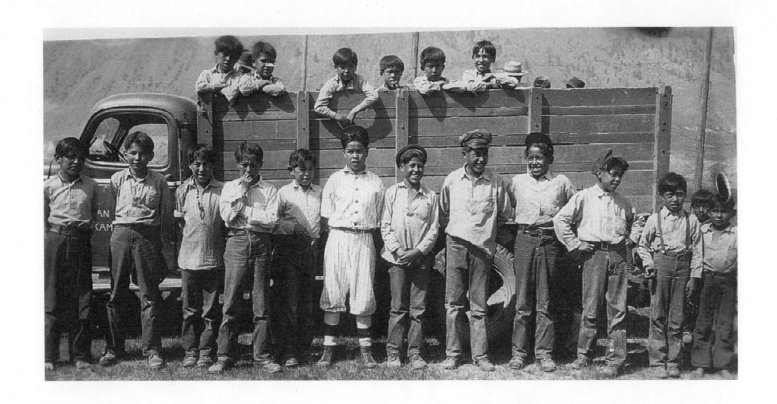

"After the summer was gone, a
huge truck pulled up with a
bunch of school girls standing up
in the back. I was put on the
truck. I guess I was afraid, I
don't know. You know you're put
on the truck and you don't know
what's going on and I don't know
where my mother and dad were
and everything was just sort of
blank."

Anonymous

Me and my brother Marvin were playing outside and this lady, I still see her to this day, she had a white shirt on and one of those plaid skirts, black and white and red and all that, and black shoes. I remember Marvin and I, we were having fun, we were playing in a field. And that nurse, I think she was a nurse, I don't know who she was, she came. I saw a car come into the yard, but I didn't think nothing of it and my mom called us. Marvin and I went running over there and she just said, "Get in the back of the car," so me and Marvin got in the back of the car. They drove us into town to where the post office is upstairs, is where we went. I don't know what they were doing, me and Marvin were just sitting out in the hallway.

When this lady and my grandmother, Margaret Camille, came out, Marvin just grabbed me and I just grabbed him, because we heard them saying that Marvin had to go to Tranquille and I was going the other way. When Marvin grabbed onto me they had a hard time taking us apart. When they got us downstairs, there was two taxis down there. That lady in a red dress went with Marvin and my mom came with me. I didn't know where I was going but I knew I wasn't going to see Marvin again. I didn't know Marvin was handicapped.

When they took him away they brought me to the residential school. I didn't know where I was going. I didn't understand what was going on and I kept asking my mom, what she was doing. Then, when we got to that building over at the residential school, the front building, and they walked us in, and she just said, "You have to go," she wouldn't look at me. She just looked straight ahead and said, "You have to go. And your brother has to go." And then, when we got to the residential school, I didn't understand, I didn't understand. And then the nuns came and I looked at my mom and she just kept telling me, "You have to go."

I didn't know where I was going. I remembered going downstairs and saw all these girls, lots of girls. Then they brought me in this one room and I had really long hair, my hair was really long. And that lady, it was a nun, she said we all had to have a shower. Well they were filling a tub up for me I guess and they were telling me how much I stink. Then they grabbed my hair and they told me to sit on a stool. So I sat on it and then they started cutting my hair and I didn't know what was going on. I just kept looking at my hair falling on the floor. I just kept saying, "I wonder why they're doing this, I wonder what's happening." I was really scared, I didn't know why they were cutting my hair, I didn't, I was really embarrassed, because they said that I stink. They took me in where the bathroom was. That lady bathed me, and they told me my number was 13. That's when they gave me my number and my clothes. It was their clothes and we all had numbers.

I didn't know what to do. I was really confused, I didn't know where my mom was and I just remembered we had to go to bed right away. And we were praying, everybody had to kneel down and pray. I never did that before.

I didn't kneel down because I didn't know what they were doing. Those nuns came over and told me I had to kneel down. She says, "You watch the girls. Whatever they do, you do." But I still didn't know why I was there, no one gave me a reason. No one told me.

I just wanted to go home and be with the horses and be with my dad and my brother again at that time, but they put me in Grade One. And I was in there for two years in Grade One, because I didn't understand. They always got mad at me because I didn't understand the English language. I didn't understand what they were saying to me and I had a hard time with that.

I just kept quiet, because I heard somebody, one of the girls maybe it was, say if you don't understand just keep quiet. I just kept quiet all the time while I was there, until they taught me to speak English. My friends helped me out a lot. Just directions, I didn't understand. If I didn't understand what they were saying and my friends would help me. They were just little, too. I don't know how we connected, we just did.

They'd just tell me ahead of time what was going to happen, they helped me with say 'yes' 'no' and they'd help me with words. What we had to learn in class I had a hard time with it. That's what they would help me with. They helped me with *Dick* or *See Dick* or whatever that book was. But that was in Grade One and I failed it, and Pauline and them ended up in another class and then I just ended up having to try harder on my own.

I met this big tall guy, I guess I was a loner there or something. I don't know what I was doing. There was a big laundry room downstairs. I was playing and I was in the hallway, I don't know what the heck I was doing in the hallway. And he came along and he said, "Come here" and I just thought "oh okay", so I followed him. When I got in the laundry room he picked me up, and put me on those things where you fold clothes. I didn't know what was going on. I don't know, my mind was blank and I don't know if I was scared or numb. I just don't have any feelings, nothings inside, and he laid me on that table and he started touching me all over and taking my clothes off. I didn't know what was going on and then he told me I wasn't allowed to tell nobody. That continued for a long time.

My girlfriend saw him call me. I don't know why I always went, I really don't because I didn't have to but I did. And then I went to a supervisor, I forgot her name, and I told her what was happening and so we went upstairs to talk to Father. They told me to go in a waiting room and I went in there and they called me back. They told me that he was working at the residential school for a long long time and that I had to keep quiet. I wasn't allowed to talk about it anymore. They told me, "You're not allowed to say anything to anybody or to your friends what has happened," and they said they'd talk to him. And I said, "Okay." I think it was two months down the road, it started all over again and he told me I got him in trouble and so he says, "Nobody will ever know because you're not allowed to say nothing and even if you do, there's nothing anybody can do." And I didn't know what to do, I was really scared.

I remember wanting to tell somebody, but I didn't know who I could tell that would help me. Then all of us girls got together, ten of us, and we all said we'd never leave each other. We made a plan that all ten of us would stick together and not leave each other anymore. If we hung out together no one would bother us, so that's what we did, because none of us were allowed to speak. All of us hung out together, ten of us, we'd always stay in a group, we'd never leave each other. We took care of each other and when he came along there was lots of us. He'd just walk the other way because there was too many us girls, we were always together. We'd all look at him, we'd all say, "Here he comes," and we'd all look and then he'd just continue on going. He didn't know what to do. He just went down in the laundry room with none of us. We all stuck together.

We started protecting each other, helping each other out. I felt really good, we ended up being friends all of us. We still keep in touch, and whenever we see each other in Kamloops, or wherever, we do stop and say hello. Then in the seniors, two of us girls there, I don't know why it happened because I was right in the middle of the dorm where I thought it would be the safest, to be in the middle. But so was my girlfriend, she was right next to me. I don't know where this guy came from, I don't even know. We were sleeping and the next thing I woke up because somebody was touching me and then there was a guy there and again I was told I was a liar. But, my girlfriend next to me saw him, he was trying to slip into bed with me. I was just cold, I didn't want to move. Then my girlfriend next to me said, "What are you doing?" and that guy just jumped out of bed and ran out the door. Then we went to get the supervisor and she just told us to go back to bed. I think it was couple weeks later, I woke up in the middle of the night and I saw him over beside my girlfriend and he was in bed with her. I slowly got up and I ran to our supervisor's door. She came out as he was running out the door. They just about caught him. Then she apologized because she said she thought I was lying the first time. I don't know if they ever caught the guy.

All our beds were lined up and every night we go to bed we'd have to kneel beside our bed and pray, every night pray, pray, that's all we did. They'd make sure we knelt down. It got to the point, I don't know what they did but, the next thing I know we were allowed to lay in bed and pray and all of us took turns saying the rosary.

But we weren't safe. I don't know why it was us he picked because I didn't know who he was, I never seen him before. My girlfriend wondered too, because we talked about it. She asked me what happened to me, what he did to me and I just told her. Then she didn't want to talk about what he did to her. I said we were right in the middle of the room. When he ran out the door he had to go down four beds and then turn, and four beds up to get out the door because our beds were all like connected in rows, and they were white beds. All the beds were white.

After that when the supervisor came out he never did come back again. It felt good that somebody believed. I guess there was nothing they could do with him, I don't know why. But I guess he was with most of us, only the seniors that I remember. I got to know him through intermediates and I guess it was happening then, but we didn't know it was happening. I don't even know how me and my friends came to talk about it, but we just all said no one believes us, like he's allowed to stay there. So we all just said every time we see him we'll just all look at him and what can he do? We didn't know if there was other girls out there he harmed, that's what was scary. After that all of us would keep an eye on him and we went by twos after that, none of us would ever be alone. That was our plan.

I don't even know how that happened. I think one of the girls was just crying and we went over there and his name came up. Then we asked each other did you guys tell Father, we all said, "Yes," we all had the same answer that we're not allowed to talk about it. We're not allowed to let anybody else know. We all realized that this one girl was really messed up and she couldn't do nothing about it, she was like us, she just came in, I think she was just a new girl. I don't know why he picked her right out of the crowd right away. She was really crying and so, the supervisors wouldn't come over and talk to her, so we all just went and sat with her. Then she told us what happened. We were all quiet for a while, and then we all just said it happened to us too. But, why did he pick you right away. The plan just came out of nowhere. We all just said none of us should be alone anymore. The plan was if anything happens we are all to be together and if he bothered any of us we'd all go and support the girl. We'd all come in together and what can he do.

We warned the other girls when they see him, don't go, we told them just let one of us know. We hung in there with each other. In the end it worked, but in the beginning it was real scary. But, I guess all of us were going through it and I didn't know, I thought I was the only one.

We never did talk about the boys, because we never did see them. We weren't allowed to talk to them or we'd get punished for going or waving at them or whatever. Well I don't think we got punished. We were just told we weren't allowed to talk to any of the boys. My girlfriends were crazier than me, because I listened. Yeah, they'd sneak over, but I wouldn't. I'd stay away from them.

When I first went to the residential school, I accepted it. But, when I first went into the dining room, there was boys there and I was really surprised. Boys on one side and girls on one side and I'm thinking, I seen my cousin in there and I said, "Oh I want to go sit with him." I was telling, I don't know who it was, behind me, "I want to go sit with my cousin. I haven't seen him in a long time." She said, "You're not allowed over there." I said, "No way." I wanted to go sit with him and I guess it was in him too, not to talk to me. I put my tray down and I went walking over towards him, to say 'hello' he just kind of avoided me. So I just went back and ate and I was wondering 'Why is he doing that?'

I used to run away from there, I ran away three times, me and my girlfriend. We were trying to go home. I think the second time I made it home and then that nurse came again and took us. But, the first time we ended up way up in the mountains, I don't know, just where Sahali is. We thought we were going. We ended up way up there. It's a wonder anybody found us.

The cops found us and they took us back. We were cold. The cops got us back to the residential school. All I remember is the two of us back in our beds with about ten blankets on us. I guess we almost died or something. They didn't find us until really late at night and it was snowing and we were way up in the mountains trying to go home. We'd see a light and we'd say we're getting home. But, I guess we were coming back this way or something I don't know. Then the cops got us and took us back to the residential school. I didn't like it, I knew they were going to bring us back. We both didn't want to go back.

But, the second time they kicked her out. That was weird I didn't understand why they wouldn't kick me out. They brought us to the office and they gave us the strap. Even the first time they gave us the strap and they told her, "One more time you run away, you're out of here." It didn't bother me that we were getting the strap, I wasn't scared. The second time they strapped me, then they told my girlfriend to get her bags packed because she was going home and I wanted to go home. And they said, "No you're not allowed to go home."

The third time I ran away and I don't know who I ran away with. They got kicked out and I still ended up there. They wouldn't let me go and I didn't understand why.

What has the residential school done to me? I hate hugs to this day. I hate hugs because no one hugged us when we were there. There was no affection at all so I didn't understand affection, I still don't. When I had my four kids, I never gave them hugs and I never told them I loved them. I never told them anything. It feels unnatural, because I was never hugged and never kissed or never cuddled or anything like that. We weren't allowed to comfort no one. If we seen somebody crying we had to stay away from there. We'd stand in a corner or kneel in a corner or we just weren't allowed to touch each other. And we were never allowed to talk to the boys because it was bad to talk to boys.

I don't even know how to hug my kids. They come and hug me sometimes and I hug them, but then I just step right away, because I don't know. I want to work on it but I don't know how. Even my grandchildren, I have four grandchildren now and I just have a hard time with it. I mean I want to give them more, but I just can't, I don't know how. It is just like bringing my kids up, I brought them up the same way I was brought up in the residential school. They had to kneel in a corner, they had to stand in a corner. If they didn't finish their food they had to go stand in a corner or kneel in a corner or do their chores. I brought them up the same way I was brought up at the residential school. And I just don't know how to give affection. I'm mostly on the go all the time. When somebody gets too close to me, I run. I am too scared to be in a relationship because I can't give them what they want.

I enjoy helping people. The people I helped last week were from the streets. I had them all in the car and I had to ask them a bunch of questions. Like why they're on the streets, right, because I was on the street, then I pulled out. I asked one guy, "Why are you here?" Like he has to have a bottle every day and I said, "Why?" And then he told me that all of them that were in my car the three men, and they were all in the residential school. One was down from Prince George, the other from Saskatoon and one was from here. They told me they were brought up in the residential school and they said if you were brought up there you'd know what we're going through and I just laughed at them. I said, "I do know what you're going through, because I was there." I said, "You can change," and they just laughed at me. And they told me their story and it got me sick. They were sexually abused at the residential school and we were all sexually abused. It was awful stories they all told me, but I

65

said, "I guess I asked for it," because I asked them questions, so I thought I better listen. But, I kind of blocked them out a little bit. One of them said they're going to try to sober up, because I told him you can change, I told them that if you put the bottle down you can change your life.

I don't know why we were ever sent there. I had a good home, I was free and I was happy and I was connected with my family and it was mostly Elders I remember, back then. I still don't know why I had to go to the residential school. I don't know why because all my other friends from the Reserve that I know of, they didn't go. And I was there right from when I was six until I was fifteen. I guess all of us that were in the residential school, we just get used to it, get used to everything there. We never starved but we had to drink spoiled milk.

I don't know why I won't tell my kids about it. Like, I see the way I brought them up. I keep looking at them every day and I keep seeing the effect that I have on them and they don't understand why. It's really clear, I see it and it's hard and I do have feelings, but I won't show it. I do have a lot of feelings but I have a hard time crying. I feel embarrassed because when we cried at the residential school we were told "why are you crying", like who cares, you keep it in, because nobody cares here.

The residential school took my culture language and my freedom. I know my language and culture and I am still scared to use it to this day. It hurts deep inside. I am willing to take it a day at a time. I know I can do it as I still have my dad to teach me and my boyfriend Chuck Louie.

Cedric Duncan

I remember when I was at home in Canoe Creek we used to go out fishing and hunting. My mom and them would go out picking berries and they would take us along and we would just play around until they're finished doing their berry picking.

We used to do a lot of horse riding and go on wagon rides. Mom and Dad had a team and wagon. They used to take us out on wagon rides and they'd camp out for awhile. And go to places where they could catch trout and stuff, then down to the Fraser and camp down there and go fishing there.

I started school out there in Canoe Creek, then I came down to Kamloops after that. Some people came out there and they brought us down here. We were just playing around outside and they came along and we got called back to our house and we got picked up and hauled away from there down to here. There must have been about eight or ten of us. Like some of the Sargent boys and Evelyn, Thelma, Patsy, my three sisters were down here, but they weren't down here that long and they all got taken home. I was the youngest out of the whole works. I was wondering where they were taking us and I thought they were going to just take us back home. I thought they were just taking us down here for some sort of trip and then we ended up staying down here. They just didn't say nothing to us. They just drove their car down here and gave us a ride down here and that was it, they never even stopped or nothing, just dropped us off and left us here. After they hauled us down here, we were asking those people that were bringing us down here where they were taking us and they were saying they were taking us to a better place to learn. I was by myself and the other boys that came down with me were in a different place. Taking us away from home.

There was some kids playing around outside and some inside. It was really strange to me because it was the first time away and it was first time at something like this and I was just wondering what it was going to be like. Then after some of them younger kids started wanting to fight and stuff like that because I was a different person.

I always got along with everybody back home. They told us where all our clothes were and we had to pick out some clothes. They never let us bring any clothes from home when we left, more or less just got us in a car and drove us away. I remember getting here. It seemed strange for a while because we didn't know anybody around here. We were too young to really know anyone. I was just wondering what they were doing to us when they brought us down here, how long we were going to be here.

I was treated sort of mean I guess. They didn't know who I was and the ones that knew each other they sort of ganged up on one person like me. A lot of them had younger brothers in here and stuff like that. But, I was just by myself. I could remember my sisters being down here for a little while but they all went home and I was down here by myself. A lot of times I wished I could just write back home and ask for money from my folks when they used to have the goodie store open for buying snacks and pop and all that. I didn't have money and the other kids used to have money and I was just wishing I could get some.

It seemed like the staff kind of just ignored me and I got punished quite a bit. They had me kneeling in the corners and holding books up above my head and if the books touched my head then they'd make me lift it up and they'd add some more books on there. I got strapped a few times by the priest with a leather strap, a few times on each hand. I don't know why the priest threw me in the pool, I just about drowned in there. Then he came in and got me out of there. Because I could taste all that water going into my mouth and I was like right down in the bottom of the pool. I don't know why he threw me in there.

It seemed like we had to do a lot of work every weekend cleaning up and mopping floors and waxing floors and all that stuff. If they figured it wasn't done right we had to do it all over again. It used to take us about three hours to do it and if it wasn't done right then we'd have to do it over again, the way they wanted it. When one of us got punished they made us all sit down and be quiet too. Everybody in the whole room had to sit down. Sometimes one person got punished for whatever and I'd get punished for not doing all my school work because I needed help doing it and they wouldn't help me.

I skipped out on a few grades. It seemed they would tell me, whenever I would go to a school they would say, "Oh you look like a person that should be in this classroom." So they'd put me in that classroom and then I couldn't do the work the other kids were doing in there and the teachers would strap me in there, spank me or whatever. And then there's times when I was sick when I went to school and they didn't believe me. They thought I was just wanting to go home, missing my parents and they thought that was what it was, but I was sick and they'd still send me to school.

Yeah I did do kindergarten. Well I started some of it at home and they brought me down here. But when I was in kindergarten at home the teacher used to help me do things there. They'd sit down there beside me and help me. But here it was different. They didn't. It seemed like they would just stand over there and they would just start telling me what I should be doing, from way back. They wouldn't come close to me.

I went home a few times, but things seemed to change a lot after I started going home. I didn't really know my parents much after being down here for seven years. It seemed like they changed quite a bit. Our home was getting wrecked every time I went home, there was something wrong with our house there. Then my folks weren't staying there anymore and then pretty soon we had no house at all out there. People ripping our house down and whatever they were doing with the lumber they got out of the house, I don't know. I just didn't have a home to go back to after I got older.

Then they broke up, my mom was living by herself. Then my dad was staying with his mom, when his mom was still alive. And while I was down here, too, one of my sisters went missing. I never ever did see her again. She was about two years older than I am. It must have been September I guess, her and her boyfriend brought me back down here and that was the last time I ever saw her. We used to spend a lot of time going to church and stuff like that. They used to make sure that our shoes were all polished right and if they weren't, then we had to do them all over again. We had a tie and everything, then everybody had all the same colours, the suits were all the same colour. Seemed like they just wanted us to learn about praying and all that stuff quite a bit. They didn't really care about our schoolwork, you know and help us with that. They wanted us to go to church quite a bit. In the morning we'd get up and they'd have us kneeling down by our beds praying. At night before we go to bed we'd be doing the same.

I'm not sure if he was working here, if he was just a caretaker of the place or something. But he used to walk around the hallways. Everybody would get called in the rec room. Sometimes I would be the last one going in and he would always punch me on top of the head. It seemed like I was always hit by him every time I'd see him if I was by myself. I can remember the places he would do that to me, coming down them stairs, sometimes going up the stairs. It seemed like he would try and block me and he'd hit me on the head, I couldn't tell anybody cause I figured they wouldn't believe me if I told them. Just about every time he was around I used to be scared of him. I'd try and go by some other kids or something because I knew he was going to hit me if I went by him. It seemed like he used to always pick on me, maybe he did that to other kids but I never ever seen him doing that to anybody else. Every time he saw me by myself he used to punch me on top of the head. He would make a fist and hit me like this, right on top of the head. Make my eyes water sometimes, but I wouldn't cry when he'd hit me. It used to hurt me quite a bit.

I'd get sent into the office and they'd ask me how come I wouldn't do my work and I'd try tell them I couldn't do it. But, then they'd just look at me I guess and figure I should be in that classroom or whatever grade. I couldn't do the work that the other kids were doing. I'd get strapped for that, probably about ten or fifteen times for each hand. They sent me back to the rec room and I just had to sit in there by the TV. I wasn't allowed to do anything until I quit crying. That time it happened to me it just made me wish I could go home with my folks. I didn't want to be around there. But there was nothing I could do to get home.

I wasn't allowed to talk to my sisters too much because everybody would get into trouble if they were seen talking to girls there. In one of those playgrounds, one time I got hurt there and my sister came over and she was checking me out. She got scared to be beside me after I got hurt there. She took off, she said I better get out of here before I got in trouble. I got hurt on one of those teeter-totters. It hit me on top of the head. I was just laying on the ground crying and she came over there for a little while then she took off because she was scared to get in trouble. Nobody came over. I just quit crying on my own and then I went back. They never did nothing about it. I had a real big bump on top of my head. Those things were all iron. I tried walking around it, that's what hit me on top of the head, that little seat. When I was at home, too, my folks used to speak Shuswap to me. I learned quite a bit while

I was young. I probably could be speaking it now, but I don't. Like a lot of it I could but I couldn't say the words.

It was strange. It seemed like they just didn't want anything to do with me. It's like we were just here being in a prison or something. They were always scared that somebody was going to run away or that you were going to run away and they used to always walk around counting everybody every night. Like pretty near every hour, every couple of hours somebody would be walking by our beds every night checking us out.

I'm not sure what they ever did to anyone that ran away. I remember some people from my reserve ran away. That person was telling me, he passed away now, Larry. He was one friend that I had but he shot himself. He was from Merritt, Douglas Lake area.

I wished I could learn how to write, so I could write back to my folks back home. I was watching other kids younger than me they were writing back home. But they never helped me to learn how to write. If I would ask them, they wouldn't help me to write a letter. It seemed to take time to help a person. I don't know if they just didn't want me to learn or how come they did that. I used to wish I could write back home to my folks, I would ask my folks if they were coming down to pick me up for the holidays or something because sometimes they would tell us that we weren't going home for the holidays.

Sometimes my dad was working for the Kosters up in Canoe. One of the Kosters would come down and give me a ride back home for the holidays. It seemed different as if I didn't know my brothers and sisters. It seemed like they didn't want to be around me and it seemed like I didn't want to be around them because they were different after being down here for a long time. It seemed hard too because after I got back home I was supposed to learn quite a bit down there and like all my brothers and sisters. They didn't really know that I couldn't write or read. I never ever did talk to them about it. Ernest and all them. All the things I did was more or less on my own. Sometimes I'd be brave and ask different people to help me. Today, even my brothers and sisters don't know that I can't read and write. They all figure that I know how to read and write. They used to ask me how come I don't write this and write and I never told them that I didn't know how to read and write. Somebody else has to help me applying for work and stuff like that. Then finally I talked to Gerald about it and he's the only one that really knows, out of our family, that I couldn't read and write. He's my nephew.

I wanted to do lots of different kinds of work but I can't do it because of my lack of education. A lot of things, different things, I wouldn't mind to try but I can't read and write. Like for my fire fighting, I can get. I tried getting my fire suppression for fire fighting but I couldn't spell all the words and I couldn't get it. I managed to get on a lot of fires through the Rocky Forest Management, they helped me get on the fires. That was pretty hard telling my family that I couldn't read and write. It seems like they might just laugh at me or something.

I don't feel too happy about it because I figured they should have helped me and they shouldn't have ignored me while I was here. They made me skip all those grades: two, three, and four and they just put me into Grade Five from

Grade One, then skipping out Grade Six, then they just threw me into Grade Seven. And I didn't really learn nothing and why did they do that? They let me go through all the other grades they skipped me out on. I used to wish I could get more education from all them years I was down there. Maybe if I would have stayed home with my parents I might have got a better education. It just seemed like when I was at home the teachers were trying to help me out there, and after I came down here everything changed and it seemed like I was just being ignored, all the years I was down here.

I think they were some sort of welfare people or something. That's all they wanted to do was just bring us here and just leave us here. They didn't want to have nothing else to do with us after they got us out of their car.

Well I've been trying to find work and stay sober and stay away from drugs and all that stuff. After I felt like I was being ignored in the schools, I turned to alcohol and stuff and whatever I could find just because I didn't know how to read and write.

I got back on the bus with my brother. I told him that I didn't want to come back over here and he brought me home. He hid me away for about two weeks up at Clinton until my dad found out I was back and he came looking for me. He was asking me how come I didn't go back to school. I just told him that I didn't go back because they didn't have room for me. I didn't want to go back because of the way I was treated and I wasn't being helped in school. I wanted to stay home after that and my dad got me into a school in Clinton. That was my last year in school. I must have been in Grade Seven. They never helped me there either because they thought I was too old to be in that school. After that I just started hitchhiking around and going from place to place. I more or less started being on my own.

I done some training over at Fish Lake and I learned how to run power saws and stuff from my brother-in-law. I went through tree spacing training for twenty-six weeks with Tom Hunt. I learned about the different kinds of trees and how far apart they wanted them spaced and all that kind of stuff. I went to a treatment centre in Round Lake, but I never really talked about residitential school while I was there.

I used to want to talk about it sometimes but I didn't know who to talk to. I didn't know who to ask for help. I'm feeling a little better about it now after talking about it.

Eddy Jules

Before the residential school I remember that there were about fifteen or twenty of us living in a little two-bedroom house. The guys all slept in one room, and the girls in another. I used to live with my grandmother. Life was a lot of fun. I never got a spanking until I got older. When my grandmother wanted me to do something she just told me.

When I first started school, I went to the day school on our reserve, Deadman's Creek. I was really excited about going to school because my older brother was there. My sister and I were going to get to meet the rest of the community because there was just us and our cousins next door living up the creek. I thought our family, the Jules family, was my whole world. That was life, and then I went to school. The first day was really scary because we were downstairs in the school, and the teacher was white. I never, ever saw a white person before in my life. That was scary.

My older brother showed me where to hang my coat and what I was supposed to do. I was probably five or six years old at the time, and it was great. In Grade One I did really good, I thought anyhow, and I passed. We walked every day from my grandmother's place, about two miles from the main community. The day school on the Reserve didn't compare with the schools like Savona Elementary. I stayed at the day school for two years, and at Savona Elementary they put me back into Grade Two. I was still living with my grandmother. I was in Grade Five when I left from there. I loved it there.

I don't know why they made me go to the residential school. I was doing great. I know I had good grades in Savona School. I look back and I think the Chief was trying to get a quota for the Department of Indian Affairs. Anyway, the Chief came and told my mom and my grandmother that I had to go to the residential school, and they didn't have a say. I look back and I wonder how come all of his kids never went? The only one that went there was the eldest daughter that they adopted. The chief's wife was my aunt and he was my uncle. They had two boys who never went to the residential school. It's just not fair.

I came to the residential school in September 1969. I remember being dropped off by the Chief, and that was hard. He brought about eight of us. We were taken up to meet Father Noonan. The Chief didn't tell us that we couldn't come home for Christmas or anything like that. We had to learn all of this stuff ourselves. I really loved my grandmother, and at the time I thought I did something horribly wrong for my grandmother to ship me out of her life. I couldn't figure it out. Being here, we lost touch with the people we really loved. I knew the language when I went to school in 1969. My grandmother taught us in Shuswap, I could speak it. But the first year here was hard. I figured maybe I wasn't learning enough at home. I didn't even try speaking in Shuswap when I was here. There were other kids from other communities that spoke it really well. But they wanted me to learn the white man's ways.

The first thing they did to us when we walked in the door is they cut our hair. I had long hair, and that is why I thought I did something wrong because they took each of us into a room and they shaved our heads. That was the worst thing that happened to me there. I cried and cried when everybody laughed. Nobody even said this was going to happen, we were all in different groups. My older brother was there, but he was down in another building.

The first year was self-preservation. After the haircut you were assigned a locker, and you had to fight over it, because somebody else had that locker the year before and they wanted it back. So the first thing that happened, I got into a fight, and the guy I was fighting with is now one of my friends. He's from Pavillion.

When I lived at home, I never ever wet my bed, but the first year I started wetting the bed. What was really bad about it was I couldn't stop. I wanted to. I tried everything. They would take our sheets and wrap them around our heads and make us walk past all the other kids. After a while it didn't even affect me. When I was at home, I was always warm. I slept with my brothers in one bed. I think that's what the problem was, I needed that family. Here we didn't have it because we each had a bed and we were all in perfect rows. We had to make our bed perfectly, or they'd rip it out and we would have to do it again. We had to tuck the sheets in and tuck it around the pillow, it was like an army bed.

I never had to do that when I was at my grandmother's. She'd always tell me, "No, you don't need to make your bed. Just get up, eat, wash your face, and get on the bus and go to Savona School. Get out of Granny's hair." She never made me do all that stuff. Once a year, Granny used to take a whole bunch of stuff and make this medicine. She'd give our mouth a cleaning and I guess it protected us against all of the diseases. But at the residential school we started to learn to brush our teeth. That became a chore after awhile.

We had to clean all of the nuns' or supervisors' rooms every Saturday night. This meant scrubbing everything, mopping the bathrooms, scrubbing off the toilet bowls. That's the job I got stuck with the first year because I was a newcomer. And they were the dirtiest toilets you could ever find, because you get thirty-five or forty boys going in there and having a pee and not giving a care. And the regular guy that cleaned up, he didn't do a very good job, anyhow.

Because of the lack of food and the bad food they fed us, we found ways to break into the kitchen to feed ourselves. One of us would just tell the guys, "It's time to go," and we would just go. We knew we had to do it within a certain amount of time, because the supervisors were drunk. They drank every night. The supervisors would go upstairs to one of the rooms and they would drink beer or whiskey or whatever. We would go down to the kitchen and break in and take bananas and apples. If we had enough time, we would take sandwiches for the intermediates and juniors and put them in boxes and run up the fire escapes.

We always looked for meat. Something that those kids needed was a lot of meat. What really amazed me was the amount of meat we would find in there: ham, baloney, Prem, and all of those different kinds of lunch meat that we never got in our lunches. Who got it, I don't know, the supervisors maybe. Two guys would be watching, one in the kitchen and one in the back door and two of us would be in there making sandwiches like crazy. We knew we needed about sixty sandwiches and that's one apiece for those kids. If we could make more, great, because then those kids would have more to eat. Then we would grab a whole bunch of bananas, oranges and grapes or whatever they had for the supervisors. Away we would go to feed the kids, and make sure each one of them got a sandwich and everyone got an orange and a banana. We'd sit there until they were finished and then take the garbage and put them in our boxes and away we would go. Sometimes we would get so close to being caught!

There were weekends when I wouldn't go home and we did this all weekend long. They would try to catch us. They tried, but we always knew when they were going to have their snort because it was a ritual with the supervisors, except Brother Heysel. He was another one that never really watched us, he was an excellent supervisor. He was fair and if we got into trouble we would get a whack on the head by his knuckles but he didn't do anything that made him look bad. You know he was one of those supervisors that was there for us but we didn't expect him to baby us. I guess everybody there was his favorite. It wasn't just one kid that he would single out. If you wanted to go and play over town, no problem, he would come and pick us up. We didn't have to worry about anything happening because he wasn't that type of guy. He used to love building airplanes, model airplanes with motors. Sundays, if we were lucky, he would spend a few hours with us flying these planes.

When I was in Senior B I used to hear about girls getting pregnant down the other end of the building. They'd get pregnant, but they would never have kids, you know. And the thing was, they'd bring somebody in from over town who'd do an abortion, I guess. We used to hear it. It used to be really scary, hearing them open up the incinerator after what was going on. They'd open up the incinerator in the big boiler, and we would hear this big clang, and we'd know they would be getting rid of the evidence. Ninety percent of it, I think, was from the supervisor, knocking up our people because to them we were nothing. That happened when I was in the second or third year of Senior B. I was starting to know what sex was. In my mind I thought that mainly white girls were more promiscuous. I figured they knew what sex was, even though I never had sex with them, but they just talked about it.

I figured out that's what happened to the young Indian girls here that got pregnant by the supervisor, or I don't know who, they would have an abortion. Not very many were sent home when I was going to school here. There were some that were sent home who didn't tell the nun or the supervisor they got pregnant until they started showing. But I remember it clearly, and it was a very, very scary thing. We'd wonder how many kids got thrown in that incinerator. We'd hear a clang and then they cranked the fire up. The incinerator is still in the middle of the big red brick building. It has a sign on it that says 'furnace room'. When they started up the incinerator, it was always at night. There wasn't too many times you saw different white people come over. It would be the same night we heard that thing cranked full blast and it would be spring, when you don't need heat. They would fire it up, and I was scared. I

74

think most of the kids realized what was going on, but there was nothing we could do. We couldn't say anything because nobody would believe us. All of us that were going to school would hear the clang, and we would say, "Oh, that's probably so and so's friend, and they gave her an abortion." We'd talk about it, you know. Fire in September or October or November when it's not cold. December was when we had to fire up the heater to warm up the building.

The other thing I didn't like was when we showered with everybody. There were thirty kids that would shower. I didn't mind washing with them, washing your face. But I didn't like having to shower with them, exposing myself. When I lived with my grandmother we did sweats. But doing these showers here, we had no privacy. When I was a kid we'd have a sweat and it was all guys. We never even thought about nudity, it was a natural thing. But when you're with a bunch of strangers, man, you get pretty embarrassed, especially when they start laughing at you. You know, when you're twelve years old, and you have no pubic hairs and they're "aaahhh, you're a girl!" It hurts, and it's a form of mental abuse. It was the older boys that did that, even some of the supervisors, they'd tease us.

When I was there the supervisor was Brother Heysel and there were a couple of others that weren't there very long, one was an alcoholic and he was Native, another one was there for a year. I found the second one mean and abusive to the boys. He was a young guy. He wasn't with the church, they just hired him to fill in because one of the brothers left. Another one that used to come and watch us was a guy by the name of Hawkeye. That was what they always called him, because of that one really scary eye. They had bad habits. All of them used to hit me on the head with their fingers, kind of their knuckles, right on the soft spot of my head, and that was for anything. Even if we looked at them wrong, they'd hit you in the head. Sometimes they told me I was dumb, because I wasn't doing really good in school the first year. They should have expected that because I wasn't in a good environment and I didn't want to have nothing to do with this godforsaken place, and my grades dropped. The supervisors did nothing to stop the torment. When we got picked on by other kids they laughed.

One supervisor was always drunk and coming after us for something. Maybe it was the booze, or maybe we were bad, but I don't remember being that bad! He would come and use a broom on us. A lot of times when we'd be walking down the hallway and he'd come out of nowhere and just give us a smack with the broom. What the heck was that about? We didn't say anything but went and sat down. I think it had a lot to do with his alcohol. Then they transferred him to the intermediates, you know one level down, a demotion sort of thing. Another good one when I got into the annex was Doug Broadfoot. My last year was his training experience and he sort of followed Brother Heysel around when he came to the annex. He was really a nice guy. Then there was John Primeau. He was a Frenchman and a pervert. He used to join the boys when they had a girl downstairs in the room where spare mattresses were stored.

They took us across Canada on a trip. It was funded by the Department of Indian Affairs and we raised about $76,000 dollars. They took sixty of us students, four supervisors I think it was. We felt like we were on top of the world. That was the icing on the cake, a cherry and icing on the cake. We worked really hard to raise that money. This was our last year there, I guess in 1976-77. In the Fall of 1975 we started raising money. We started beading and doing leather work and bake sales and car washes and bannock sales and it just went on and on. Making purses, necklaces, wallets. They had two kilns down in the annex. They were brought in when we had a teacher come in and teach us how to do ceramics, and we were selling ceramics. We had slave auctions where we would be sold to the highest bidder. Sometimes it was to people on the Reserve and sometimes it was over in town and we went and cleaned their house, cut their lawn, whatever they wanted.

We used to have a little thing in the supervisor's office, and every week we would go and mark how much was in there. It took us a long time to get that first thousand dollars. Then all of those other things started happening. Then man, we would just start climbing up there and we flew. We drove from here to Calgary and then took a flight out to Toronto Pearson Airport and got on another flight to Quebec and went to a residential school there called La Touque. Those poor guys. We thought we had it bad here but they had it worse. Their milk was watered down, you couldn't even compare it to what we had. Their mush was water. There was mush in the water if you could find it, you know. Their food wasn't very good.

The other thing was we had to get in a line to go have breakfast and if we so much as moved, or got in between the wrong people we could have a wreck because everybody would line up so they were matched up with their girlfriend. If we happened to be in the wrong position, you know, they thought we were trying to step in with their girl and there would be a fight.

There were two gangs when I went there, one was from Lillooet area and one was the Shuswap gang. They used to have some deadly fights, like fights where there was blood on the walls and on the floor. Clayton was the leader of one, and Richard was the leader of the other. They were the two toughest in Senior B. They had all of their clan, and I happened to be in the Lillooet clan because the Shuswap didn't like me. The third year I was in the Shuswap clan, maybe because I was a little tougher.

The longer you stayed in the Senior B the less stuff we had to do. I got an allowance the second year. We worked and we got an allowance. The first year I worked all year and I didn't get anything. Everybody would be eating chips and having pop, you know, watching the hockey game, eating candy and I didn't have nothing. The money I would get from my grandmother, I couldn't use it until I went home, which I didn't think was fair but it was a set procedure with the supervisor. The second year, I got an allowance. I was working and did all kinds of stuff. We'd get pop and chips and we would show off to the new kids and put them in their place because we're cooler.

The best years I guess were when Nathan Matthew first took over from Father Noonan. The first Native administrator, Nathan, came in and it was like a dream come true. He came in when we were still doing the mush thing and spaghetti. I think it was about 1974. The first day he ate with us and the second day he ate with the supervisors. We despised the mealtimes because in the morning the supervisors had bacon and eggs. In the evening, they had steaks and probably prawns and lobsters. We would see all of this fancy stuff, and here we were eating spaghetti or macaroni or something with no taste.

What he did, he had them come and eat breakfast and dinner or supper with us. In three days he changed that place just like you would snap your fingers. We were having waffles and boiled eggs, bacon and eggs, you name it. We thought we had just died and went to heaven. Milk was real milk, you know. It was wild, it was totally wild, he was a godsend. To this day I have so much respect for that man. He put his job on the line in just one month to do what he did. They must have saved tons of money on food, and he did what he did, he ate with us, and got in the line with us.

Nathan changed the whole feeling of going to school here. When he took over he changed our menu. He made them get rid of the mush. It was gross when we added powered milk and it had hard lumps. All we did was soften up the lumps so we could wolf it down. When Nathan changed it, we started eating like kings. He came in 1972, and in 1974 he took over from Father Noonan, that was so cool. He made things feel like home. We were home at last, we functioned as a family.

By the time Nathan got there it was my last year as a Senior B, and then I went to the annex where you were spoiled. We're the elite of the kids because we are now in Grade Ten. The clothing we had when we went on to the Senior B for the first year were uniforms which I didn't like. We had blue shirts with blue cords and if it was brown cords we wore a brown shirt. We all looked the same everywhere we went and that was sad. Nathan changed that too. I look back at what Nathan did, how he changed the place, and I wish they could've done that way back in the 60s when the things that went on in the evenings with the Brothers were happening. I think Nathan went to school there and he knew about this stuff.

We had a supervisor, or a janitor in the boys' dorm. His name was Anthony. The way he got to us was he'd take us hunting. I caught on really quick, and I would never go with him again. He would take us hunting and treat us really nice and give us a special gift, candies or whatever. The second or third time he took us hunting, he would start to teach us how to shoot, just so he could hold us from behind. I already knew how to shoot. The first time that happened to me was the last time. He wanted to hold me, and say, "This is how you shoot," and pull me right in. And I said, "No, no, I know how to shoot, you just stay over there and I will show you." He did that to some of the boys, I guess they were scared. One of them turned gay, but we all knew that boy was different. He is dead now. He was different but we never ostracized him. He was a friend of ours. We took him under our wings. We all tried to protect him, but he always went hunting with that janitor, and there was nothing we could do. He would go hunting with him because he wanted to. That was really sad, because he was thirteen or fourteen and there was this guy in his 50s doing whatever he was doing.

I think Nathan got rid of him too, and fired a couple of other people. He was like a godsend to the school. He came out of nowhere and changed the place into a homelike atmosphere. I wanted to go to school and I wanted to learn. I guess that's when my grades started picking up, when I was in Grade Ten.

Anonymous

I stayed with my grandmother and my grandfather for ten years up in Skeetchestn, then my grandfather passed away in 1960. So my grandmother raised me for three or four years, and then she couldn't look after us because she was getting on in age. She told me I had to go the Kamloops Indian Residential School, the priest was coming to pick me up. I didn't want to go, I wanted to stay with her, and she said, "No you have to go." She explained it in Shuswap, then in English that I had to go. Because the welfare people will come in and take you and move me into a foster home in Kamloops or wherever. She thought it best to try the residential school instead of going to a foster home. I couldn't hardly understand it at first for the longest time. She explained it to me the best she could that I had to go to the Kamloops Indian Residential School.

There was a lot of pain involved, not really understanding what it was all about. To this day I don't remember exactly what happened. All I remember is my granny told me you got to go and that was it. And the next thing I know I was in the residential school. At that time, that black part out there, that leaving part, leaving my grandmother, was painful.

But anyways, well I waited and, as we were lining up to go in to have some supper Wilfred Ledoux came over. I don't know if the priest told them to help the new guys out, show them the ropes. And he helped me out quite a bit, showed me where I had to line up and what to do, things and stuff.

I was in the old building, at that time we had to wear red t-shirts and black slacks, and black boots, black shoes. I had to cut my hair off short. That part I didn't like too much. I know it felt ugly, because, I couldn't do nothing much about it. I had to just follow what the other kids did in the mornings. Whatever they were doing I would do the same things. Wilfred would show me where the bedrooms were and stuff. I don't remember the rest. I think he maybe showed me the pool outside and the baseball field and the soccer field. We played sports.

I can't remember, there was a few other parts. I met another friend. He's now the Chief of Neskonlith. I think his name is Art Manuel. I remember him as Art Manuel, but I know he is the Chief out there. He went all the way through school but I didn't, I only went to Grade Nine. In '67 I quit. Well Father Noonan told me to quit and go get a job and stick to it. I figured that he was letting me leave there. I did run away couple times but I got caught and was brought back again.

It was like a jail, because I saw kids my age lined up, I think it was in the principal's office. My friend was in front of me and he was crying, because he didn't want to get strapped. I believe that was what was happening, but there was a big line up of us. They were getting strapped. I could hear them crying in there or screaming in there, behind the closed door and my friend was ahead of me and he was crying, his name was Kenny. I can't remember exactly if he was from Merritt or from Lillooet. But he didn't want to get strapped and he was just really crying harder and I was trying to calm him down, trying to comfort him so he won't be so sad. We got strapped for running away, that was the whole thing. They took me and Kenny, we had run away and we got caught and we were brought back. They got us in downtown Kamloops and they put us in a van. There was already two or three other kids in the van, they had run away. They rounded up whoever ran away, then we had to go back, it was a beginning of a lot of hard stuff for me. It was because my marks weren't good at school that I had more work, harder labour work, like mowing around both buildings. I guess that's what you call it.

Of course we were told not to speak our language, not even one word, I couldn't say one word in our Shuswap language. For ten years, my grandmother, that's all she could speak was Shuswap. I mean she could speak a little English but not that good and so she could speak Shuswap better. But, my grandfather spoke more English than Shuswap. He could say a few words in Shuswap, but my aunt and my grandmother they was always speaking in Shuswap.

They said I had to do a lot of different types of work, hard like, labour work, you know, I had to clean the whole school yard, stuff like that. I had to stack boxes of apples. I didn't want to ask any questions about what was going on. Plus what do you call that, stacking potatoes, sacks of potatoes? Big bags of potatoes, holy smokes. All that time I didn't want to be there. Every day, I hated to be there because I was so used to being in Skeetchestn and going to school here and all of a sudden I had to go there.

I heard stories that are really bad stories of other people that I talked to my age. They told me pieces of what was going on there. It was real worse than what I went through. They went through hell compared to what I went through. The only thing that happened to me was I got strapped.

Saturday's people would go to town, but these are the ones that had the good marks. You could go to town all day Saturday. I don't think I was allowed at all to go into town on Saturday. You know, I had to work that morning and I had to study until suppertime. So things got worse and worse after that, for all four years I was there. Just for that once, for running away that one time and they brought us back and ever since then it was worse than jail.

I rebelled a lot against what was going on. The feelings I felt from the nuns and brothers wasn't all that good. They weren't friendly, their glares were like you weren't there. I was fearful of them. I wouldn't want to be alone with them. And then I went and tried to fight against them somehow, the best of my ability tried to go against them. Anyways the harder I fought against them the worse things got.

The painful part was when my grandmother had come to see me. She had managed to get from Skeetchestn to there, because we never had vehicles then. She must have hitchhiked or caught the bus or something. It was so hard, I was down in the basement with the other kids my age and I looked out the window and I saw her, I didn't see her coming in, but I saw her going away and I ran out the door and I managed to get as far as the outside door and then I saw her walking down the road. Two nuns grabbed me and pulled me back in and I was told not to do that and I thought I must have been punished again. I had to do some more work. They knew of my work detail, so they added another thing to the list. They were figuring I was running away.

Grandmother wasn't allowed to visit and that was the hard part, I didn't like that. If she had to use the old buggy and wagon ways, it took three days from here to there on a horse. If you had two horses and a buggy, it would take three days to travel that distance one way.

For the whole four years she didn't want to go back there again, because she got turned away when she came to visit me. I don't know how she made it from here to there but she got there and they turned her away and I didn't like that. So I just about went off the deep end after that. I was already in hell, but this was making it worse for me.

She managed to give me two dollars, I could live with that much. My grandmother, she couldn't have been drunk, because I saw her walking by, she was walking, she wasn't staggering. They didn't turn her away because she was drunk. They turned her away because she spoke Shuswap only. She spoke very little English. I had no way of knowing. I probably would have asked the nuns about it, but they wouldn't have told me the right answer. I think that was probably what happened, they couldn't understand her. She must have handed them the money so they knew to give me the money and they told me you're not allowed to go with your grandmother or something like that.

I felt a lot of pain, a lot of hurt. I kind of blacked it out. I couldn't think, could hardly move. Other people my age in there, they got to see some of their family. I remember some people coming in to talk to boys my age and their parents, uncles, aunts, whatever. I could see they had visitors and I guess it's because I rebelled against the whole thing, they turned my grandmother away, just to punish me more. I guess that was the whole idea. All this time I kept holding on to whatever inside of me. And hopefully get out of there one day. After four years I was out of there. I was glad.

I guess a lot of people call it worse names. I just call it a hellhole or a jail. Because they're very strict people, the nuns and priests, because they were always scolding. Not only me, there was a lot of other boys that were getting worse treatment than I was. Like Victor, he's from up North. He was in the next bed to me, he had a problem wetting his bed all the time, they would strap him, they'd get him up by the ears, drag him down the hall, the nuns, and slam the door. You could hear him crying in the hallway. I used to try to help him change the sheet, if he wet his bed, I would help him rush, I knew where the bedsheets were. I'd change his bed before the nuns get back, so he wouldn't get punished. Not only me but my other friend, that other guy in the next bed over would help, too, because we didn't want him getting punished or getting his ears pulled or whatever. Because he was just a little guy.

I remember one time being really sick with pneumonia and I almost died. And all they did was give me a little thin blanket and that's it and one or two aspirins, the whole time, must of been a week I was sick, one whole week laying in bed with just, you know hot and cold sweats. They would come in and check once or twice a day, they'd peek in and the nuns would go about whatever they were doing. It was cold, real cold in there. Then they would bring me a little cup of orange juice with a plain aspirin and that was it. Well I pulled out of that, I was better.

In Grade Nine I had to move into the annex building. It was a little better in the annex or I guess you could say a lot better than the old building. The food was a lot better and I met a lot of people my age, again. I got along real good there.

I think it was last year I had a sweat with *Sheni7* and Eddy and they mentioned about doing this book. So me and my cousin decided to do this together, we were talking and I asked him if he was going to do it and he said, yeah. I said I'll do it too, then. I didn't want to talk about it. Because all these years I blocked out pushed it in the back of my mind and forgot about it, the horror stories I heard from other people. I can't remember who they were. But I heard stories or rumours about people, like being molested, being beaten and stuff like that even when they were little kids and teenagers. Other people were in there ten, eleven years and I couldn't believe it. I was in there four years and I was wondering how they managed to last ten, eleven years. When I was in there, there were boys my age that were orphans, they had to go there, they had nowhere to go. I was feeling bad about that too. I know Kenny he didn't like it there, he wanted to leave. There was a few other boys my age there wishing they could get away from there, but they can't no matter what they do. They were stuck there.

I felt kind of lost, I was thinking I was never going to see my grandmother again, ever. She might die and they'd bury her and that would be it. I was thinking about stuff like that. I watched my grandfather die in 1960, I was the only one there when he died. Because my older brother, he passed away now, and my younger cousin, I told them to go for help because he was sick, he was having a heart attack. But I had to stay beside him 'till they got back, by the time they got back with help, like we were way off the Reserve. By the time they ran across and got help, by the time the truck got down or the Chief got down to see him he was gone.

My life after that was just lost, really out, gone, completely. I went to alcohol off and on to cover up the pain. A lot of problems just because of alcohol, too. But, that's when I went to Indian school. I didn't want my grandmother dying and me not being there, she was sick. She was getting on in age and my mother had gone away somewhere and I never knew my mother that good because she was always away. Anyways that's why my grandmother and grandfather raised us for twenty years because my grandmother passed away in 1970. There was a lot of alcohol related deaths in my family. I went to Round Lake Treatment Centre in 1980. We did what you call a collage and writing why people died, then you had to put a cross beside it and a bottle with a cross and skull. I could see there was cross, bones and skull and a bottle on, by every grave. I don't think that would have happened if I would have stayed in Skeetchestn, went to school here instead of going to school over there. My cousin Randy, he went there about four years and there was a lot of drinking going on at that time he was staying in the annex. There was people about to graduate, so they would celebrate and they'd bring in alcohol, hard liquor and because they were just leaving in a day or two so they'd get real drunk staggering in the hallways or laying in the beds passed out from drinking too much. I could see that happening as I grew up with a lot of alcohol around me. You know from age one to fifteen, sixteen somewhere around there.

Every time the priest or the welfare people or whoever would come to look for the kids here that were still missing that had to go to the Indian school. My brother, he's a good runner so he'd run to the mountains and hide. I can clearly remember, like we had tall alfalfa in the field, he'd run and hide in there, lay down in there and they can't see him. He was two or three years older, he must have heard about it and that was probably one of the reasons that he would run and hide.

I want to let people know that it was one thing losing all our language, our Shuswap language. We lost it because of that. We were brought there and told not to speak in Shuswap, not even one word, or get strapped if you spoke one word of Shuswap.

I had given up trying to understand anything and everything that was going on around me. I was almost like a zombie, just do what I was told and hope to get out of there, and that was about it. I was mostly really confused and upset, of course, and angry and you know, all the bad feelings, because I really couldn't understand why they were doing that. "Why do I have to go through this," I kept asking, "Why, Why is this happening to me?"

I was sure glad when they said I had to leave though, when father told me I had to leave, go get a job and stick to it. "You're not doing no good in school, here." I didn't even go back to the annex to get my stuff. I was, out the door and down the road, I was gone. I didn't even want to look back after that. I was just happy to get out of there. I was waiting, when I was walking down the road I was looking over my shoulder waiting for that blue van to pull up that drove back to, like I called it, a jail. Didn't want to see that blue van up the road, because I didn't want to go back to that jail. I just kept thinking that as I was walking away. I was scared Father Noonan might change his mind, say, "No you better stay for three more years or whatever." When I left there sixteen or seventeen something like that, I did ranch work, I have been working ever since, off and on.

If I didn't go I'd be a totally different person. I would have finished school for one thing.

I would have done better in life. I probably wouldn't have went to alcohol. In the twenty years or from the time I went in school until after that and then do the three or four years there. There was a whole lot of mix-ups because of alcohol and drugs at that time. Well I was confused when I was there, but when I came out I was more confused. Because a lot of things were happening, everything was happening so fast. Two years later after I got out of the Indian school, my grandmother passed away. I got to see my grandmother when I came out of school, I was happy. There's no more pain, no more worry like I was right sick cause she was not feeling very good when I left. There was no word from any member of the family to say she was all right or anything and that was the hard part. Well there was a lot of things happening with her, in her life too. My grandfather passed away so she mentally fell apart, and then slowly physically she was falling apart, so that was when she told me to go to the residential school. Because my mom was not there and a lot of alcohol going on and then maybe she thought if I go to residential school that it would be a better life for me. I just remember telling Grandma, "No I don't want to go there", I kept saying, "no, no, I don't want to go anywhere, I just want to be with you."

Speaking English is nothing, it doesn't mean nothing to me now it didn't mean anything to me then. I was wishing my grandfather and grandmother would stay alive longer to be able to be like my Aunt Marie who is blessed with the Shuswap language. She can speak it fluently. Well she teaches it now I think. She used to teach me. She listened to granny and grandpa on the language as she was growing up. It must have stayed with her solid, she can speak English and Shuswap. I heard people say that the younger people don't understand why we're not good parents. We didn't have parents. They didn't teach us parenting skills in the residential school. That was one thing missing right there. They really beat into us the Catholic religion, it was a number one thing.

The meanness, you could hear it as it come out. They wouldn't just whisper it. They'd, almost like a scream, screaming right in the face thing. They would say don't talk about chokecherries or *sxu'sem* or bannock or stuff, not allowed to say words like that. That was just part of it. There was a lot of other things like hunting, fishing, we weren't allowed to talk about how we hunted or fished.

There are times I'd block these things out of my mind because I know there's going to be a lot of pain. I protected myself by blocking it out. It worked the first time so I kept doing that and it would go to a point where I'd block out a whole day or whole week. I'd be reading or in school studying, writing stuff down. That was what mostly upset me a lot of times, fighting it and being hungry.

I'm glad to be able to tell the story. I've told some of it to some people, just what I remember. Because when I'm talking to other people, my relatives and friends, the pain would come back so I'd block it out again. Then next thing I know, it would be like stumbling along, as I was all mixed up and confused again. I told my family about it, but lost interest, part way through my whole experience at the residential school. And the alcohol abuse when I returned to Skeetchestn was too much.

Dorothy Joseph

Before I ever went to the residential school we were happy. We didn't have all the necessities but we were pretty happy. My dad went hunting and we went fishing; it was a lot of fun. My mom had a garden and I ran around barefooted. Then my dad said I was going to go to a different school. I just started at a little school house on the reserve, so I thought I was going to a bigger, better school. I was so happy. I hollered to the kids "I'm going to a bigger, better school than you guys." So exciting, you know. My dad got mad, "Dorothy don't say that."

My first year at the residential school, I was afraid. There was a lot of young girls there, but I was scared because I was the only one from my reserve. I got to know some of the girls, but I felt I was treated differently because I was the only one from my reserve.

If you lost a sock or even one of your clothing, you got a strap. It seemed like I was the one targeted for losing my socks. I didn't lose it, I put it in the laundry, both my socks, I know I did. It always came up with one side of my sock missing. They called me up there, I put my hands out, got my strap. It seemed like it was routine for me going up there. Almost every day I got a strap because of something.

When I was younger there was a chubby nun, I don't remember her name, she gave me the strap on my hand. At that time they were using some sort of belt. I remember I knew a bit of Indian and I only knew it in Indian, these certain words. I said it and they hit me. They said, "What did you say? Do you want some more?" I said it in Indian again, I was trying to say it in English. I only knew that little bit in Indian. They made me put out my hand for some more. I thought, "I'm not going to say anything." I just shook my head, okay. I wasn't going to say no more. These other girls from Stoney Reserve they kept speaking mostly Indian. They kept getting strap after strap, all the time because they kept on talking their language. I was like, "Don't say your language, be quiet, just do what I do, shake your head," and so they did that. I felt bad for some of them because sometimes they just blurted out their Native language and then they'd get in trouble.

The food was gross. I couldn't' stand the food, porridge every morning, porridge, porridge, porridge, I got so sick of porridge. And macaroni and cheese; they made their cheese so clumpy. I was sitting in front of my dish and was looking down at it. I didn't want to eat it, it looked gross. Some of the young girls liked macaroni and cheese and I couldn't stand the smell of it. The supervisor would come by, tap the table, "Start eating!" So I grabbed a whole bunch on my fork and I stuffed it in my mouth and I grabbed my milk and I just swallowed it.

I didn't chew it or nothing because I knew I would have gotten sick. It was just about ready to come up. Soon as she was gone, I grabbed my milk and I downed it. My friend across from me, her name was Delores, she liked macaroni and cheese, I whispered, "Do you want it?" She goes "Yeah." I poured most of mine in her plate and I got the last few clumps and the supervisor never knew what we did.

The teachers called us savages. I remember that, called us, "Dirty savage, you'll learn," stuff like that. I felt bad, I felt real dirty. I thought the nuns were so pure and clean. I went outside, I didn't want to play. There was this big thing on the back of the Indian school. I used to go underneath there. I used to get picked on a lot because I was the only one from my reserve. So I used to go under there and pray as hard as I could hoping he'd answer my prayers, but it didn't work.

One time we were playing ball and the ball went and rolled down the hill to the river. I was like, "Oh gosh, we're going to get a real big strap for this one." I just about started crying. I was looking down there, my cousin Jeff Seymour came by and he asked, "What's the matter?" I said, "The ball is going down there, we're going to be in trouble now." He ran down the hill and jumped in the river, I was so scared because he went under, the current pulled him down and I was screaming, "Never mind that ball, come up, come up. I don't care if I get in trouble." I didn't want him to drown. His head popped back up again. I was like, "Come on out," I was trying to get him out of there. Then his head went back under again and we ran all the way down by the side of the river bank. There was a part that sticks out down below there where the old orchard was. We ran all the way. I was oh so scared and he came up, "I got your ball, you won't get in trouble." I don't know if he got in trouble for being soaking wet. I felt so bad, I didn't care if I got in trouble. He almost drowned, so we wouldn't get in trouble. That was awful.

There was some other times when I ran away. This one girl wanted to run away, so I said, "Yeah okay let's run away." Then Rena, she comes over, shakes me, she said, "I thought we were going to go run away." I said, "I was just kidding, I'm tired, I want to go to sleep." I was scared to get in trouble. She started crying so I said, "Okay, let's go then." I was still dressed under the blankets. I got up and we went down the fire escape. There was some snow on the ground. I think it was just getting to winter time. We were walking and it started snowing again. We kept going, we went up between Peter and Paul. There's a ravine there and she rolled all the way down the ravine and I ran all around the outside of it trying to catch her at the end, her legs were all scraped up and bloody. She said, "Let's go back." I said, "I'm not going back now." I knew what was waiting for me back there. I was going to get in real deep trouble. I had a bit of scratches on me too. So, far as we got was down in Kamloops Park and cops came by early in the morning. I told her, "The cops are coming, jump up the tree, I'll give you a boost and you pull me up." The cops came by before we had a chance to get up there. We were covering up with the little bit of clothing that we had, it was so cold out there early in the morning, freezing. Those cops said, "Where do you live?" "Oh we just live up here in these houses." At that time there were no Natives in town. So he says, "Oh yeah okay, hop in, we'll bring you home." So I was wondering if he's going to bring us to one of these houses. He brought us right back to the residential school. I was so scared, "How does he know we live here?".

We were marched up to the dormitory, Sister Superior was waiting upstairs. She said, "Get in there, pull down your pants." My eyes almost popped out of my head, pull down my pants? She said, "Take your pants down, down below your knees." I was so scared. "Everything, underwear, too." "Oh my God what are they going to do to me?" So I pulled my pants down and she said, "Lean over that bed." I leaned over the bed and she pulled out a whip, looked like a horse whip. I didn't really look at it until after she hit me with it; she hit me a few times on my butt with this whip. I turned around and looked at it, it was a horse whip alright, because I remember what a horse whip looks like because my dad used to have one of those. I just sat there and I was crying, my butt was sore. "Put your pants back on," I put them back on. I just sat on the bed rubbing my butt. "I'll have your sister come over and talk to you."

I was afraid of my older sister because she was brought up real prim and proper. I was sitting there crying and Delores comes walking in. My heart jumped out of my chest because I knew she would scold me. She came in and she said, "Holy cow you have the guts to do what I've always wanted to do." She asked me how far I got. I told her and she made me laugh a bit. Anyway, I sat up there for awhile, came down, and then I sort of forgot about it. I just erased it out of my mind after that. I was Grade One, I was pretty young yet. I think I was maybe about seven years old at the time. The other girls never knew about it because they were downstairs in the recreation room, doing whatever.

I don't know if anyone else ever got the strap. I felt like I was singled out to get the straps all the time. That's what it felt like to me. Sometimes they just told me it was because I lost one side of my sock. They were trying to teach us the ways of God and they called us savages and dirty Indians.

When I'd go for baths I'd get real stressed out when I was younger. I just remember they'd run our water and they'd come in there while you're in the bath tub, scrub your back or whatever, right. I don't know why I used to get so stressed out, but my bowels would move. I would have a stomach ache every time bath time came around. I would go in the bath tub and then they would get mad at me and I'd have to clean out the tub, put some more water in again. I don't know what that was caused from, probably being so scared. Every bath time I used to get so tense and get scared because I knew I'd get a strap for some reason.

We'd go for walks a few miles down the road, even in the wintertime. The cold air used to hurt my chest really bad. I could hardly breath so I used to put my jacket over top of my mouth, it would get so bad. I went to see the nurse and I told her I had bad chest pain when I went for a walk. She sort of laughed at me, "You're probably running." I told her, "No I wasn't running, I was just walking." She didn't believe me. There was a lot of pain in my chest, back then. Ever since then, I covered my mouth all the time.

I found out a few years down the line, from a doctor that I have asthma. I told him I was having these chest pains. I told him I used to always put my mitts or my coat over my mouth, so I could breath because it hurt so much. He just shook his head and he told me I had asthma and said, "You're lucky. That could have killed you. You were smart enough to cover up your mouth like that because that cold would have hit right there. That thing would have seized and you would have just fell and you would have died."

Only once I remember being in a hospital. I had my tonsils out, and ate ice cream. That was a treat, get out of the school to go get my tonsils out. This other time I don't know what I had. Anyways I was in a black room, they had curtains around me. I don't know what was wrong with me but they wouldn't let me see daylight. They wouldn't tell me what was wrong with me.

There was this great big guy, he was a janitor or whatever. They called him Anthony and he used to work down in the basement. I always grabbed on his hand, we were tiny and we used to grab on his hand and swing on his big arms. I was swinging and my sister got mad and she says, "Dorothy come here, come here!" And she says, "I don't want you ever being around that guy. Do you hear me?" And I go, "Why?" "Just do as you're told, you stay away from him," she says, "He has these girls, he gets them by themself and he sexually molests them downstairs in the basement." I got scared. I go, "Are you serious?" She goes, "Yeah, I don't want you near him, you don't go near him ever again." I said, "Okay." I never did go near him again. There was a lot of young girls that were getting molested by him.

There was this other time when I was in the junior's dormitory. They had this older girl in the room with us, I thought she was just there to help keep an eye on us. Jennifer Camille, she said, "Dorothy, Come with me to the bathroom." I go, "No I don't want to go, I'm too nice and cozy in my blankets, already." She says, "But I'm scared, there's somebody in there." So I went walking with her, and she says there's a guy down there. So we went walking down towards the bathroom, and I just saw this white butt sticking up in the air, moving away. We didn't want to make any noise, so we crept along and then we ran down the hall to use the washroom. Next day I went to Betty Arnouse, the supervisor, and I had a hard time telling her what we saw. She asked, "Are you telling me the truth?" and I said, "We all seen him, me and Jennifer and Delores." I guess that girl must have gotten kicked out of school or something, she wasn't around anymore, but I don't know.

Our beds had to be perfect. If it was messy they'd pull it all apart again, you had to redo it over again. I don't know how many times I fixed my bed because there was a wrinkle in it. It looked nice and neat to me. They'd yank it all off and make us do it all over. Our towels had to be folded a certain way; our bundles and everything had to be all nice and neat and tidy. If it was messy we had to do it over.

It affected my life. I was being a neat freak in Vancouver. I had to have the table nice and clean, floors had to be clean. One speck on there and I had to sweep the whole thing over. I kept on being late. My relations would come over, they came a long way to visit me, and I was downstairs cleaning up, clean up my bathroom, fixing the bed making sure the kids' toys were put away. I would not leave downstairs until it was clean, folding up the towels, measuring them and everything. My brother came downstairs, he just shook his head. He goes, "You better come up and visit your family, they're only here for a little while, you're going to miss them. You can do that after." I go, "I'm trying to rush around to get it done." Then I realized, "Geez he's right." I don't even have time for my family because I'm busy trying to get my house clean. So I went upstairs and I visited with my family for a bit, but then I went back to being that neat freak for awhile. I did that for quite a few years, being a neat freak.

When I went back home after that one year at the residential school, I told my mom and dad, "I'm not going back, no way. I am not going back there, you're not making me go back there." Then they told me, "If you don't go back to school, we will be charged." So I went to school, but I didn't like it there. My brother didn't like it there, he ran away. He didn't want to go back to that Indian school. My brother told me a few things of what happened in his dormitory. He'd pretend to sleep at nighttime and I guess one of the brothers, they came out, got a couple of the boys, two or three of them, brought them in this room and then they'd come back crying early in the morning.

They told my mom that she was incapable of looking after us after my dad passed away. They told her she was retarded and she couldn't look after all of us kids. We were put in a foster home, we weren't allowed to stay with our mom. I used to think my mom didn't want us, why doesn't she want us, doesn't she love us. I guess she used to think the same thing, that we didn't love her and we didn't want to stay with her. I was in Grade Five when she told me not to cry that she would be going to the happy place and she died. So I didn't cry and I was wondering why my sisters were crying; I didn't cry at all. I was trying to be strong, but now when I think about my mom, I cry for her, you know. All the time I could have spent with her; instead the residential school put us in foster homes and foster homes weren't that good either.

I was put in a foster home where I got molested, I got raped. I didn't know how I was supposed to walk, because they said I walked too slow and I walked too fast. This other foster home I went into was just as bad. They wanted me to look after their kids. And the neighbour's boy would come over and rape me and I felt so dirty. Then I stayed in this other foster home where these other boys were trying to have sex with me and my sisters when we were small. He said, "If you tell anybody, then we'll beat you up," really threatening us.

One of my foster parents put me back in the residential school and I ran away. I said I wasn't going back there, so I left. All my friends from the residential school were trying to talk me into going back there. I remember the last time I ran away I got strapped and that's what was in my mind. I said, "I'm not going back there even if it was different." I ended up in a school for girls who are unmanageable, because I wasn't going to stay in no foster homes.

My sister passed away at the residential school because of some diagnosis they did. They didn't bring her to a doctor or the doctor they had there diagnosed her wrong, I don't know. She was only seventeen when she died. She had yellow jaundice and they said it was something else. I never got to see my sister, I remember a part of her when I was younger. I was still little at that time; I don't remember going to a funeral. I never went to my dad's funeral neither. I was at home when he died on a Christmas.

We had to stay at the residential school for Christmas because I guess they didn't find a foster home to put us in for the holidays and they wouldn't let us stay with our mom. My sister did run away though, she wanted to get out of there for Christmas. She jumped on that Lillooet bus, she went to Lillooet for Christmas. She kept on going back to Lillooet after that.

When we were allowed outside, there was the girl's side and there was the boy's side, we were separated. I'd get to see my brother, I was so happy to go down there and play with my brother. Then there would be, "Okay line up we're going to go back." And we were like, "Ahh do we have to?" "Don't talk back, get going." I'd wave to my brother, sometimes I'd think he was crying and I wanted to ask him what was wrong. He looked like he was ready to cry all the time. I'd look at him, "That's okay I'll see you tomorrow." I was trying to make him feel better because I knew there was something bothering him but I didn't know what it was, he wouldn't tell me. I knew there was something going on. He told me there was stuff going on in the boy's dormitory at night time. He doesn't want anybody to know because it's too embarrassing to let anybody know. So many stories that I have from there and that's about all that I can remember.

On first seeing the photograph above one would think the boys were in a military academy. This photograph taken in the 1920's was depicted on a postcard.

The picture below was taken with Father O'Grady and a group of intermediate girls in the 1950's.

The photo on the right was taken in the 1960's, it is quite a contrast to the one on the opposite page. Nonetheless the boys are still sporting crew cuts and still wear the same clothes as one another.

These happy little girls have their picture taken with one of the teachers. There were happy times at the school, although it is the memories of the not so good times that need to be talked about today in order for our people to begin to really enjoy their lives.

Anonymous

I think the anger is gone now. Now it's probably just memories and the sadness of what all happened. I think there was one Christmas that they never picked me up. I think that was the saddest time of the year for me because I remember that one year. There were other kids there that also the families didn't come and pick them up.

I'd go for walks or I'd go jogging, then I'd let the emotions out, so nobody knew about it. I didn't know why but you know now I wish there was somebody there to comfort me. I cried a lot of times, crying alone, alone.

We would have no choice about it, no. Again you know you're going through all the emotions, different emotions and to leave your parents, they're probably heartbroken too. It would probably break me if I saw my daughters leave and go to a place like that.

There's something missing there from your life, something that's been taken away from you. There's probably a lot of things out there that needs to be said or people want to say it or maybe they're afraid of saying anything.

I never really talked to my daughters about it. But they're curious now, they want to know. You know I'd tell them now that hopefully we never go through an experience like that again where families are forced to break up, and I hope you kids never experience something like that again.

I used to do a lot of art when I was in Indian school, I did a lot of carvings and the one thing that kind of stood out for me was trying to make a flag. It went through the whole process, through a visit to the premier it went, yeah it went all the way up to him. I don't really know what really happened to it. I remember doing a lot of work on it, I think it was probably me and another few guys with our supervisor at the residential school. It was really big and it was an eagle on top of what was a union jack on the bottom, I think it was. I think they brought the flag to the premier and I think they might have showed it to him. It must have been rejected because I never heard anything about it. I think I made two flags and I don't really know what happened to them, maybe they're stored away somewhere, I'm not sure.

My carving work, I did have it shown in the Gallery in town, I had my own show which was really neat. I sold them all which was amazing. I used to like reading a lot then, you know I'd get into the books, go to the library and get ideas from there. It was different Native works from around B.C. Back then there was not too many books on it and it was really hard to come by. I think my supervisor used to help me, like he used to do some travelling and he used to like picking up books here and there for me which was great. I can still draw pretty good but I never went to school for it or anything like that, but I remember I used to get straight A's. I stopped doing art and carving and then I got interested in something else which was music.

I started taking music classes. I dropped the art and drawing and grabbed the guitar. I do other people's music and dances and what not. But I do have my own music, but I've never really showed it to anyone. I'm the lead singer with a guitar, and when I get up there I'm a totally different person. You know very talkative, I talk and joke with the crowd and they really enjoy it. And when I get off stage I'm really quiet. But when I get on stage I'm a totally different, to me anyway, you know I just have fun up there.

I think maybe there is some bad stuff that went on, you know, maybe my mind blanked some of that out and maybe that's where my memory loss came from. I'm not sure. To me I don't really think about it. I mean sometime I can get concerned and sit down and really try to think about it. Some of it does come back, some of it doesn't.

Right now I'm playing in a band. Charles Etienne, he went through it before I did and there is another guy that I play with and he was there when I was there and he has a good memory about everything there. You know I'd sit down and talk to him and I'd be amazed about what he remembers. And I was there too and I don't remember and he'd come up with names and faces and I'd say, "Oh yeah", and it'll start coming back to me. But you know we'd sit down and the three of us would talk about it and we'd talk about what happened to so and so, did you ever see him or her or whatever and we'd start coming up with names and I'd say, "Yes now I remember the person's name."

I remember during the summer they had a swimming pool there. I used to be a pretty good swimmer, I got a few ribbons for swimming or medals. I used to enjoy that, doing a lot of swimming there. And not only there like we'd go on trips or whatever. Yeah we'd go to swim competitions. That was fun back then.

To me it wasn't all that bad, but maybe I had fun. Like there were other people with different experiences. They'd never talk about it and I didn't pry. Everything wasn't all that right. There was probably things going on around me that I didn't even realize. I just sat back and said, "Whoa, did that happen, really?" I was curious I guess, I wasn't shocked, not really. I don't think I thought they were just BSing around or joking around. I never thought any of it was true but like I said people, different people went through different experiences than I did, maybe worse, maybe better, I'm not sure.

My motto is I don't say nothing, I don't hear nothing. I did learn it from somebody, oh it was an older fella and he passed away and I just remember him saying that. You'd try to get something out of him, you know and he was a musician and I used to try to get things off of him. "I want to learn this song, can you teach me that."

As you grow older you change. But back then I think maybe I wasn't such a good person when I came out, maybe I did change. Because when you're that age I guess you're trying to absorb everything and you could pick up on anything and everything. Age sixteen, seventeen, eighteen and maybe some of it ain't good. So yeah I probably did change through the Indian school. You know there's so many other kids there and you learn off them, you learn to watch them and they're not so good kids so you absorb all that. I guess it's just behaviour, because I wasn't used to kids behaving like that, you know. Maybe they're more aggressive, maybe they had more anger than I did. Then I started absorbing that too, hey. I kind of stayed off to the side and watched all this.

It was really confusing. You come from a little community like this and go into town where everything is huge. I felt like I was lost. I think things got worse in our community and you know like I said it took twenty, thirty years for everything to improve.

When I came out I didn't have a family left, I didn't have anybody to come to. So I was all alone when I came out. So I didn't have a home to come home to. That was hard on me you know to have no family to come home to. Because all my family was gone, they moved away. Soon as I left they left too, like all my brothers and sisters left.

I did find out probably couple a years before I came home that there was nobody here. So you know, what was the use of coming back if there was nobody here. I did come back for awhile, then I moved away for ten, fifteen years, moved off the Reserve, went to work and just the recent years I moved back. There was other families too that split up. So I guess I probably wasn't the only one.

But the part I remember is where I had two younger brothers that also went to the residential school for about a year and we were older then, but we got to know each other again. Then they left and I think I stayed on a little longer.

I was just trying to think about what I did after I came out because I was still a teenager yet, I'm pretty sure I was eighteen, nineteen I think after I came out I did a lot of travelling. About two or three years of travelling around before I settled down. That's all I wanted to do was just travel.

After twenty years then everybody started returning back to Skeetchestn and now there's people here I don't even know, I don't even know their names. Now the community is getting larger and there's people here I don't even know.

It was just I felt like a total loss at that time. I felt lost when I came out, that's why I said I traveled, I did a lot of travelling because I didn't have nothing to come home to anymore. I was probably angered by it, saddened, you know, when you come out there's nobody there. I just talked about it to other people and I wanted to know their experiences, too. And their's were different than mine and we talked about it. Or I'd bump into old friends that I made during the Indian school and we'd talk about it too. Now people are starting to open up to it a little bit more. I think it took maybe twenty years for them to do that, now they're not angered so much about it or whatever. I think people are starting to open up about it now. I think it's going to be a great difference you finally speak freely of it, and you can get it out. I think once you get it out, then you'll feel much better about yourself. I think they can put that experience to rest and move on.

A few of my friends talk about it and maybe they wanted to get it out, too. But we'll both listen to each other, hey. And a good way of doing it is to laugh and talk about it. We'll just sit around and just joke about it and you know just laugh and that's, I think it's a good healing in itself is to laugh about it now.

Myself I've calmed down really a lot after twenty years, and I'm not so angered about it anymore, you know. I think I'd be six feet under if I didn't talk about it. It would be inside of me forever and it would be too hard to live with. Like right now I talk about it you know it feels really good to let it all out. And talking to my friends I feel the same way, we'd laugh and talk about it. And it feels like there's something lifting off your shoulders.

Allan Mitchell

We lived over here at Salmon River with my dad and I don't remember my mom. She died when I was about four years old. I remember always going down to Aggassiz and we'd stay with my auntie down there. I guess that's when my mom was sick in Vancouver. My dad would always go down and visit. Over here at Salmon River we used to run all over the place. We lived about a quarter of a mile from my aunt and she had a bunch of boys the same age as us so we used to always run over there and get them, then run up into the range and be up there all day. It was fun the adults said, "Get out of the house," so we got out of the house.

I remember being with my cousins from Lillooet all year, whereas before I used to see them just in the summer time or just when we went over there to visit Grandpa. I didn't think it was much different than at home. I don't know, it just didn't seem to be much different to me. To me it was almost a little bit better because I saw my cousins more. But the cousins from Lillooet I saw more because they were going to school there.

The meals were terrible. A lot of it looked like the food we were feeding to the pigs. Being able to eat the food and wanting to eat the food are two different things. When we went to Lillooet to visit Grandpa, he always had fish and another kind of meat on the table, always canned vegetables, canned fruit for dessert, all this everyday, every meal. Then you get to Kamloops Indian Residential School and it's just very bland stuff. Can't even say it tasted bad because it didn't even have a taste.

One of the things I remember is there was an early mass and it was voluntarily if you wanted to go into it or not. I remember it was advantageous to go to it because then you got to the breakfast line up earlier than the rest of the kids. So I think that most of the guys I knew that were going to the morning mass, that's why they went, to get breakfast earlier. Not to go to mass, they didn't care about that, couldn't care less about that because they were always speaking Latin. We never understood what the hell they were saying anyway.

The only other thing I remember is I don't use salt any more because of that salt and pepper. There was only one salt and pepper for like about a dozen kids or more. And by the time it got around to you to use it your food was cold and I'd rather eat hot food than cold food so I just quit using it, it was easier. They used to feed us split pea soup. To this day I can't stand the smell of split pea soup. One good thing I remember about the meals on Sunday, we always had dessert on Sunday and it was usually ice cream. And there was a girl, I can't remember if she was from Lillooet Band or from Fountain Band, she was from that way anyway. She used to serve the ice cream and if you were right near the end of the line, you got more ice cream. So breakfast was a fight to get at the beginning. Sunday, supper was a fight to get to the end, because you didn't really care what else was there, because you usually didn't really eat it.

I don't remember a whole lot of the schoolwork. About the only one I really remember is in math class. I love math. I hated English, I always did. Social studies I could take it or leave it. But math is something that really interested me. I don't know why it just intrigued me and I've always been good at it. There was a couple of them that were pretty good.

I remember this one old nun she cried really easy. I don't know why but she cried really easy and all the guys that was their challenge when they went into her class, was to make her cry. Because if you made her cry then you didn't have to spend the whole period learning whatever subject she was teaching. You didn't have to do anything, really major. Like you could just talk back to her sometimes and make her cry. I don't know why she was crying so much. I remember this one math teacher, a nun, she could tell you what kind of gum you were chewing as you passed her desk. We tried all kinds of ways to fool her, that was a big challenge, trying to fool her. Well what kind of gum do you have? Or that you had gum at all. She had a nose on her though. Like you could sit way at the back in the far corner of the room and she'd still know that you had gum and knew what kind it was and she'd say, "Allan spit out that peppermint gum, okay." Like she wouldn't really get mad at you or anything, she'd just tell you to spit it out, go back to your table.

I remember, I don't know what subject it was, I think it was in the math class, but this one nun, you had to sit straight up in her class. This one guy didn't like sitting straight up, he liked going down in his chair. He was a big guy for his age I remember and the nun would just harass the poor guy about sitting up straight. One day she put a yard stick down the back of his shirt to try to make him sit up straight. He just sat there all the way through class. He sat there trying to break it, slouching over, by the end of class he did break it. The only thing that this did though is he never heard anything else that went on in the class cause all he was concentrating on was breaking that yardstick. And we all knew he was trying to do it.

I don't remember any bullies so much, but I had like a protector. I don't know why this guy, maybe because I was so small, hey. I was always small for my age and this one guy from Kamloops, he was always looking out for me. If he seen somebody big picking on somebody small he didn't like that. If you want to pick on somebody pick on somebody your own size or bigger. I don't even know where he is anymore. I kind of knew what was happening but I kind of always thought I could look after myself.

One of the things I developed there is that I could throw a rock, I could hit anything I aimed at with a rock. And once the rest of the guys found that out they kind of stayed away because there's lots of rocks around Kamloops. I remember me and my cousin from Lillooet getting into rock fights with other boys, quite often. One time there was him and there was about five other guys against him. I said, "Can't have that," so I ran up. He could throw with both hands, not accurate, but he could throw with both hands. And he'd get it in the general direction, he was not too bad. So I'd go up to him and I'd say pepper them Skeeter so he'd pepper them with both hands and as they were ducking his,

I'd be nailing them. I remember winning more rock fights than we lost. And this other time I remember this one bigger guy was going to beat me up for some reason, I can't remember why. But he came up behind me and grabbed me and dropped to the ground. I squirmed and I got out from under and I started running for the road and he got up and started chasing me and I was just reaching the road and he was still running after me and one of his friends was yelling at him, leave him alone. And I just remember reaching down and grabbing a rock and spinning and throwing it at him and I hit him right on the back of the head, dropped him.

All I could remember about Dad is him being drunk all the time, even when he came to visit us at the school. You'd smell it on his breath. I remember two or three times a year anyway. It was good to see him, like it was really good to see him because we were all happy. Because when a parent came to visit in Kamloops there was a little room they had set aside. You could all go in there, like the girls would be there and all the guys would be, us guys would be there and my sisters. Other than that I hardly ever saw my sisters. Well if it was meal time like sometimes you'd catch a glance of them in the line ups, but if it was between periods at school then you could talk to them. I remember talking to one of my older sisters between classes. If you tried to talk to each other, even talking in line up, if I was talking to another guy in the meal line up they'd come along and discipline.

One time the whole dorm got a strap. We all stayed up on the hill too long. Because usually on a Sunday, I think it was, we'd all get to go play up on the hills behind the school and we'd stay there until dark. I remember that one time we all came down all at the same time, just as it was getting dark. We all came back into the school and brother was really mad because we all missed supper but we didn't care. We were having fun. And so I think just about the whole dorm got a strap, so we all knew we were going to get it. So what the big guys did was when they lined up, the bigger guys in the dorm said, "Okay!" They'd be laughing at the brother. Just to make them hit harder. So by the time it got to the little guys he wouldn't have so much energy strength to hit. I remember that happening a couple of times actually. So those big guys were looking after the little ones.

I remember they always use to punish in front, like they never took it in a room and did it. I remember one of my cousins getting caught chewing snuff and he had to eat a whole can of Copenhagen. There was two or three of them that got caught and they all had to eat a can of Copenhagen.

I remember our grandpa use to send us dried fish and everybody wanted it. My brother said we cut it into strips. We'd cut it into individual strips and sell individual strips for a quarter. My brother used to say we used to sell as much as we wanted and they had, I remember they had a candy store there, it was one of those, just a tiny room and they had one of those doors that the top half would open. I remember going to that cause the top half would be open and the store was open. That's where the profits went, to the candy. I don't remember going into town, into Kamloops, much. I know we used to once in a while but I don't really remember going in.

I remember one thing they used to get all of us to go pick asparagus. Some farm I can't remember where, but they'd bring in a truck, not a bus, a truck, load us up and we'd all jump in the back. We thought it was great fun to jump in the back of this truck. I just remember going to pick asparagus and at the end of the day we had a break. This guy would have cases of coke and he would be popping them without using a bottle opener, but using another coke bottle and I remember those caps would just fly. He was good at it. I don't remember who he was. I don't think he had anything to do with the school. He must have owned the asparagus farm. I don't remember getting paid. Shipped us out, give them pop, they'll be happy. We were.

I remember going down by the river and looking for wild asparagus. There was a plant, I can't remember what it was, I remember it was red, the new shoots were red and we always use to cut it off right at the ground level, peel it and eat it and I remember liking that. I've been trying to remember and I've asked other people what it was. They remember eating it too and they can't remember what it was. I know it was down by the river and we have a river here and I don't remember ever seeing it here because we all were always down by the river.

We ate cactus. We loved cactus, that little tiny cactus that they have all over the hills. We used to eat those all the time. Peel them and eat them. Usually when we were up in the hills, that's what we did because we didn't have water up there. But the cactus we used to always eat them. Somebody always had a jack knife around, always.

Well the residential school taught me how not to love. Because there was no affection shown. There was a lot of discipline. No affection, none whatsoever. I don't ever remember getting a hug from them, even on my birthdays or anything. It kind of reinforced what some of the other people enforced on me before is 'men don't cry.' So I don't ever remember crying in public or in front of anybody. Once in a while I cried when I was alone, but even then it's hard. I don't remember crying at night as a child because there was so many people around. There was other people that would hear you and what was drilled into me was, "Cowboys don't cry." My brother, my older brother, my dad, the, well the brothers indirectly because if you cried it got them madder. So crying was something you just didn't do, so you didn't do it.

I still don't cry very much, it's still hard for me. I remember my dad's funeral. I remember looking around and seeing everyone crying and wondering well why are they crying. Okay I can understand the girls crying, because girls can cry, but why are these guys crying, cowboys don't cry. I remember looking at my brother and thinking that, cowboys don't cry. I was a cowboy, through and through. What they call the cowboy philosophy of life, I still kind of believe in that. Like treating any woman like it's your mother, being as tough as you want to be but don't be mean and stuff like that. And always shoot a rattlesnake, you know that kind of stuff. To me a cowboy is somebody that really respects nature because they're always out there in it and they live with it instead of trying to fight it.

I always wanted to be the cowboy, Indians always lost. Because look at some of those movies. John Wayne would be shooting a six shooter, standing there for half an hour shooting a six shooter, you'd never see him reload. He takes one shot and six Indians would die. Indians were always the bad guys. I remember Thursday or Friday night, they always showed a movie. I had a good sleep, I slept through most of the movie. Because they showed it in the gym and the girls would be on one side and they'd shut the lights off. Well shut the lights off on me, I'm going to sleep, no matter what time of the day it is.

One of the things that I keep thinking back about now is that they always used to give us cod liver oil pills and sometimes I think well that's a good thing. We may not have liked it, but you know it probably kept us healthy. You know, not only in that period while we were there but for years after. I remember hating taking those things, the cod liver oil pills were better than the cod liver oil that we use to have to take. So I remember being happy that we were getting those pills instead of liquid. They were black, semi-transparent like you could see light through them. You don't chew those buggers, right down, just like an oyster, you don't want to chew an oyster.

My relationship with my sisters and brothers - sometimes I think we kind of had an advantage over other brothers and sisters, because we didn't live together. After my dad died we all went to my Uncle John's, then some of the older ones just left. So the only one that I remember growing up there the most was me and my sister, my youngest sister. So we're really close, we're really close. My oldest brother, I remember some of the times when he went to Kamloops for a little while but he kept running away. So he was ten years or more older than I am. My other two sisters, we get along pretty good but we're not as close like me and my youngest sister are really close and my brother that's a little older than me, we get along really good.

The proceeds from this book should probably go to the communities. Especially for the older people because I think they had it a lot harder than I did. Because I was right near the tail end of the residential schools and they were toning it down more. In listening, hearing some of the other, some of the older guys from Vernon that went, it was horrendous, way harder than I had it. I had it easy compared to them.

You see, as long as I could see my cousins, I was happy, you know it reminded me, it still connected me back with Lillooet and Grandpa. So as long as I could see them, you could put me through hell and I didn't care. My grandpa always told me and I always remember that whenever I start getting into trouble is, "Just be your own man, stand up on your own two feet, don't let anybody push you." I've lived that way. My grandpa was an inspiration to me. More so than anybody else, because he was his own man, he had his own business, he didn't rely on welfare or the Indian department or anybody. I used to laugh and go with him, anywhere he went, let's go, can I come, can I come. If he needed food, he put food on the table. He was a very good role model whether he knew it or not, whether he tried to be or not, he was. It was more a part of me, you know. I don't remember ever sitting down and talking to grandpa.

On the left are little boys and girls having received their first communion at six or seven years of age. The Catholic religion with its rituals and prayers played a big part in the children's daily activities.

This is the original industrial school which was later replaced by the red brick structure that can be seen on the site today.
The boys did the farming and the girls did the domestic chores that were taught by the nuns and priests.

Survival

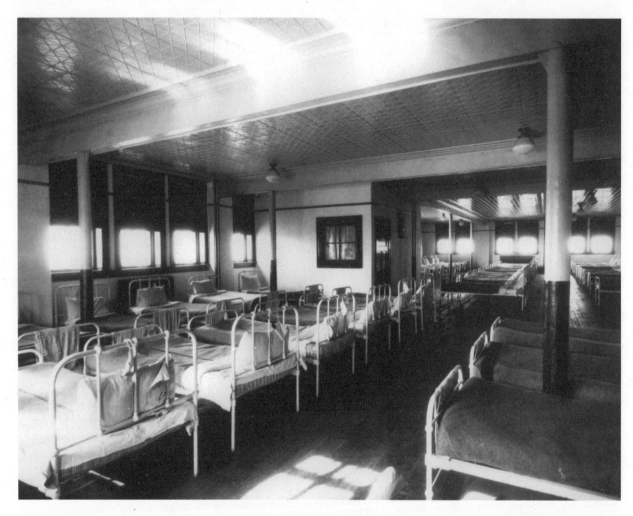

This photo depicts a dormitory from the residential school. All of the dormitories were laid out in similar fashion. It was here that many children suffered various abuses by their caregivers.

Robert Simon

I'm from the Skeetchestn Indian Band. My mother is Christine Simon from Skeetchestn and my father is Emery Louis from the Okanagan Indian Band. I was, for the most part, raised by my grandparents and for part of my life as a child, I was in the residential school system. I remember my life before better than I do the residential school itself. As near as I can tell I was five going on six. We also had a day school at Skeetchestn, so I was there for awhile, then they may have closed it so I ended up back at the residential school for another year or so.

We had a small ranch in the community, so we took care of it as a hay ranch and we had a lot of vegetables and horses and some cattle. I spent most of my time in the small ranch house with my grandparents and it was pretty good. We had everything we could ask for. We had all the food we wanted, freedom to go fishing or play outside. I was taught from my grandparents, about sweathousing. They'd tell me stories about the people, about the land and how to fish and hunt and how to take care of stuff. They also taught me how to be a good person in the family or in the community. They spent a lot of time teaching me those things.

My grandmother was insistent that I get an education. She was concerned that I be able to live in the *seme7* world, so early on she encouraged my mom and the other family members not to talk to me too much in Secwepemc and spent a lot of time teaching me how to count, how to do ABC's and a lot of time talking to me or reading to me. So it was kind of interesting.

My grandfather was strong in the culture and traditions, he was big in sweathousing and he liked to play stick games. I spent a lot of time with him and he taught me a lot. My grandmother was religious, spiritual. She knew a lot about our own spiritualism, but she was also very attached to the Roman Catholic teaching so she was kind of split. She talked about the religion and how important it was to pray and she'd do the rosary. On the other hand she was very fluent in our own spiritualism and she did that once in a while. But she tried not to do that very much because she considered it a sin; it's too bad.

I remember what it felt like when I got to the residential school. I was frightened for a long time. There seemed to be continually new frightening things happening. I was on my own. It was the first time in my life that I had ever been separated for any length of time from my grandparents or my family or my mother.

Until I got to the residential school, I had no idea about violence. I didn't understand fear. You're trying to go to sleep at night and everybody is told to be quiet, so they can go to sleep. Well it's tough because first of all you're alone and you've been accustomed to people saying goodnight to you, giving you a hug, talking to you for a while, reading to you or something like that. It wasn't like that. You listen to children cry and you'd get scared because they'd be scared, not much you could do about it. So you'd lay in bed and think to yourself, "How can I ever get out of here? What did I ever do to get in here? Who did I offend so badly or who did I make so upset that I would be here and if it is so who do I talk to about promising that I would never do it again?" You'd ask yourself all these kind of questions.

I'd go to sleep. Sometimes the children would still be crying and that was really sad. I'd cry once in a while, too. It was just pure loneliness. My grandfather used to sing a song. There's different versions, it's called the 'Lonely Song.' I remember when I heard it as a child, the 'Lonely Song' was an expression of yourself being alone and needing love and care. My grandfather sang it with a real lonely sound and it always tore your heart to listen to him. That was a good feeling to recognize you had that kind of sadness and understanding of loneliness. When I was in the residential school I understood what lonely was without the song and there was no end to that song. The loneliness was there when you were trying to sleep, when you went to sleep. When you got up in the morning, you were still lonely.

I learned early on to be caring about people around you, by watching my family how they took care of each other, how the older ones took care of the younger ones. And I was like five or six and trying to comfort other children who were maybe a little bit older or younger. They'd be really scared. I'd say, "Don't cry it'll be okay." I remember trying to comfort the children, saying, "Don't cry, you'll be alright" and they'd be saying, "No, I can't stop because I miss my family." You know you can understand that even as a child and you say, "But you have to sleep." There is not much you can do. You can pat them on the head and then you have to get back into your bed and then you have to try to close your ears to them crying, and they don't stop. I remember that.

There was a lot of bullying and fighting that went on. It was like sorting out pecking orders. People came from different backgrounds. Some I think, came from pretty rough homes. They had no way to deal with their fear and their loneliness, except by finding somebody weaker and taking their anger or frustration out on that person, or that little child. I didn't like that, I stood up for myself early on. I was fortunate, I had my uncle who was three years older. Every now and again he was able to spend time with me and he was somewhat of a protector. But, a lot of times you were on your own because they always separated you.

I remember little children hanging around with me because I stood out. You know I wouldn't back down from bullies, telling them to stop it. You have a couple of fights with them, they usually back away and try to find somebody weaker. I had two or three friends who got picked on. They saw that I stood up for myself so I ended up becoming a protector and I'd tell the bullies to stay away, you know, go pick on somebody else, but leave this one alone. I would fight and sometimes that's all it took, win or lose you just stand up and try to take care of yourself. I had several pretty good fights with some of the bigger ones or the more meaner spirited children. Then they started leaving me alone and I had to defend some of the little ones. After a month or two they learned it's not worth it to pick on them because Robert will fight back so they'd go. You end up with a happy little crew then, because at least you don't have anybody picking on them and all you do is play and be children again.

I was as scared as any one of them. I just couldn't see any other way out of it. I couldn't just not fight, I had to stand up. I knew from the time I was walking down the hallway, being led away from my mother, that I didn't like the school. I knew it then. I started saying as early as I could, as many times as I could that, "I don't like it here, I don't want to be here, I want to be home." If there was ever a broken record, that would have been me. I was very insistent about that, I would tell everybody, anybody. I didn't like it there, I didn't want to be there, I wanted to be home.

My family taught me ABCs and how to read and write and by the time I was five, I was able to do quite a bit of that. So when I got in there, I was thought to be a pretty bright child. It didn't take me long and I learned how to write and then I understood. You watch some of the older children and they get mail and you ask what's that and my uncle would say this is from the family. So he'd read it, wow, and then he'd write back. So it was important for me to learn how to write, because I wanted to be involved with writing back to the family. The thing I wanted to tell them was I didn't like it there, I wanted to be out of there. I reported the things I didn't like about it and who I didn't like. The priests or whoever, they would open the mail and review it before it went out. They would have a talk with me and say, "Robert you've written this letter again and it says bad things about us, you're not supposed to say bad things about us." I said, "It's the truth. I want to go home, I don't like it here," and they'd say, "No, you can't write this and we can't let it go." So they'd figure out a punishment for me. It started out with like no dessert, miss movie night, little things designed to stop me from standing up for what I wanted, which was to get out of there. I never did stop writing the letters, I don't know how many I wrote. I kept writing and the punishments they were dishing out to me escalated. They were trying to find a way to stop me.

Where I finally stopped was when they took me down to Father Noonan's office and there were desks there and letters there and they said, "Robert, look, don't write these letters. We cannot let these letters go home to your family because you're writing bad things about us, you know we've done this to you, and you're not listening, this is not reaching you, so now we have to stop you." Then they would strap me, God I hated that. That's how high it had to get and so I don't know how many times that happened. I would stop for awhile, then I'd write again and end up back there again to be strapped. And at Christmas and Easter I visited with the family and pleaded with them to get me out of here. I remember the letters. I remember reading one and learning how to write, because I had to tell my family you have to get me out of here.

I always listened with great interest about people who had escaped. Even if they were caught it didn't matter. They were my heroes, I always thought, "Wow! I wonder if I can make it." I don't know what else it would be described as other than a jail. Any place that holds you against your will, punishes you and sets up rules to totally retrain your thinking. I don't know what else to describe it as, it wasn't a friendly educational process. It was severe with extremely harsh rules, changing who you were because they wanted a different person to come out than what came in. It wasn't until years later, at college or university, before I started realizing what had happened. I always took it as one of the worst times of my life. There were so many of us around that had the worst times of our lives that I knew about and we used to share that. We knew we didn't like it.

I went to a psychologist and was talking to him about the residential school, just making sure I was okay. You have to do that now, because this kind of experience in your life twists you up so that sometimes you can't see when you're doing yourself wrong. You're hurting yourself, so you have to check with somebody outside to see that you're taking care of yourself properly. We went through the whole process of reviewing my experience with the residential school and the impacts of it, how it reverberated through my life. His conclusion was, if I didn't have the five good years that I had as a child at my grandparent's place with my family, he said it is highly unlikely I would have survived. I would have self-destructed at a much younger age, because that's how powerful that experience is in terms of damaging a person and their ability to cope with life.

I'm glad that we are here today, writing this book, because it is important for people to understand how this affects them. There has to be a permanent record of it and only then you can see how it has weaved its way through families, through a person's life, through a community, through a nation. That's why I wanted to put something down that would last for a long long time. It is going to take a long time for this to work itself back out of our communities again.

Alcoholism is such a rampant issue and still is in our communities but it is clearly rooted in the residential school system. All the abuses are there, sexual abuse, physical abuse. Those things pass on, not only generational but intergenerational and the residential school was the major contributor. It took away people's ability to be parents. My mother didn't understand how to be a parent, so I never understood how to be a parent to my children or to be a spouse. My first relationship survived some fifteen years which is totally amazing.

How do you capture the lives of these people who are dead now. It doesn't seem to be possible. Our boardroom, I think it was the boys' common area, when I sit in the meetings, sometimes I get up and walk to the window. I'll look down on the window sill. I'll see little etchings that say the name of the student, the month and the year and it's sad because at least one of them I knew well. He went to the residential school. He's not able to come here and talk and tell his story because he's dead.

His life seemed to be extremely tough. He couldn't figure out what the heck to do with himself, it seemed. He was always in trouble, he couldn't fit in with the world. He was young when he died. I guess he was seriously working on killing himself, he drank way too much, way too often. The first car accident he got into, he was in the hospital, he got out. After a near death experience most people would be extremely careful where they walked, not this young guy. Next time I saw him in Vancouver, he was drinking again, riding in a vehicle and it crashed and he broke his neck, just about died. I saw him around. He was still determined to kill himself, that's my opinion. He kept on drinking. Then the final car accident, he didn't survive that one. That's a legacy of the residential school that can't get into this, because he can't come in and sit down and tell it. His name is still there and it'll be there for a long long time. I'll probably be one of the few people who will remember him or why he died.

That's one of the sad things. There are so many people who have not made it. There are so many out there who are suffering. There are so many parents having crisis in their lives whether it's: inability to hold a job, inability to finish an education, inability to commit to a relationship, inability to mature, inability to hold any kind of responsibility, inability to understand parenting, or interest in learning. All those things are legacies of the residential school system. A lot of them just don't understand the reason they're having such a hard time in their life today is in good part because the residential school screwed up that part of their family and its been passed on.

So the churches have a fundamental responsibility. When it comes to paying the costs, they don't want to have anything to do with. They hire the most high priced lawyers to defend their actions and to excuse them. You see that today in court. The churches are adamantly denying they have any responsibility for the damage that their brothers, priests, or nuns did or what has happened. They say, "Oh that's not us," but it is them. They are directly responsible, I don't know how we are ever going to get them to live up to their responsibility. That may never come about.

I found that spirituality has been a big help in resolving a lot of our social problems. The people who are able to pull themselves out of that difficult place, usually it is in good part because they've somehow found spirituality within themselves. It starts to help them find the strength and to find purpose to live again and to work their way out of their problems. Our spirituality is one of our ways of helping ourselves.

In 1981, I competed for the position of Tribal Director for the Shuswap Nation Tribal Council. My first office, (in the old building) was the waiting room. I don't know what's the worst thing I can say about that place. It was terrible. As far as memories go, that was the last place I used to see my mother before I had to go down the long hallway. So, that had some pretty funny memories to have my office in that place. I had to get over that.

We then moved up one flight and my office was where Father Noonan's bedroom was and his kitchen became my secretary's office, the dining room was our reception room. When I got there I used to hear echos of the children, echos of my childhood and I'd feel a real sense of sorrow and frustration and anger and a lot of other emotions. It was scary. We started developing the tribal council and laying out our goals which was a lot more control over our lives and we started to form the Secwepemc Cultural Education Society. I knew that we were reversing the effects of the residential school system, and every day that we created something new, I knew we were changing the impacts of that.

I started to appreciate myself. Self-destruction to me didn't mean a whole lot because I didn't value who I was. I couldn't deal with abandonment. I never knew the word until 1989, I learned it quick then. Affection in my life, not only was I losing my wife, but I was losing my children. Even though I couldn't express the love, I did feel it. So abandonment came into my life like a train down a track. It was high speed and it hit me. I felt so lost, I was five years old again and I was walking down that hallway and there wasn't a thing I could do about it. Every where I turned, nobody could help me and I couldn't help myself and I was frustrated again. Like the days when my mom would leave and I'd be stuck and I had that exact same feeling I had as when I was five years old.

It took a while before I started to think about going to school again. I spent time with an Elder and she's really a strong spiritual Secwepemc person. She lives in Chilliwack and I spent six months with her. I had no where I wanted to go and I had nothing I wanted to achieve in life. She could see I was spiraling down. She told me, "I want you to stay with me, you'll drive me to my meetings. In return I'll teach you a little bit about our customs, our culture and our spiritualism." I said fine; it was really a good feeling to be around her anyway. She took me to spiritual practices and slowly I started to find value in life. Again it took a while and then the days got better for me.

Over the years since then, I've put together a prayer that I say almost every day. It's about gratitude, it is being thankful for the year that I've experienced or that I'm experiencing, then the day I'm currently in, and I'm thankful for another day without drinking and another day without smoking. Then I say thanks for balance in my life, the mental, emotional, spiritual and physical and I check to see inside of myself if any of those are out. If one of them is out, then I need to know why. My prayer goes on to say "Thanks" for all the gifts in my life, my wife, children, grandson, mother, friends, ex-wife and so forth.

I look back on my own life and I can see how my experiences in the residential school affected me. The way I related to my children, I was distant. I couldn't express myself, I couldn't say, "I love you" very well, couldn't hug them. Whenever they cried too much, I couldn't deal with that. Because I couldn't cry, I didn't know what crying was. I was brought up in the school, we were taught never to cry.

When I was there, there was no affection between the supervisors and the children. There's only rules. So it's not like a home situation, you don't have the adult in your life saying to you; "I care about you, I love you, I think highly of you, go do this, we're behind you, if you hurt tell us what's wrong, we'll help you sort it out." None of that happened in a residential school system. So growing up in that system you have no way of passing on that knowledge, unless you acquired it later on.

You don't know what happens if you express affection or care or love. In the residential school your primary concern is survival, taking care of yourself somehow. So you can't have space in there for caring about anybody or anything around you. You become what they used to call a lone wolf, very self-supporting. And to reach you, there's layers and layers of protection inside, so that you don't ever get hurt as much as you were hurt at the residential school. There are lots of things I could have done a lot better if I didn't have this experience with the residential school.

I have a hard time putting into words, how did that happen that a generation of people didn't know how to show affection? What kind of influence is it that the school could create that generation, what happened? The model of the residential school in good part is based on military models, everybody had the same uniform, same rules, same regulations. You get up the same time, you go to sleep at the same time, you eat at the same time, you all do everything the same. There is one standard for all; in the military, there is no room for freedom of thought. A good soldier is the one who follows orders. It's not about independent thought and especially at the times they were running these schools. A good military operation drums out all the feelings inside, and you have no feelings about what you're doing. And they repeat over and over and over again until you're a machine. In a sense you do things without question, without thought and then after a while you learn how to be like that. It is a highly established system, an old system, and you apply that same kind of system to children five, six, and seven years old. You can be certain those minds and emotions are vulnerable. It's going to take, it's going to hold. Then you add in the violence, then you add in the sexual abuse, then you add in the focus solely on church or religion. And the coldness, the distance and then twelve years, five years, three years, probably even a year after that kind of treatment you get out on the other side. You are no longer a full human being. You've been modified.

The courts will try not to look at that. The governments will deny that. The churches will deny it as well. But if you step back and you get away from all the defensive positions and you see the residential school as a way of modifying people and you compare it to what the armies do, in terms of developing and redeveloping minds and people, you'll see it is very similar. They programmed us to assimilate or die.

Anonymous

The life that I had as a child growing up, I was raised by my mother because I lost my father when I was three years old. What I know about my mother is she had a lot of love for me, not only for me, but for everyone she raised, big family, she had seventeen of us kids. And there was about thirteen brothers and sisters that passed away. I felt so secure growing up with her and she never showed any abuse to us children. And she had a lot of teachings that she passed down to me.

I came to the residential school when I was seven years old. And when I first got there I was so afraid and I didn't speak much English because I was brought up by my mother and lived close to my Elders and that was all that I spoke was mostly Shuswap. I was brought to the residential school by my uncle, he was the only one that owned a vehicle on this reserve, so he, Mom and Frank, took me up there.

The first day, I felt a lot of fear because I didn't know too many people there and my sister was older than I was, and always in a different area than from where I was. I was a junior there so it took me a while to be able to make friends.

The first day I was really scared, I cried, I just wanted to go home because I didn't know what I was going to do because even having to leave my mom, it was hard, but she told me that I had to. I was there. I was being sent to school to learn to read and write and to speak English. So I had to stay there if that was what I was supposed to do. And learning for me was pretty hard all through those years.

Because there was so many of us in a class and I couldn't get the help that I needed, and because I spoke mostly Shuswap when I got there, and trying to learn English. You know I wasn't grown up around English much so it was even harder for me when I got there. And I needed more help with my homework. I actually didn't learn to tell time 'till I came back home for my summer holiday. It was my dad that showed me how to tell the time just by counting in our own language. He'd move the clock around and then when I went back to school, that's how I found out, how to tell time. I learned faster by them teaching me in our own language than I did in English.

At first just knowing I had to stay there, I found it kind of hard. Getting up early in the morning and doing chores wasn't new to me because that's what I did at home. You know helping my mom out while she was working. I was hungry sometimes. I used to faint because we used to have to go to church before we could go for breakfast. Sometimes I used to faint in church.

They used to take me out and make me go and lay down in bed there 'till it was time for us to eat, then I'd go when I was told to go downstairs. They never once checked me out to see if anything else might have been wrong.

In residential school it was just the daily routines. I used to get up in the morning, go wash up, then we'd have to fix our bed and we'd have to go down to church and after church we'd have our breakfast. Some of us were servers so we'd have to serve the bread. After our breakfast then we had to do chores. Our chores were cleaning the hallways, cleaning the bathrooms or doing laundry, something like that.

We either had to listen or we would get the strap. I could remember getting the strap this one time when I was only about Grade Three by this nun. She had a real big thick strap and I got strapped for nothing. These others, the ones that were in the same class (as me) went and threw little notes. That note landed right on my desk and it was supposed to have been for somebody else. She didn't even look at that note or anything, she just called me in the back and I had ten straps on each side of my hand. I had to put my hands straight out, ten straps and I was crying and I didn't want to come back into the class. But I had to come back and everybody was just looking at me and I was so embarrassed. I just felt like running away and hiding because I was being laughed at because you know I was called a baby for crying.

Some kids in class, we always had smarty kids. We called them bullies then. We always had to take care of ourselves in there because we never know what might happen, getting beat up by other kids that were bigger than us. We were all age groups, we weren't all the same in age, some were bigger than us. That's why I always had to try to listen to what other people had to say.

There was another time I had to kneel; I was kneeling down for hours in the hallways. And if we were caught chewing gum even, we'd have to kneel with our gum put right on... they'd stick the gum right on our nose and make us kneel down. We'd be kneeling down for quite some time, 'till they figured it was enough of our punishment and that's the only time that I've really known what they called punishment. And sometimes the other girls I've seen knelt for so long that it seemed like sometimes they were forgotten. I remember one time my older sister, she got punished and she got locked up in one of these rooms in the school there. They didn't even feed her all day, that was her punishment. But what me and my sister and my other cousins, what we did with the apple they gave us, we put it all together. She was looking out the window, looking down at us when we were just outside playing so we noticed she was up there and we asked her, "What's wrong?" and she said, she got punished and she had to be there locked up in that room. So when we got our lunch we put it all together and then one of my older cousins was throwing it up in the window and she tried to catch it. She caught a few before we were called back in, that was our recess. That was my Auntie Doreen.

Another discipline was where we get hit on the head, sometimes with that stick, the willow stick. One of our teachers always had that. And sometimes when she got intoxicated we'd have to run away from her, because she'd scream and holler at us in our class just for nothing. Sometimes we'd have to run away to get out of her way, if we didn't want to get hit we had to run away from her.

I more or less lived in a lot of fear right from the time that I got there. After seeing what might happen. I just listened and after getting the strap for nothing and some of the other ones used to get hit on the head, slapped on the head sometimes if they didn't listen. But, it was mostly for kneeling down in the hallways, and that's all cement floor that we knelt on too.

The thing I remember most about residential school is I was always afraid. I know right through my life I was filled with a lot of fear, I had to overcome that. I was afraid of people there. The only time I felt really good was when I came back for holidays and being around my mother, my dad and my Elders, that was where I felt all the love was there. At the school I remember loneliness, lots of loneliness and I used to cry a lot.

I guess how I survived that, was as a child mom always told me that praying would get me through anything. She told me that what I was going to go through, it wasn't going to be easy going through life, so she just told me to pray, never give up praying. She said it is the only thing that will pull me through and it still has today.

I guess what I really didn't like was being there. We were always given whatever food that they dished out and I worked in the dining room where the priests and nuns all ate and they had all good food. But, what we were given it wasn't as good as theirs. It made me feel really bad, I guess that's another thing that I noticed, you know like I wasn't brought up to feed others different than what was put on the table.

When I went there, there was actually fighting going on amongst other girls. But I can't really say what kind of abuse they got because they pulled them out away from us and we never knew what happened. When they were caught fighting or something they just took them right out. We were in really big areas where the juniors and intermediates, where they'd have us all get together and darn socks or do whatever we were supposed to do to, clean out our little closets that we were given to put our clothes away. Sometimes when we were all together like that, some fighting went on.

Another thing I didn't like about that place was they always favoured some children other than the rest. I had friends and this one girl friend of mine had a hair lip and everybody used to laugh at her and make fun of her. I used to catch her crying all the time and then I became her friend. That really hurt me to see other kids being laughed at. There was another girl in my class, her one side of her face was all burnt up. They used to make fun of her too and there was nobody around to, you know when that happened and... Now I better stop – my stomach is starting to turn...

Sheni7

In 1965, Grandpa was looking after us and I remember waking up to a bunch of commotion going on. I tried to ask my older brother but he didn't understand what was going on either. That's when we heard the folks passed away, they got in a car accident down at Savona Bridge. We lost my mom and dad, aunt and uncle and my cousin.

Until then life was so beautiful. I used to go up to the logging camp with my dad. We used to do things together and my mom, you know, she was always around. We used to live in a house with a dirt floor. I thought it was just awesome, a little shack, I guess it was a tar shack. Then we moved, my dad built a really nice big house.

I remember going to day school at Skeetchestn, where we had a one room school. We used to ride our old horse to school – Old Tony. Used to be ten of us kids riding that horse, two to three miles to school everyday. Then all of a sudden things changed and we went to Savona Elementary and I was living with these *seme7* in Savona. I guess they tried to adopt me. I kept running away. Me and Jackie Taylor and Benny Peters and the boys, we would sneak away back to the community. Of course he would come and pick me up.

In '68 or '69, or somewhere in there, I remember being driven into Kamloops. They said that I was going to a new school. I figured maybe I'll be bussed back and forth. I was always homesick going to Savona School. I was always homesick. But back then there were pretty lean days, and all my aunts and uncles were already preoccupied with their families so they had no room for us.

Anyways, Bob drove me there, and he said "You are going to a new school." I said "Oh, do I get off the bus where and when?" All of a sudden he dropped me off and said goodbye and then he left. I was dropped off here (residential school), I couldn't figure that out. All of a sudden there were all these routines and all this praying and praying and praying, it was just really weird.

I knew then that it would be awhile before I would ever see home again. I knew I was lost then, I had that feeling in me. I spent a good part of my young life here. I saw a lot of guys and a lot of girls suffer in a lot of areas with all these things that were put upon us as soon as we got here, all that religion stuff was just entrenched in us.

When the folks went on there was seven in my family and thirteen in the other, we are just kids, you know. We were all shipped all over. I lost my sisters until I was about seventeen or eighteen years old and I finally found out where they were. That's when I was going to high school, I graduated out of Kam High.

In those days it seems like you were always in trouble in here no matter what you did. For some unknown reason I was always kept here, whether it was the weekends or Christmas. I remember spending Christmas over in that other building, just me and the nuns you know. To this day I can't understand why.

I was polishing floors Christmas day one year. I was going up and down those hallways. On Christmas day they called me and said that they had Christmas dinner for me. I didn't know what the heck it was but it was turkey, I couldn't believe it. I was surprised, you know. The next thing I knew my aunt came in and she was shocked, she was so angry that they did that to me.

I was punished for some things and I can't remember what. Punishment was for petty little things, like whether your bed was made right, they would flip a quarter on your bed and it had to bounce. Your shoes had to be shiny and oh, my God, all these other things, shirt buttoned right up to the neck. Then on the weekends they would keep me in, it was just like jail. I was glad when all my friends came back from their holidays because at least I had company besides all those nuns, brothers, sisters, priests. I spent Christmas, day in and day out, praying while my friends were at home with their relatives for Christmas holidays.

Now, it gives you funny feelings. You saw a lot of things that kids shouldn't have seen when they're growing up, you know the abuse. The things we were put through, these things shouldn't have happened. We were so young, we didn't know where to turn for help. I was whipped so many times that eventually you get so tough that you block those things out and you can't feel things, you'd get hit and you can't feel it no more. That's how it was here.

I held on to all those beatings, all the put downs and other things were entrenched in us. My adult life has been nothing but ups and downs really. Over the last few years it's been on a rise so I look back and I see a lot of effects from what happened, what they done to me here. It rolled right into my adult life, and I'm trying to shake a lot of it right now. I think I'm doing a good job.

I always lost my privileges here. I don't know, you do so good, you get out of study night, you get to go to movies or you get to go over to town and do something with basketball or movies. We used to run everyday down this darn Harper Road, for miles and back and all the way down to that cement factory way down the end there. I would call it a privilege, otherwise if you didn't do that you were back here doing dishes or mopping floor, or making beds or washing or doing something, so running was good.

You knew you were in trouble when you went to the supervisor's office. I used to go there pretty often for reasons I thought I didn't deserve. You could take his lickings but when you went further up into the principal's office, that is when you knew you were in really big trouble.

I saw kids drug out from their beds into the bathroom. They got drug in there and you could hear them getting beat up. You could hear them crying and screaming. Either because they pissed their bed or they were talking after the lights were out and stuff like that. We used to sneak around after lights were out and visit friends. If the lights came on you knew something was going on. Kids were getting beat up and or slapped around. You could hear that happening in the bathroom. They didn't have the guts to do it in front of everybody. That used to really anger me. You know there was nothing you could do about it. You're so little. You are trying to think of many things to do and try to help your buddies but you just couldn't do it. They would be fifteen years old, some of them even younger. I used to hate standing in a corner for hours. While you're standing you're holding a book. I remember doing that a lot of times.

I witnessed a lot of things over in the annex in terms of abuse. The supervisors they seemed meaner. There was times when I saw girls that were abused downstairs in that one room in the annex. There used to be mattresses there. I don't know if the girls liked it or not but they were always down there, you could hear what they were doing. The supervisors would be there too you know. That's when I got into the booze, I was there, I saw it. I never was involved, I never personally went down there with a girl or anything like that. I remember those girls either being taken down there or maybe on their own will, I don't know. I saw what was going on with those girls. Nobody wants to talk about it.

During the high school days I got out of here during the fall times or early springs. I got involved in rodeo, bull riding and bareback. I started riding bulls first. I was nervous at first and then I started thinking about a lot of things that were happening in my life. I rode bulls so good, I could ride any bull they put under me. Skinny little Indian kid, he would come out there and ride like nothing.

I used to get so mad, so angry behind those bucking chutes. What happened to me here, I used to find ways of taking it out on somebody. I was always in fights here, I was a good scrapper too. I used to put it all in that bull, that bull used to be a victim of my anger. After that eight seconds was up I used to feel so good, it was such an awesome feeling.

My grandpa Mike Simon used to come here and say, "I come to get my grandson." He always told that Father Noonan, "I come to get my grandson." I would always be happy to see my grandpa, oh, was I ever so happy. He would come to Kamloops in a beat up car or someone would drive him in and he would take me out in the summer. He would take me, and son of a gun, he would go right past the Reserve and I'd say, "Grandpa, where we going?" "Going to work," he would say. I said, "Going to work?" He'd say, "Yep, we're going to work." Okay, so away we went and we would stop up at this one ranch and pick up old Polly and Sugar and we would ride from there to the camp up at X-J country. We would stay there all summer, just him and I.

Grandpa could get any kind of deer or rabbits, that's what we lived on. My relationship with my grandpa is something that no one in this world will ever give me. The things that my grandpa and I did, that feeling of family you know, feeling of being wanted, feeling of someone out there loves you. I knew that old man did, he's the one that gave me my Indian name and everybody in the community calls me that.

We would sit in that mountain day in and day out and all he spoke was Shuswap. That's where I learned my Shuswap. Then I got back here and I wasn't allowed to use it. When I got older, you know, we started sneaking around and speaking our language as much as we could when nobody was around. We could communicate with ourselves, like the southern and the northern Shuswap back then, we would communicate through our language. They used a lot of discipline, they would whip you or make you stand in a corner or they would make you do more work to get that language out of you.

We prayed in the morning, we prayed at lunch, we prayed at evening, oh man, we prayed so much you know, we prayed, and prayed and prayed. We were robots it seemed like. We knew when to fall into line, we knew when to go to certain places. The one part I hated was being an altar boy. I was chosen by Brother Heysel. He thought that I would make a good altar boy. Being an alter boy, it was an honour or something. I don't even know what it meant. I don't even know what an altar boy means today.

To this day I have no feelings for church. I honestly hate to say it, but I really don't. I have been doing a lot of work on myself, spiritually in my own way, dealing with a lot of things and I think I'm doing okay in that area. My grandpa taught me a lot. We did sweats, hunting ceremonies, berry picking ceremonies, we did all these ceremonies in the mountain. Grandpa always called them white suits hey. "When you going to go back to the white suits?" I'd say, "I don't know it's up to you Grandpa." He says, "Well, pretty near time look at the leaves are turning color." He always knew the signs of the mountain. "It's time for the white suits." Oh, man I hated that feeling, down the mountain we came on old Polly and old Sugar.

I valued my friends so much here. At any cost I would protect my own relatives. We did that, we looked after one another here as best we could. I remember a lot of tough times with my cousins here and used to hate it when I was over there and my brother was over there and I always saw him fighting. He would lose a lot, win a lot too, but I used to always hate to see him fighting. I don't know, it's just a God awful feeling. A little thing would happen and all of a sudden you would have to take on all these other tribal groups. Like all the Skeetchestns, we stayed in one of these rooms all together. We looked after one another really good. I thought we did. To this day I have friends saying thank you for being there for them. I was so happy to be there for them because I had nobody else really, you know, they were my family.

I strive to be as good as the next man and always try and help him if he's stuck. I do a lot of sharing, my stories, my traditions, my hunting, everything that I get from the mountain, I share it within the community and I look after my family, of course. I make sure my sisters, my aunts and all the old people always have something fresh to eat. I'm a hunter, I hunt in the mountain all the time. I love doing that because when we were here, I used to hate that sound of the kids crying all the time because they were hungry, they were always hungry.

As young as I was, I formed a little group - I don't know if Eddy Jules was there, Yogi Jules, old Football, a couple of my old buds. I said, "We are going to go down, find a way into that damned kitchen and we are going to steal things and bring them up to those younger ones that are crying all the time." They were always hungry, God that was sick.

We had to do something, those kids had to eat. They were going to get sick. I don't know for how long we got away with this, I don't think they ever knew. We would break into that kitchen and lock it up the same way we broke in. We would get oranges, apples and all these other goodies. We would sneak down to those kids, give them an apple and tell them to eat everything right to the core. I guess that's why I eat apples and oranges, I love orange peelings and I eat the cores of the apples, leave no evidence. The kids were so happy. They were full for the night and they could sleep better.

The nuns were different I thought. To this day it still haunts me. The way they could walk down that hall and look like they were floating. What a freaky feeling. I get nightmares of this place, about nun's clothing, about swimming, you know, we used to pretty near drown because we didn't know how to swim. I don't know how to swim to this day. I love being down at the river, I hated that pool, I don't know why, I guess, the way they tortured us in there. It's just a weird ugly feeling. You still get nightmares of those people that you know.

You got good memories too, you know. Brother Heysel, he tried to help a lot of us kids back then. He was the father we never had. I thought, anyways, because he used to do a lot of things with us. He would take us on little bus trips or he'd teach us how to make different things or how to get into model airplanes, all these awesome little things that you enjoy as a kid. I don't know about some of the other kids but I felt pretty damn good when I was near him because like I said earlier, this was home to me. I accepted it you know, considering our treatment here, this was home.

If you said you were hungry they would probably starve you even more, take you away from your supper table, take you from your breakfast you know. It was endurance between us and them. Maybe it was a way of breaking us down even further, trying to break that spirit we had in us, of who we were. I would never bow down to let them be the winners.

Me and Jackie and David, we got in trouble because we snuck up to the girl's dorms to see our sweethearts. It was late at night and somehow they found out about it and I remember they always strap you until you cry you know, whack, whack, whack. Just strapping the piss out of us. I finally got tired of being hit. The supervisor grabbed my arm, and I pulled my arm away and 'whack' he hit himself. I said, "You ever touch me or you ever touch my cousin Jack ever again, I'm going to go to see the welfare." I'll be damned if I knew what welfare was. After that he never really hit me. I didn't know what the hell welfare was. I heard it somewhere, someone talking about protection, or somebody said that there's people that try to help people that are in trouble.

I think that you're born somebody, you are born with a language and that language I was born with was Shuswap. English is not our language, it's never been. We have a great responsibility to our children and to ourselves to provide the language. We have to revive the language because if we lose that, we lose all identity of who we are as Shuswap people.

I think guys like myself, we have so much to say. It gives me strength to let out what I have been holding for many years. It makes me feel better. I think that within our communities that these stories are going to help. The things that are happening in our community, we are on a dangerous path right now. We are not centered yet and it's because of the things that happened here in my life, my aunt's, my mom's, my dad's life, all that happened here. We were denied so many things, these stories are going to be passed on to our children so they can also thank the Creator that they have never experienced what we did here.

The young traditionalists, they have a great opportunity to revive our culture and our traditions, and our language because they have the opportunity to be at home with their relatives. They have that opportunity to learn more about who they are. We were denied that from one end to the other here. I hope that these stories we tell today benefit our children and they see and learn about who they are and about the strength of our people.

There's some questions that I was kind of hesitant to talk about. To be honest with you, there's a hell of a lot more that went on here than I'm letting out. There's stuff within me that I'm scared to let out. A lot of stuff that was entrenched in me here, whether it's religion, or whether it's other things that happened. It's never got to a point where I couldn't control it. I could control it, I know I could and I love that. What I have in me has brought me back the desire to look at my own self and start understanding my traditional ways and my spiritual ways as a Shuswap man. I've been on that path, I've been sober now for fourteen years and when my son came around I swore that he would never in his life time see me drunk and he probably never will because I have no desire to drink.

It's just a strong urge to overcome what happened here, I think if I ever lost that, I know what would happen. I've witnessed in my time, all my friends that went here have died violently. They're all gone now and whether it's drinking, or suicide, or drugs, or whatever the case may be, it could have been because of this school. They could have been abused sexually. I can't say I've been abused sexually, there has been attempts, but I fought it off. I remember down at this one room down here. I fought it off. I told the boys what happened and they said what should we do about it. I said, "We're all going to get bicycle chains, we're going to get clubs, and we're going to kill them." I don't know it's spooky, it's everything horrible thrown into one bag I guess.

I hated seeing people with nowhere to turn. I hated that with a passion I hated seeing my friends get hit in the head and walk around in a circle and stay that way until they dug a ten foot hole. Oh I hated that! I hated not being able to do something for them. I swore no matter what the case may be, if somebody needed help, there's always a way, whether it's financially, or food or whatever. There's always a way to help that person.

I hated them for what they have done to all my people and yet I put my hand out the other way too. I thank them for me being alive today, and proving that there is another Shuswap guy out there that went through the system. A guy that is more willing and capable of standing up and challenging what has been entrenched in us and carrying that torch for our kids so they could learn. I look forward to that one day where we will be self-sufficient. So we don't have to think ever again about what happened here. I'll be long gone before that day comes where they can hear these words 'what is an Indian school?' But it's going to take a few more generations to heal what happened. I think that the churches should step forward, the priests should step forward, all the supervisors should step forward, all the Chiefs should step forward, the communities should step forward and address what happened here.

Pauline Arnouse

What I remember about the residential school, I was about five years old when I was taken away from my home and moved to the residential school. I just remembered it was quite difficult during those first few months/year. I remember that the school was so huge and at night it was just so dark and lonely. When I was young my Aunt Ethel worked at the school and I was able to talk to her and see her for short periods of time. I don't remember who brought me to school on my first day. I don't remember if I was fluent in the Shuswap language when I first attended school. I understood the language, from my Elders. They said I was good at making birch bark baskets when I was a little girl at home before Kamloops Indian Residential School.

I remember being in Grade One and Grade Two, our teacher at the time was Miss Finen and I remember when we couldn't get our additions and subtractions right, I remember her using the whip on our knuckles. I remember my knuckles being black and blue and sore. Another thing I remembered about her was she used to duck under her desk to take a drink of alcohol. She wasn't a very good role model.

I remember going to church a lot. Everything was on a rigid schedule. Because I wasn't one of the dancers, I remember staying at the school and being one of the cleaner uppers that would wash and scrub and clean, clean the place. I guess it had a good effect because I learned how to be clean, to be neat and to be tidy.

We all wore uniforms. Our own home clothes were stored away. We wore blue tunics, white blouses, oxford shoes and undies provided by the school. All the years of school.

I went to school about a year at home and a good eleven years was spent at the residential school. In Grade Nine or Ten we went to St. Ann's Academy in town. I remember we used to have a lot of current events in socials because we didn't get the paper or didn't get to listen to the news very much. I thought it was unfair. How I made out in marks at that time I can't remember but I just remember being held back because, you know, we didn't get all the conveniences that other white children got. I also remembered putting my hands up to ask a question in English, the teacher always preferred the Caucasian students over myself or other Native students. I remember getting very discouraged.

For breakfast we had porridge, sometimes it would be cold, sometimes old, sometimes sour, sometimes sticky. For lunch a sandwich, and an apple for a snack after school. In high school we had an evening study to do our homework.

After study it was time for bed. We didn't really have much time for anything else. I guess we had more time on the weekend to do what we wanted to do – wash our hair, curl our hair, go for a walk. If we did go for a walk it was for everybody, it wasn't just for one person. Sometimes we would walk to town or across the bridge to a little corner store to buy candy or just to go for a walk. That was our exciting outing for the weekend.

I remember my grandfather coming at times to join us on a Sunday picnic and he would bring goodies, fruit, candies and chips. He got his grandchildren together and we would have a little picnic together. I could remember my mom coming sometimes but sometimes she would be drinking so I didn't want to see her. At the time I thought quite harshly about my mom drinking, but as I grew older I realized their responsibilities were taken away. How were they supposed to fill their time. A lot of them drank and it was so much a way of life for a lot of people.

I was treated fairly. I don't remember being abused, like how others have been mistreated, physically or sexually. I got along with the priests, nuns and everyone at the school.

At the school I had my cousins Joyce, Bertha, Julia and my sister Betty, as well as some of the other Chase girls. Some of my younger brothers and sister, Elizabeth, Tommy and Wilson, I didn't know until much later. When I left school they were living and going to school in the Fraser Valley. I hardly ever seen them.

When I was older instead of going home summers, Christmas or Easter break I used to work as a kitchen helper, baby sitter or work in Woolworths Department Store in and around Kamloops. I didn't want to be around drinking-people so I didn't spend very much time at home. When I was about eleven or twelve years old my sister and I went to live with Uncle Bill and Aunt Mary. That was the year we went to school in Chase. When we stayed with them they plunked us on a berry farm and we stayed there all summer. We earned enough money to buy ourselves some of our own clothes before returning back.

Learning how to sew is one of the positives in my life. I was quite young when my mom tried to teach me how to hand sew. She used to do a lot of hand sewing and embroidering. She sort of started my desire to sew. In those days no one had sewing machines because they couldn't afford it.

I took some Home Ec in high school. I remember making a blouse and an outfit. I don't remember finishing and wearing the projects I worked on. Sewing to this day remains my hobby. I do custom sewing orders for various people. I sew graduation dresses, brides and bridesmaid dresses and so on.

I guess I enjoyed my schooling there. The only thing I didn't appreciate is I don't know my culture, my heritage, and I lost my family ties. I had moved away to work and now live on Vancouver Island. What I know is through my Aunt Ethel and my sister that I lost most of what I knew of the language. I couldn't speak it fluently but I did know some words when somebody was talking but now I have a more difficult time to pick it up.

When I think back when I was about eleven or twelve years old I had a toothache. The Indian office had a dentist, he pulled my tooth out and broke my front tooth. To this day I have trouble with that tooth. It has a plastic cover on it now and the plastic yellows over the years. I don't have good thoughts about that old so called dentist.

I and my girlfriend who is also a licensed practical nurse, we applied for a job at the Victoria Jubilee Hospital in 1965. I moved to Victoria to work and then I got married. I stayed home with my two daughters. I looked after my family, my house, my garden and helped the kids' dad with his construction business. I kept busy in the community.

I work as a teacher's assistant for First Nations kindergarten. I work Monday to Friday at Tillicum Schools and I have been there for eleven years. I love my job and I love the children who come and go. It's also nice to rekindle our friendships as they get older. And I'm sure glad they don't have to be taken away from their families like what I went through years ago. I'm also a home support worker in Sydney.

I lost my son four years and eight months ago. It devastated me. He died in a car accident because the driver was drunk. I buried myself in my jobs, keeping busy helped me through my difficult time. It's been a struggle and I made it this far. I guess I'm a survivor. I continue to look after my own inner healing and try to help others that are going through a loss. I attend my Monday night group meetings and I also attend Compassionate Friends meeting once a month to continue to help me in my life's journey.

Senior girls in the early 50s with principal, Father O'Grady, and two nuns. The photos from this period are not as formally set as those in earlier years, when there were group photos taken of the entire school.

The chapel where the children prayed at least twice a day, seven days a week. The boys were seated on one side and the girls on the other. They were not allowed to speak to one another even if they were siblings.

The interior of the chapel at Kamloops Indian Residential School (KIRS).

The boys and girls from kindergarten to highschool spent a lot of time here attending services or going to confession.

Today it is used as a conference room for the Chief Louis Centre.

One of the classrooms at KIRS. The teachers, many of them nuns, were found to be very strict.

Forms of punishment in the classroom varied, from belt strappings, rapped with a wooden ruler on the knuckles to standing in the corner with arms stretched out with text books in each hand.

Ralph Sandy

I only went three years to Kamloops Indian Residential School. When we were getting hauled in the cattle truck, I didn't know what was going on. They took the boys to one side and girls to the other side and you couldn't speak to them. You had to learn, find out who you could hang around with that's your cousin or something like that, that could look after you. I can remember crying my head off, because my sister Doreen went the other way, then I went the other way. My dad died in 1947 so I ended up going to school pretty young in '48, I guess it was.

In the school, if you didn't work, do the job that they asked you to do, you get punished for that or get a whipping. Especially during tomato harvest everybody has got to be out there when it's ready.

You go to school only three hours a day and the rest of the time you're out working, milking cows. You had to be up at five o' clock in the morning. Work until eight o' clock, then there was the breakfast. Some went to classes, some went to work, so age ten and eleven I was working out there like a slave. You figure it out when you're nine, ten, and eleven and working and slaving out there, it's very hard for a person. I don't go to bed until after midnight, out there flooding rinks and if I didn't do it, I'd get punished for it. People used to get punished for everything that we didn't do.

I figure, well, when I was thirteen years old instead of working for the school, I might as well come home and stay, start working with the people. Might be cheap wages but they're getting paid everyday for the work you do. Besides there was a lot of things going on there that you see with your own eyes. Now that the Elders talk to you, even I'm an Elder, but I always talk to older Elders than me. They tell you, your eyes never lie, so the things that you see that happened there was kind of, wasn't a very good feeling to me at the time, but they never got a hold of me. I had some good friends that was pretty tough and stayed with me, like my brother in-law's brother, Huey, you call him Hubert. He used to kind of look after us, because we were smaller. If something went wrong he was there to protect us. Like you kind of stay close by his bed all the time.

I see some kids getting dragged in the rooms, some of them boys getting dragged in the supervisor's room. Mr. Vielle, was our supervisor. If you didn't do anything that he wanted you to do, he'll be giving you some punishment. I see a lot of younger kids getting dragged in there, with my own eyes I see it during the night time. A lot of guys went in that room with him.

I was one of the fortunate ones that never did get dragged. If something happened I used to wake up Huey, because we stayed close to him all the time. I don't know how come the other boys, I don't know what happens to them, either they were afraid or get punished or something like that. I used to see Mr. Vielle hit some of them kids in the head with a flash light or his key chain or something like that, a big key chain. I see some of them getting hit with that on the head and around the face. I don't know the other supervisors, I imagine they were about that kind of people too because they were pretty hard with us like what I say.

Even our school teacher Miss Finen used to whip us if we didn't do something. Some of them guys they were pretty small and they wanted to go to sleep, because this day and age now your kids go to sleep even at five and six. Them kids go to sleep but Miss Finen used to wake them up with a ruler, getting hit with a ruler if they fall asleep in there. They never let you sleep. If you did go to sleep, they'd stand you in the corner, part of the school hours, if you didn't do what they tell you to do.

So, anyway I got promoted to Grade Five, in the three years that I done schooling. After I came out I took some correspondence, I learned a little more. I'd say that I am a pretty good reader now that I can pass things that I'm doing, qualify for everything that I'm doing.

People have a lot of hard feelings about the school part though. When you get older that's hard to forget, I guess. You just have to do a lot of things to forget what happened in school, like I see one of my friends who live on the Reserve here, he is one of the boys used to get dragged in that room, there. And he's still walking like he's not all there, yet, I see him walking all the time on the road. He don't have nothing to do with making a family or having a family of his own, I don't know. Yet when you look at him it's pretty hard to, pretty hard to look at him, like you know he's a good friend of mine. But, he don't realize that when you don't have nobody for a family, it's pretty hard. Well he's got lot of brothers and sisters, but I mean have a family of your own, like a son and a daughter. You think that your name is not going to go on. I look at him sometimes, I think about that situation what we got ourselves into.

That was the saddest part of all, missing your mom and dad. You don't see them maybe ten months at a time. Some of them guys during the holidays they never see their mom and dad, because some of them didn't have no money like for Christmas. You had to stay in school if your mom and dad didn't come and get you. That was kind of hard for a person staying in school during the holidays. But we were pretty fortunate, my mom and stepfather used to make it there and come and visit us, so that wasn't too bad.

The funniest part about going to school is when you're having fun and when you're playing cowboys and Indians. They used to have some kind of guns for playing cowboys and Indians with. When they chase you and catch you and then touch you, you're supposed to be dead, so they take you and they bury you in the tumbleweeds. You're supposed to stay there 'till all the fighting was over, I guess. I don't know they see that in the Lone Ranger shows and Gabby Hayes shows. Once a week we had a movie, everybody knew, we learned how to play cowboys and Indians from Rowdy Yates (Clint Eastwood), I guess, Gene Autry and Gabby Hayes.

The best time I had in school was learning how to ride the cows, that's where everybody come, my partner Huey used to make us some bareback riggin, so you can stay on the milk cows, there. That was the best part of it, learning how to ride. In order to survive in that school we had to learn how to steal, too. If you didn't steal, boy I'm telling you, you starved.

We had some good Native people used to work with us there that used to when they go to town they used to get some things for us. I guess I learned how to chew snoose and everybody learned how to do that.

You always had to have a protector when you're in there. Like you had an older boy to look after you all the time. We looked for the oldest person that come from Bonaparte to look after us, seemed like we stuck close to him. There was Huey and there was Vincent. And there was kind of, seems to me, there was kind of gang leaders, too, you're kind of afraid of them gang leaders there. When they ask you for something, if you don't give them a chew there they'll slap you around or punch you out, plus you had to play toughie in there. Had to learn how to protect yourself. That was the best part of life in there, learning.

Once a week we had a movie and we had dances. When I was working during winter hours, the high school people used to take me to their parties when they have a big party on weekends, so that was pretty good. I learned how to dance with the older girls there. The high school girls would drag me out, I guess because I was too small to say no. That was a good part about it. Most of them were my relatives, the ones that used to drag me out there, if I say no, they drag me out anyway. I just couldn't fight back so I stay out and dance. That's the best part of the learning, I guess. Oh there was all different kind of dances. There was no such thing as waltzes, was mostly we all learned how to jive and everything like that. I just knew there was no such thing as two step, them days, all the conventional style dance I guess.

I wasn't no sport addict, there was lot of sports and, hockey, we played hockey. I was goalie for a while and jeez like I was saying it was mostly working. By the time you come back from work you were pretty tired and some guys would play and some guys would just go and sit around or go look for the food that they stole and go eat apples.

You had to hide away to go talk to your girlfriend or something like that. Funny about the staff members. If they see you talking to a girl, boy I'm telling you they sure didn't like that. But they can do a lot of things themselves like that. Like they can whip you or give you a punishment if they catch you talking to a girl, so that was kind of pretty strict order that one. So best part of it is when you had to go hide away to go see your girlfriend. Fighting over girls that was the other part, best part, too.

There was lots of people in a dorm, but them guys used to get dragged when everybody was sleeping, you know, about one o' clock, two o' clock in the morning, get dragged. The supervisors used to have their own bedroom in a corner on one side of the room. But, sometimes maybe, them guys would get a hold of you. I know they tried that a few times. Huey was close to us all the time, if something happened, I'd wake him up. It was good that way, but the other people had no protectors. All the reserves had their own different gangs, if you come from a different reserve you stay with that gang. Sometime each gang, from a different reserves they'd fight out one another in a boxing match or something like that, see who is tougher. But we sometime used to beat them, we had a pretty tough gang. There is lot of guys tried to get even with the staff members. The only thing they do is they get themselves in trouble. Then when they came out of school, they go back there and tried to wipe out the guy that was doing things, trying to give him some punishment. They just get themselves in trouble with the law.

I see them old guys here and I remember when they were so small. So I can remember them guys, Peter Sekora was the tough person, he was the heavy-duty guy. He uses a harness tug as a whip, boy when he's going to punish you. You get punished if you do something really badly and you turn around and they use a wet towel over your butt, take your clothes off, put on bed and use a harness tug on your butt, that was your punishment.

Miss Finen used to hit you on the wrist here if it don't hurt on you they'll use your hands like that and then if you don't cry, they'll hit you right here with a ruler. So you pretend to cry before you get hit, just so you can survive. I was fortunate enough I didn't get hit with the harness tug. But I did see some guys get punished with the harness tug. Sometimes they get thirty of them boys getting hit to show you when somebody does something wrong, how they use that harness tug on you. They put them out in the dormitory or out in the general recreation room where the gym is, they call everybody there. When everybody is looking this guy gets punished and they just show you what happened if you want to do something.

If you run away from school, when you get caught they cut all your hair off and sometimes they put books on each arm when it's church time. In the church your punishment was with your hands out with the heavy books on each arm and you had to keep your hands out there until church was over. Sometime the church maybe take an hour or so, holding something pretty heavy, pretty tired boy. If you dropped your arms, they give you a longer time and when you go back to church they give you longer time. After church maybe you still have to do their punishment in holding the arms out. They shave all the hair and they give you short pants and they make you kneel down in the church altar in front of everybody that's in the church, there. Don't matter who's in the church, but you had to kneel down in front and let everybody see you.

So, that was their punishment. I don't know what the other boys done, some of them were just in the church area there, too, they were standing in the corner, they were facing the other way. I don't know what they were punished for though, I never did ask them what it was for. But every time it was church services them guys had to go in their corner and stand there until the church was over or something like that.

I see some of them guys that run away, depends on how many days you been out, maybe you been out a week, so you get a weeks punishments, with them or something on each arm, holding it out like that and if you drop it you have to do more time on it.

I hope things goes good for everybody now. When people try and for those things it seems like it's always coming back up anyway, if they're healing theirself, something always seems to come up.

Think about that, but it's good to talk it over. There's lot of things that happened in there, I guess. I keep wondering what happened to them girls they never come back to school. You hear stories so and so got pregnant by one of the staff members. So I guess that was what happened there, they wouldn't come back.

Some of them guys there, too, some of them my friends that was going to school they never show up, they never come back. They don't like coming back.

They take you to jail or to something like fire fighters. They tell you to go fighting fire, they put you in jail for so many days or something like that. Maybe that's the way it was the government had to control you, so they had to do what they do. I never forgot the Indian words, but to learn the *seme7*, they try to teach you. If you talk your language too, they think you're talking about them. I see some guys getting strapped for just talking the language, they might think you're swearing at them in your own language. Most of them kids do that too sometime, just use their own language and swear at the principal that was there. So then even if you say a good word to them, you still get punished for that. But I was pretty fortunate, I knew how to write my name and count up to 100, before I went to school. My cousin Eva taught me that when she used to be on holidays from school so I was pretty good at it. I knew how to count and write my name before I went to school.

My dad died in 1947 and '48 I went to school, so I must have been eight years old. I was eleven when I come out and I started working when I was thirteen. 1952 when I quit, in the fall time I didn't go back. They couldn't catch me then, jump on a horse and took off up in the mountains, there you couldn't catch me then. Yeah, well working in there might as well stay home and work. Pretty lucky I found a job as cowboy when I was only thirteen years old I started working for four dollars a day.

Sometimes we'd get up at five o' clock in the morning and go milk cows, I think they only gave me half an hours lunch, that was all. Half an hour to eat your lunch, by the time you come out of there, the dining room you have to line up again. They let you know who's out working so you can change in your work boots and get your coat. Never had no time to yourself, you just come out of the dining room and you had to start doing that. If you took your time at it you, I don't know if they punish you or something like that, they lock you up somewhere.

I was pretty fortunate to have somebody that was older than me to look after me, Hubert and Vincent were the ones that was there for us when we were younger and smaller. They taught us how to survive during the school. Some people don't agree with that, some of them people hurt more than I did, because like I said they never got a hold of me. But I sure think about it now, the people that staff got a hold of, they must have something on their mind. Because you look at them and you can just tell. Now I bet I can tell the person that's been abused in there. Some of them got in car wrecks and some of them died from alcohol poisoning and I don't know what. Not too many guys left that I went to school with, just the ones that sobered up. I guess, like Johnny Dick Billy and Joe Stanley Michel and Elders. They never got into heavy boozing, I guess. But some of them guys died when they came out. You don't see them no more, like no more school mates.

I'd rather keep it to myself. I don't want to think about the few bad things that happened in there. It's kind of personal, I don't like swearing. If I start swearing, maybe I'll never stop swearing, so I'd rather keep it to myself.

I think the important thing is whatever a guy can use nowadays is pray, pray for a lot of things, but it's good for you anyhow. Now, if you don't understand things you pray for some kind of help, sometime that prayer gets answered from the Creator.

I don't regret going to school there the few years that I went to school. I don't know, maybe people got abused too much in there. It was more like a jail, if you didn't do things what they tell you sure get punished for everything. In jail I don't know if they ever did have what you call a black hole, if you're a bad person they put you in a black hole with bread and water, that's all. I don't know if they had that in school. I never heard anybody talk about that, but maybe they did have some kind of thing like that. Because sometime you didn't see guys, if you didn't want to work, I was wondering where they put them. Maybe they just give them that, I don't know. There's so many of us that you don't miss your partners, but as you get a little older you look for them if he's not there, you wonder what happened to him, you know. So, they might have a deal like that in school, if you didn't want to work.

Oh yes, the best part was cooking potatoes down in the pigpen. One of our good friends, Lally used to work at the pigpen down there, him and Huey used to work down there. Eat all the potatoes you want. Yeah, pig potatoes that they saved for the pigs, roast them and eat them yourself, that was pretty good.

Things that people do now, forgetting is a pretty hard situation. You have to pray a lot. I know I still use my prayers what I learned in school. By praying and doing the healing yourself, you need a lot of people to discover who you are. When you're trying to heal yourself, you talk to a lot of people. I'm pretty fortunate I go talk to smart people who go in the spiritual way and everything like that. Healing myself in a Sweatlodge and people help me if I don't understand what I get myself into sometime. But there is good ways, I sobered up, it's nine years this September, so I'm pretty fortunate. I done what I'm doing with my life now, so, hope everything goes good for everybody that is doing that too. All my relations.

Like I said I don't want to talk about it too much. For anybody who went to school and is having problems all I can say is pray hard and wish the Creator to help them. And the Sweatlodge is where a person can go and do their thing or go do their thoughts in the mountains. I think a Sweatlodge because grandfather is the one that always helps a person out. So I hope people who want to learn, get it, there is always some teachers around to show you, because there are sisters around there all the time to help us out and to survive in this day and age. So All My Relations. Ho!

Edna Gregoire

We had a lot of happy days before residential school. We lived on a farm by White Man's Creek on the Westside Road, just by Okanagan Lake. We used to have a lot of fun, especially through the summer months and Fall and Winter, it was really good days.

We used to help take care of the cattle and there was things to do, like help our grandparents. We'd feed little calves and give them water and we would go and get the milk cows, and our grandparents would do the milking. When they were done we let the cows out for pasture, you know, out on the range. Then, late in the afternoon, maybe around 4:30 or 5 o' clock, we'd have to be going up the roadway to look for the milk cows. There were times when they wouldn't be by the gate waiting to come in, so we'd go looking for them and the way we used to find them was by looking on the ground to see if we could see their tracks, what way they went. That's how we used to find them and see which way they went. We'd have a little dog with us, and we'd go walking, looking for the milk cows.

My mother didn't really speak Okanagan. Her mother died when she was a little girl and she didn't really get to learn how to speak but she could understand. Her dad was from Kamloops, but he was living at Lytton. He moved away from there when he was just a young fellow, so he was working at O'Keefe Ranch. That's when he got to meet our grandmother.

I do know about our grandfather, he spoke Shuswap and Okanagan. But, I didn't really get to know our grandfather, Isaac Harry, because he died in 1930 and we didn't really get to know who he was. Mother said we did go and visit him when we were little but we didn't remember.

When did I go to Kamloops School? I was just thinking this over to myself the other day. Let's see, I was nine, ten years old then, that was 1934, when I was over there. I'd have to have been eleven years old. I was born in 1923.

We got to ride in a big truck. It had sides on it and they had benches to sit on. They had been down to Westbank, because there was some children already in the truck when we got on. My sister was with me, and our cousins, they went to the school at that time too. I went to school in the new part (the big red brick building). They say that part there, was built the same year I was born in 1923.

I wasn't afraid when I went to Kamloops school, but I didn't know the children there. It took me awhile to get used to them. The other thing was to be in a different place, it was hard to get used to being away from home. I did miss home for awhile.

After I got sick that time, things really changed. I was in bed this one day and I usually got up and went to the washroom and things like that, do what we had to do. I got up and went to the washroom and went to the wash basin to wash my hands up and everything. Then before I went back to bed, I was just washing up there and my nose started to bleed. It started bleeding more and more. I called a sister. I had to use a lot of tissue and my nose was really bleeding fast. They put a pack right there on my neck, I think it was, and on my forehead, and that didn't stop the bleeding either. It was just about choking me, because it thickened up. I had to look at the basin of blood. All that thick blood, it was really clotting and I got that out of my mouth and I was still bleeding. The sisters, they emptied the basin out for me and they put a bit more water in there and had to clean my nose and everything. So they called the doctor to come out there, check me out and they took me right to the hospital. That was nighttime then but this happened to me in the early part of the afternoon. Then, even in the hospital it was like that most of the night before it stopped. How they looked after me in the hospital is just like what they did in the school there, the way the sisters looked after me. I had to call on the nurses, too, just like I did with the sisters. It was scary to see all that blood. That time I was just glad when my nose did stop bleeding and it was daylight again. I was about eleven years old when that happened.

I was in there (the hospital) way before Christmas. I wasn't even in school that long, must have been there for maybe a month or so. I spent most of my time in the hospital and I didn't get home until the Spring. While I was in the hospital, the doctor would give me a needle on my hip on one side and next week it would be on this side. I never found out what was wrong with me. I found out there's some people from this Reserve, and other different places that have been having nose bleeds and some of them died. Because, you know, they couldn't stop it. Well I think if I was at home, maybe I wouldn't have made it. I'm grateful to the sisters and the nurses.

When I was in there, I found they had times when you got up. When we were at home too, we had hours, a certain time to get up in the mornings and to get out and do things. Like chores and whatever we had to do and at the school it was like that too. You had to do something at a certain time of the morning get ready then to go to the classes. I can remember. They had certain classes we had to go to in the mornings and other ones would be in the afternoon.

They had one room for sewing. They had all their sewing machines. I was just very little. I didn't really get to do very much at that time. My sisters and me would cut out some pieces of material and they would teach us how to do some sewing, but I knew how to sew already. They were just helping out and sewing some pieces of cloth. I knew how to do all that, because I seen my mother sewing. They also had a sewing class. Mostly in the morning and then afternoons they had school for the beginners.

Then some girls would have to do the clean-up, all the dusting and all that. The older ones, they had to do the sweeping and the dishes and some of them worked in the kitchen and in the laundry.

They had navy blue uniforms and they wore white blouses and some wore a pullover with it and they had nice shoes to wear. They didn't all have white socks, some of them were black or navy blue or whatever. And they would have these other colors, too, a sort of beige color. They wore that when they went to class. When they weren't going to class they would put on some other clothes. Dresses, they were a beige color, and they had sort of a grayish color dresses they had to wear. We wore a uniform to church too. They had these little pom poms and they were different colors. My Auntie Irene got ours, I think it was a reddish color. They had different colors, I remember blue and white. I didn't have a blazer or a jacket.

Oh, the food was nice, we had home baked bread, and they would make toast out of it, and they had cereal in the morning with nice fresh milk, because they had milk cows there. So I was happy with the food. We had fish every Friday, and it was good. Oh yes, we had fruit, too. It was either fruit or we'd have jam or jello or else a berry pudding or rice pudding or custard, now and then.

We went to church in the mornings, not every day, some days you didn't have to go. We always made sure we went on Fridays and every Sunday, of course, we'd go to mass.

My sisters, Carolyn and Bertha, they went to school there too. They're younger, Carolyn was just about two years younger than I am and Bertha was born in 1928. She didn't go to school with us. She's much younger, she went to school later when I wasn't there. My sister, I got to see her everyday. She was right with me there.

I don't know exactly how many kids were there, but there were lots. It was alright being with all those kids. I got to talk with them and things like that and they were from different reserves. Some of them would be right from Penticton, Westbank, Winfield and some from Enderby, Salmon Arm, Adams Lake, Chase and Squilax and from around Kamloops, Lytton and Lillooet. I don't know if there were any from the north, I didn't hear of anybody.

They had boys there too, but they had one side to themselves and the same with the girls. We got to see them (the boys) when they came in for the meals but we never did play with them or anything. We could talk with them but we weren't allowed to play with them or anything. Then we get to see them in the classrooms and things like that. The same thing in the church, they had their own side and girls on their own side, one for the boys and one for the girls. The sisters looked after the girls, and the boys they had the brothers. Sometimes they would have the help of a sister too.

The playground was close to the river. It wasn't even fenced off, we could go down there. We didn't have to go too far to get down to the river. I don't remember the orchard, but I remember going on walks. We didn't really go that far either, but we always went out in the field there to play. There was a big playground that we had there, they had swings and teeter-totters. The older ones, I guess, they did play and all that. They had certain games to play and the boys, helped out in the gardens, taking care of the milking of the cows and feeding them.

My experience at the residential school was good. There's one thing I'll tell you, it was really good to be able to go to school and to learn how to read and write. And the other thing, the best of all, I was happy to learn about God.

I think it's the prayers of the sisters and the priests that helped me to get well. The sisters, they prayed through the night, because it was at night sometime that I stopped bleeding.

I didn't learn everything at that time. We had catechism lessons and I learned lots from mother and dad, too, you know. My mother especially, she was a great person. I remember when we were going to the school, she said to us, "Now you make sure you treat the sisters right." She said, "You be good to them, be good girls." Hey, I think that's what helped me to obey.

Yeah, I have good memories of all those years that I went to residential school. Those years I never saw what some of the kids talked about. And my sisters, they never went through anything. We talk about our days in school and stuff like that, yeah everything was good.

Anonymous

I know when I left Kamloops school. It was February 1965, that was after my father passed away. I was born in 1955 and I remember starting what they called catechism. I guess it is equivalent to pre-school, kindergarten. I was about ten when I moved to live with Uncle John and I started at St. James. I must have been in Grade Five. So I would say I was at Kamloops school at least five or six years.

Before I went to residential school, I remember my dad being there at home. He would always make the fires and have pancakes and have the smell of coffee and we only had one or two, three bedrooms. I remember I was always sleeping right beside him. He always kept me warm, I was the youngest.

I don't remember going to school or who took us. I just remember all of a sudden being there. I remember going to bed all at once and everybody lined up at the basin. Everybody taking their turn brushing their teeth, washing their face, changing, going to the bathroom, going to bed, getting up in the morning and going to church. We had free time outside to play.

Going to breakfast there were big line-ups going down to eat. I was by myself on the one side and Eleanor and Barbie were down below with the other senior girls, I guess. Eric and Allan they were over on the boys' side, so we were all separate and I really didn't like that. If you've ever been in the Kamloops school, the boys came from one side and the girls came from the other side and they all went into the cafeteria. I guess I saw Allan or Eric and I went running towards them and they pulled me back, gave me a strap. So from then on I didn't like it, because they were keeping me away from my family.

I was even separated from my sisters because they were older and you weren't really allowed to go over and see them. I think Eleanor or Barb came over once in a while to see us and that felt good because the biggest thing for me was the loneliness. But it seemed like so long in between, they never came over very often. I used to sneak out of bed and go into the room and just cry. The loneliness was pretty difficult, to show your feelings to others.

I didn't really have too many friends there because, my brother and them are a lot darker and I have lighter skin, so I was always called a *seme7*. So nobody would really associate with me. There was one other girl, Mary Jacobs, she was the same. She had light brown hair and light skin. We talked but we weren't really close. I guess I never really let anybody get close there. I was always getting into trouble. This one girl, she was always trying to be my friend but I'd always push her away. I guess, being in a strange place, I didn't want to get hurt again.

I remember eating a lot of stew and a lot of butter, but it always had a rancid taste or a smell to it. They wouldn't let you leave until you ate everything on your plate including the butter. I remember seeing them making kids eat the butter and they'd get sick. I never gave my food away but I remember eating other kid's butter for them so they wouldn't have to get sick but, I did it. I guess in a sense I was trying to save them.

I remember the porridge. It was thick, and usually cold by the time we got there. A lot of the times, like now, you have your milk and brown sugar. I can't remember ever having that. I think there was some bread there, like homemade bread. I can't remember ever having milk with it. But I remember the stews, there was always that. I don't remember how often we had stew. Now you have different varieties of food for lunch and I don't remember ever having that.

I don't remember being hungry, but I remember different things, like Mary had an orange somebody had sent her from home and somebody took it. Little things would be sent in packages. I don't remember if I ever got a package or not.

Dad came to visit us. I remember somebody would come and call us and they'd take us up to this little room and we'd wait for him, and he'd come and visit. We were all young and he'd just start crying. I guess he couldn't work and look after us at the same time. Running out of baby-sitters too, he had six kids, that's a lot of kids to look after. We all know my older brother Ronnie escaped. He was there but he ran away, then he went to work. He might have gotten caught once or twice but I think when he ran away again, he got away. He was by himself. If he was with other people, he probably would have got caught.

I was probably too scared to try to run away, I never even thought of that. Not so much running away but from being on the little kids side, you didn't see all that excitement. I just remember hearing of people getting caught smoking or something, and that they'd make them eat a tin of tobacco or chew or something. The other thing I remember was the playground. It was all gravel. They had the swings and everything but they never used to have a fence there, so kids would go down to the river and you always heard of somebody getting swept away. Then I remember they put a fence up. I remember kids would drown and their attitude was just, "Oh well." I don't remember hearing of anyone dying in the school, just in the river. The kids would always tell each other not to go by the river. I guess the older ones didn't really care.

I remember with catechism, they always had the singing. I think that was the only thing I liked about that school, because I really enjoyed the singing. In church I liked the singing. I think it was when we were a little older and this one particular friend, Phyllis, she was kneeling beside me and she was a lot thinner. I don't know if she was sick but she was always fainting. I guess she fainted and they took her away. I think she did come back, so she had a fainting spell for some reason. But, she fell underneath, because you're sitting there, kneeling for a long time, it seemed like forever!

The only recollection I have of going to town was when there was a group of us that got to go on a bus. I don't remember them telling us where we were going. We were going to the hospital, to get our tonsils out. One other time we were all paraded into town in front of this elementary school and we had to sing.

I didn't like that. That was humiliating, I thought, even as a child. Kids were calling us names and everything.

When we went on the bus to get our tonsils out, we got to eat jello and ice cream and the whole bit. In that one hospital, there was this little window, and there were a few of us in the same room. So, all the younger girls would sleep together and I remember being so scared at night because you could hear the night watchman going up and down the stairs. Every once in a while he would open the door. You'd always hear stories about him that he used to attack girls and stuff, but I don't know if that was true or not. I didn't hear about it until after. When I was younger it made me scared just hearing it.

We were terrified to wet the bed because they'd make a big ordeal about it. I wet the bed a few times, I probably got a spanking. You're just a little kid and you're fumbling around with the sheets and dropping them and they would make you wash them again, and hang them up when I couldn't even reach the clothes-line. Why did I wet the bed? Probably the fear of not wanting to get out of bed at night.

I remember walking, like, there used to be movies or something at the gym and then walking back. It was cold but I don't think there was snow on the ground yet. They used to have movies every weekend, maybe Friday nights. They used to have a few dances too. I got to see Barbie and Eric and them, they were all dancing. I was quite young, I don't remember being in sports or dancing. I just remember going to the shows when I was smaller. I only remember going to one dance. I probably would have been about ten or eleven, before moving to Uncle John's. We used to go watch the others, like the seniors, play ball. We never did play it ourselves. We were playing outside or sometimes they brought a TV in. We used to watch the occasional Ed Sullivan Show. Sometimes they'd have drawing or printing and writing and stuff. I have a scar here from those old pens with the pen nibs. I was running. They had the tables set up in the middle. Me and my friend were running around and I tripped and fell. One of those ink things went right in my hand.

They used to have orchards down below the school and we went to go in there. I think they had a statue there. I heard stories, but not until I was older, that we shouldn't go down there alone. We weren't allowed to go down there anyway, the junior girls, I guess. I don't know why we weren't allowed to go down there. I don't know if it was because of the boys or if they were doing things down there they weren't supposed to, I don't know.

I don't recall if there was anybody offering us any fruit from the orchard, because we just went down there and did their little prayers, then went back again. To me the whole religion thing was so contradictory, it didn't make sense. They say thou shalt not do this and that and the other. Then you go back and one of the people that was in charge, I'm not sure what they use to call them, they'd hit somebody or swear at one of the kids. Or you'd see one of the nuns giving the strap to somebody else for no good reason. They were maybe in a bad mood that day. They were mean. One girl I remember there, she used to go to Venture training, Rosie. I remember her being there. I guess we were all the same age and she was mentally challenged, so she didn't understand what they wanted her to do and they would strap her for it. That was mean I thought.

I remember they always cut everybody's hair like what they call the 'page boy' look, with bangs. I don't remember wearing a uniform. I had jeans on, hand me downs, old blouses and stuff like that. We had those little tunic things with white sleeves that we wore to church. Then you had to go into confession. I didn't know what that was all about, you hadn't done anything wrong.

A fun time was when they brought the record player in. They were playing rock and roll and the older girls were teaching the younger girls how to dance and the nuns came in and had to turn off that devil's music. That was okay.

When I was older there was one incident that happened towards myself, I don't even know what you would call it, I guess, sexual abuse. There was a little room, like a porch I guess it would be, because I remember it was glass. We used to always play in there. We were playing in there one day and, I don't know, just all of a sudden, there was just two of us. This other girl, she just wanted me to lay down so I did and I don't remember feeling anything. She layed on top of me and was sort of imitating to me what she had seen, maybe what her parents did or what was done to her, I don't know. I still can't explain why she did that. I think the nuns caught us. They probably gave us a strapping, like it happened, but I was still wondering why she did that. It was weird. I didn't do that to her, she did that to me. It must have happened to her, so I guess it's a form of sexual abuse. To me it was just strange, I was just a little kid and I was looking at her, like, wondering what are you doing? She was imitating all these things, it only happened the one time.

I learned to survive by being mean to people that were trying to get close to me. Acting tough is a shield, I guess it was. Don't let anything in, don't let anybody see you, your weaknesses and that's the way a lot of people are. I don't ever show my feelings. I think everything, all together, mom passing away, being away from dad and away from all of my siblings, everything toughened me up. I was in Salmon River one minute, then all of a sudden I was in this place and I'm wondering why am I here? I wasn't blaming anybody for putting me there, I was just wondering. No one told me I was coming here, I didn't understand. That was my biggest thing was just being totally clueless and wondering why and being lonely because you couldn't see your other siblings. And that one incident with that one girl on the stairs and just being scared. I guess, that's how they controlled the little kids was they'd put the fear of God in you. They used to have that Sister Superior. She used to dress up on hallowe'en in a gorilla mask or something and run around and chase kids. At first the girls were running and playing as though it was funny but when she hit, it wasn't just a tap. And then they ran because they were scared. They even crawled up on top of the lockers and she was hitting at them and then she finally went away. This other girl and I went running into where the beds were and crawled under the furthest bed. She came in, just like one of those scary movies you see. We were just cowering and then she left. Then we came out. It was stuff like that, that was hard.

Sister Bernadette, she was always really nice, I liked her. Some of the other nuns I thought were really nasty and mean but she was always really nice. And I think her name was Teresa, she was nice, she would let us have some music. I remember the one thing I didn't like was when there was a line up to go down where the medical place was. They'd come into the bathroom where they'd have line-ups of bathtubs and they would come in there and try to scrub you clean. That part I didn't like, they used a brush with lye soap and just tried to scrub the dirt right out of you. I'd just be red or pink. I guess there, too, you didn't show your feelings because if they knew it hurt you, they would do it harder. I guess that toughened you up, but it always seemed to be a battle of wills all the time. I guess probably, you learn how to manipulate people.

When I was a teenager I did the usual drinking and drugs and the whole bit. But, luckily for me, I straightened out. We've taught this as a family, all of us trying to piece together what had happened and why it happened. I was wondering why we were always at Auntie Shirley's and I didn't like being there. Ronnie told us later, it's because I think Dad would drop us off there and then he'd go visit Mom. She had cancer and she was in Vancouver. I never knew that before. Different situations and circumstances like that toughened you up. Things always happened for a reason. I'm just glad, I kept myself together to get through that, to survive that and move on to the next stage.

When I was a teenager, when I would drink, I would get really angry and I would tell people about the residential school. They wouldn't believe me. They would say, "Well that doesn't go on in this day and age." These were friends from town. They were non-Native. I didn't like drinking because I would get really angry. I didn't like that at all. You'd get mad at different people for all the wrong reasons, they had nothing to do with what happened.

I still can't make any sense of this Catholic religion, because to me, even as a young child, it was always contradictory. They would say one thing and totally do the opposite. I've lost my trust in church religions. I know there is a higher power, a Creator, but Catholic, no. It may be a good book or whatever, but the people that were teaching it were not good people.

No, they certainly weren't good role models. You went in there and said your little Hail Marys and confession and do your 'Thou shalt not' and then you go out and beat up a kid. It just doesn't make sense. Why would you do that?

I have gone to a few healing workshops. I know I should go to more because like I said, "I still feel like the little child." There's always questions. There's something there that I need to find out but I don't know what it is yet. It does help talking to my sister Barbie, she's a drug and alcohol counselor. I go up there once in a while and when the kids are playing, then we get to talking. All the different pieces fall together once you ask questions and you get answers for them. I can talk to her about how I feel.

James Charles

I can remember clearly about my family life before the residential school. I was the oldest, so my younger brothers and sisters don't have those memories. I can remember my dad was always doing power saw work, and his youngest brother and my grandfather worked with him. It was a family business, they did logging. My dad and uncle were self-sufficient and self-employed. We were well off and had just about everything that a family would want or need. They had strong cultural values and strong family values and knowledge of our Secwepemc ways. They went to band meetings way up north and down to the Okanagan. They were well known although they weren't political leaders. They were always involved politically and they were strong in Christian beliefs. We went to church every Sunday, where my dad played the electric organ. They were all musicians. I remember when they went to a house party they'd be playing musical instruments and they were respected by the people at the house party.

I went to a public school, it was one classroom. I was in Grade One and it went up to Grade Six. There was one other large classroom and that was Grade Seven. All the students would catch the bus there in the morning and after school everyone would walk home. It was a very good school experience. After that year my dad passed away and I realized what death was then, when he passed away. It was like the whole world crumbled, went from good to bad. I watched my mom and aunts, they had to work to support the family.

I was six when I got to the residential school. I was under my grandmother's care and my younger brother was in the same boat, too. No welfare for us, so that's why she had to bring us to the residential school. We took the bus from Chase to Kamloops and then we took a cab over to the residential school and it was very hard on my youngest brother because they wouldn't take him in. They said he was too young, he was five, no, I think he was a little younger than that. I can remember my grandmother and the nuns arguing in the other room. I could hear them arguing and then my brother just broke down crying. They had to bring him back in the same room as me because he wouldn't stop crying until some time after, and then he was able to leave with our grandmother. That was pretty well the last time I saw him for a long time anyway, because he went into a foster home. Shortly after, I found out our grandmother's house burned down and her husband went up in that fire. They sent my youngest brother down the highway and all he did was remember which way Kamloops was, and he was walking towards Kamloops when the welfare picked him up. That was how he ended up in a foster home.

I was there from 1964 to 1972. On day one I can remember clearly, I had three fights, one after another. It happened when a new student got into school.

I won each time, but I got strapped twice the amount for each one. That's where I started learning fast about how strict the school was. I think my number was 365, I'm not sure. We had an apple box for a locker and I can remember clearly from 100 to 200 was not used. I don't know why. It never was explained to any of us and no one could ask questions anyway. I was placed in Grade One B. I tried to explain that I passed but they refused to believe me so they just said that I'm in Grade One B and that was that. It was like being told I failed.

The only thing I remember about the earlier years of the school was that it was very harsh and strict. I got to experience the transition the Indian school went through, from the harsh strict schooling, to integrating into the public schools. I think it was around 1969 when the students started getting bussed into public schools in Kamloops. I didn't like that at all, because it was an embarrassment to me. I didn't want to be seen in a public school while we were being segregated and isolated in the residential school. The good thing about it was that there was no more corporal punishment in the classroom. From Grade One to Grade Five, we'd get rapped on the knuckles when we answered questions wrong. After a third time we were sent to the hallway, and an oblate brother would be out there with a strap and I'd get thirty-five straps on each hand. Then it went to seventy straps on each hand. I can't remember that oblate brother's name, roaming the hallway. In the public school there was no such thing. The straps that the oblate brothers used were like a leather belt. What the principal of the Indian school used, it was twice as thick and heavier and it stung more.

I remember that strap, I threw it in a garbage can one time. I got about 500 straps on each hand and this happened through the course of about ten days in a row. Each evening I would be sent up to the principal's office. I'd get the message from one of the students, I knew it was corporal punishment. To this day I never got to learn why, although I did ask him once. He had no answer. Receiving that harsh punishment for no reason, it was an insult to me. I was trying to be just a good student and trying to get good school marks. On the tenth day, he sort of threw me around and punched me and kicked me around in the office. I fought back, I fractured his neck or something like that. I guess a lot of the students might have wondered what happened that day. After all that punishment and physical beating I took, I was going to leave the school. I don't know what happened, it seemed like amnesia or something. I was sitting on the porch of the senior school building, smoking a cigarette and then I was told to just go to the dorm. In other words I wasn't being kicked out or charged, that crossed my mind. I thought I was going to the penitentiary. When any oblate brother got so much as shoved or punched or kicked, the student would automatically go to the BC Penitentiary. I thought that's the kind of punishment I was going to be dealing with, but nothing did happen. Like the oblate brothers or supervisors, they gave only thirty-five to seventy straps, but the principal would always be twice as harsh. That one punishment I took ten days in a row, I took his strap and I put it in that one garbage can out by the front doors. I don't know if they ever found it out there. Chances are he had a whole collection of them anyway.

I remember drama acting. The thing I hated about it, it was very strict. I didn't know who the people were that ran the drama, they were from somewhere else, yet they were very strict and harsh. Any mistakes, we got strapped severely. It seems to me that even when we did the drama perfectly we got punished, and got punished twice as much if we made a mistake. That's the way it seemed.

I didn't want to have nothing to do with it.

When the public schools came into effect, I guess I tried to take advantage of it to try to advance my grades, but that never seemed to happen. Every year I'd end up with a C+. We'd get severely strapped for being a C+. The school wanted grade A+ students and maybe B's, but C's and down to E's and F's, we got severely strapped, 250 straps on each hand. We were told to improve on our grades or next year it would be twice as much. I think the reason why I always stayed with C+ was because I had no eyeglasses and I was not allowed any, so I went from Grade One to Grade Nine without proper eyeglasses.

We played basketball, softball, scrub hockey and volleyball. One of my favorites was hockey. I can remember one year it was the Indian school being challenged by the *seme7* team. They won a BC Junior Hockey Championship and a Canadian National Championship. When they came back they wanted to teach the Indians how to play hockey. At the residential school, a team had to be picked and I was the team captain. The game took place at Riverside Park and that was a good experience. Our fans outnumbered the *seme7*. There was only a handful of *seme7* to cheer for this championship team. They used hockey pads and all the gear. We were only allowed to wear just the skates and sticks. Our goalie was allowed to have all the hockey gear. We slaughtered them ten-to-one. We let them have that one goal in the dying seconds of the game but that was my best hockey experience. I can just hear that roaring crowd cheering for us. I won the MVP trophy. I made five goals and three assists in the first ten minutes of the game. They gave us a plaque for it, and I got a plaque for MVP. Then we were banned from hockey after that. We had to turn in all our skates and sticks. But I knew from experience whenever we lose one sport, we're given another. We were assigned to soccer in the Winter and students would have no choice but to participate. It would be sub-zero weather, we'd have to be out there.

Going to this school was very harsh and strict and very lonely. I always believed there was no reason for what I was going through because I was just like any other student. I didn't want that kind of treatment. I used to wonder why we were treated like this. Why were they allowed to get away with such things? I always believed there must have been a reason. That's what helped me get through all this schooling.

In all my time at this residential school there were a few suicides. The names I don't recollect. One suicide was over on the swings beside the brown building. No one could figure out how that really took place, because it happened in broad daylight, blue sky out, sun was shining. It was on a day all the students went for a school bus ride, either a Saturday or a Sunday. When we got back everyone had to fall into assembly with their own groups. They gave a head count and called out the names. One oblate brother was asking who saw that student last. He was seen hanged on that swing. It was a big surprise to all the students. We knew there were a lot of students following that suicidal path. I've been told by students that they wouldn't be back after summer and their words would ring true. I guess they couldn't handle the school system.

I was thinking of another time on the main school bell rope. We were falling in line for meal time and that student was hung on that rope. It was up by the church. The nun went to ring the bell, it was called the supper bell, but she couldn't pull on the rope. I was on the second floor and for some reason I saw that student. For seeing or finding that student I got 150 straps on each hand and everyone had to fall back in their assembly line up in their rec halls. I think we had to skip our supper meal that time. I think remembering all these suicides played a big role in a lot of my anger that I had bottled up inside. Each time something like that happened, I used to wonder why I was punished so severely. For these questions, I never got any answers yet.

Another student was believed to have run away, and they named out certain groups, and we had to board a bus. We went along the back road a ways and then we were told to search certain areas, that this one student was missing. I was placed with a small group to check the river banks towards the school. I walked along the river bank and I found that student floating in the water by the shore. He was face down. I went to check his pulse but it was no use, his body was stiff. I hollered to one other student to call a supervisor and they showed up in a private vehicle. Again, for finding that deceased person I was strapped 150 times on each hand. I think there was a few times that happened.

Over by the river bank, there was a statue of Mother Mary. Students would fall into assembly there to pray on Sundays. One of my close friends was believed to have run away. Later I was informed that he hung himself in one of the apple trees close to that statue and I was strapped severely, I went into amnesia.

When I gave that some thought in my healing journey, I must have been close to death myself when I was going through that kind of experience. I can remember that I got strapped around 150 times. We were not allowed to move our feet or hands during strapping, but I was unable to stand. I guess I was going through a broken heart experience and I just collapsed to the ground. They told a student to remove my shirt while I was on the ground and they strapped me on the back. I guess that's where I went into amnesia for a while. That really took a chunk out of my life. I was never the same after that experience. I must have forgot about everything. My schooling. I didn't really participate in sports and I didn't associate with other students and things like that. I even skipped meals. I struggled in grades and eventually I forgot all about it.

One time I was asleep and the supervisor picked me to go grab this garbage can by the back gym door. That garbage can was never supposed to be there. I was kind of angry because there were other students awake, but when I went over to that garbage can my heart started pounding very heavily for some reason I didn't know. Then I turned around, this was early in the morning, and I saw this girl hanging. I ran up the stairs and checked her pulse and she was dead. I catapulted down the side of the steps to the ground. I was hysterical. I wanted to run back to my side, then one girl came out and I told her to call the supervisor. That nun ordered the girls to stay in their dorm and the boys had to form an assembly. One nun was going hysterical telling the students to pray, then she told us to look away from her. Eventually the Mounties got there and removed her. Then the boys were ordered back to their rec hall to form an assembly lineup. No supervisor came in our rec hall for a long time and finally an oblate brother came in and announced that no one was to talk about what happened.

I think that went for a lot of things like that, no talking was allowed about it. Even accidental deaths or if someone was sent to the BC Penitentiary, it was never to be talked about. One student shoved an oblate brother by accident when he was getting strapped. He slipped and shoved that oblate brother just to catch his balance. He was removed at midnight by a cop who came to the front door. Everyone expected that. We knew what punishments to expect when the cops came to the front door at midnight and they drove him straight to that penitentiary. Actions like that, I'd really be outraged, because where were that student's rights.

I remember it was a Saturday night, everyone got to see a show in the gymnasium. It was a comical show, everyone was laughing and I realized there was one section that no one was laughing, so I asked the student on my right, "What's going on up there?" That student said, "Ignore what's going on up there." I said, "I'll go find out myself." I walked across the gymnasium floor, to the corner section by the projector room. When that group saw me approaching, some of them tried to tell me to forget what I saw. I just said, "I want to know what's going on."

An oblate brother must have took some boys in that projector room and he was sexually molesting them up there. I went in that projector room, the door swung shut like a saloon door, by itself. When I was in that projector room I got my eyes used to the dark, there was a part of me that was scared, but another part was enraged. That oblate brother was saying, "What goes on in this room stays in here." Then he asked, "Who is that at the door?" I said my name and he said, "Oh, a new boy." Then he told me to go beside them other boys. I told him, "There is a problem brother," and he said, "What is the problem?" He turned towards me and I grabbed him. I guess that surprised them other students and they went cart wheeling out of the projector room.

As I walked out, there was a mop close to the door, I grabbed that mop and when he was standing up I broke the mop handle over his forehead, split his forehead open. By then other staff were running around, they ordered the front lights turned on, just one of the row of lights in the middle were turned on. There was a pay phone by the door, I ordered a student who was in the projector room to phone his parents. One nun confronted me and said, "Father is going to be very angry at you." I screamed in her face, I told her to shut up and they all said, "No one is to move and no one is to say nothing." In about an hour or so their parents came and they were outraged at what had happened. There was four involved, but they died or committed suicide, and that oblate I think he was charged in Williams Lake.

In later years the media would say something like he was attacked for no reason. I just got out of prison, I'd see that on the TV and I'd go into a rampage. But that's how these things were dealt with, they were covered up, even by the media. The days after that I was strapped severely and no one was to talk about that incident. That was what I can remember of that experience.

My last year was 1972. Three days before summer holidays, my younger brother and another close friend of ours, we decided to celebrate the summer holidays coming on. We got a bottle of whiskey and we got carried away with our celebrations. That was the day I took off. I didn't want to stick around for corporal punishment, because I had word that I was kicked out. I can remember walking down that highway and I felt free. I could feel all that burden being lifted from my shoulders. It was like getting out of prison, I guess. Just knowing I could go home and stay home and never look back.

I didn't know that I would be going in and out of prison, though, and be a ten time loser. I managed to quit getting into trouble with the law and then it was another ten years of alcoholism. I went through a fifty-fifty chance operation on my 18th birthday and in 1980 I went to Round Lake. Since that time I have been sober. I'm still working on my Grade Twelve and working on my healing journey.

At the present time I'm finishing my Grade Eleven and Twelve math and hopefully by next fall I may be in some university course, forestry or Native politics or Secwepemtsin. Those are the three big steps. I just feel it's a challenge to myself, because it's something I missed out on because of the nine years in residential school and all that I went through. I went in and out of prison ten times. That was mainly because of the residential school and then ten more years of alcoholism. That was mainly because of the residential school. I feel like I'm a step ahead, but there's a long ways to go yet.

Highschool graduates were seen as proof the school was successful in educating the Indians as spelled out in the government's assimilation policy. Until the 60s the children only went up to Grade Eight.

Healing

"We used to go home for two months in the summer and two weeks during Christmas. The kids really looked forward to that. It was just such a happy time and every time we went home my parents were still there, still carrying on, never ever being away."

Anonymous

I remember just being real lonely, missing my mom and my dad. I was quite young and didn't really understand what was happening. All of a sudden I was taken away from my mom and my grandmother, whom I was very close with. I remember being really lonely and clinging to my brother Kenny because we were real close in age, and it really bothered me that they took my sisters away from me. Back then, as a family, we lived in a two bedroom house, and there was approximately ten of us in that house, so we were really close all the time.

That was one of my first times away from home. When I was a kid there was hardly any vehicles and I was really excited to actually go for a ride. But, the thing that really bothered me was that I got to the school there, and it was really strange for me. It was a big place and all I really remember is wanting to go back home, back to my mom and my granny, but I couldn't do that.

At that time I could only understand Shuswap because I was raised with my grandmother. She raised me because there was so many of us in our family. All of the kids were about a year apart and our grandmother took three of us and my mother had the rest.

The thing I found troublesome for me was learning English. I remember getting beat for using my language but I didn't really understand anything else.

We were forced to learn to pray in their way. It was really difficult because back then prayers were done in Latin, and we were taught English in class and we were still trying to hold the Shuswap language.

When we got up in the morning the first thing we did was we prayed and then we cleaned up our beds, then after that it was breakfast, then it was praying again, then class, then praying, then we'd pray again and, seemed like we were praying more than we were actually learning.

The clothing was basically everybody wore the same like we had work boots and black pants and a gray and white or sometimes a white and black shirt. And we all had the same haircuts. When we got there, they took our hair right off of us.

The beds were very close. They were dormitory style and people were maybe about two, maybe about four feet apart. All up and down in rows. I would say about sixty to a room.

We had to shower and do our teeth and at that time we were always what they called deloused, and they put this stuff for bed lice. At that time there was a lot of bed lice, and there was scabbies and there was bed bugs.

Discipline was very harsh. We weren't allowed to talk unless it was play time. If we were talking in class we were beat on and we were made to stand in a corner, and a lot of times we were strapped for speaking other than in class. I was beat on a lot for using my language because I didn't understand any English until I was in about the third grade. The thing about being there that is really important for me, is that I got an education. I feel I've also got discipline in my life.

We had to fight to survive and a lot of times some of the guys even stole too. A lot of the guys would go down to the orchard and steal, or go down to the cellars and steal, or go into the kitchen, because at that time the food there was awful. A lot of times the older kids would, I don't know what they had to prove, but it seemed like they were always picking on the younger kids.

The thing that really helped me along through my years was yearning, I guess, to get back to my grandmother. I was a very young age when my mom passed away. I was about seven years old and I didn't even know my mom passed away and my grandmother came and picked us up and brought us back home to Bonaparte. We asked where our mom was. No one would tell us and during the funeral, I realized it was my mother's funeral. Then I learned I had to be strong, not only for myself, but for my younger brothers and sisters because we only had the one parent and then our grandmother took over the parenting role.

When I first left the residential school I really had a difficult time trying to fit back into my family, because I felt they didn't understand where I was coming from, because I had a little education. When I came back and my father didn't understand what I was talking about and then he'd speak to me in the language, I really couldn't understand him.

The thing I've found with myself was that I had a lot of hurt, because of the things that had been taken away from my family and I did a lot of drinking. I became an alcoholic. I still am an alcoholic because of the things I've gone through from that school, I tried to, more or less, wash my sorrows away in a bottle but I found that doesn't help.

Today I try and watch what I eat, because I'm a diabetic and I walk twenty minutes sometimes a half-hour a day. I go to the Sweatlodge and I try to keep an open mind, like I've gone back to our ways. I don't go to church, I leave that part alone. I don't knock it either because some of our people still use that way. I've decided to take myself back and do our own, our own thing, our own ways.

I feel I'm on a real good road if I stay within the circles like the Sweatlodge, the Pow wow circle, the Native American Church where we sit and pray all night. That's the things I do on a regular basis and everyday when I get up I always give thanks for what I have. I never take anything for granted anymore and I always give thanks for the food that I have, the water that I have to drink, give thanks for my family and I try and take care of myself the best I can.

When I first started my adult education journey this lady came to the school, her name was Shirley Sterling and she had this book she wrote called *My Name is Seepeetza*. All that time I thought it was just myself and my brothers. I envisioned just us going through all the things that happened in the school. But as I listened to this lady speaking about her experiences I thought about my sisters. All this time I thought it was just us that had gone through all that. As I listened to this lady it really made me feel hurt inside for my sisters and my relatives to hear the things they've also gone through.

As I listened to this lady talk about the residential school and her recollections, it really made me feel for my sisters. That they were being beat on also and going without food and getting abused physically and mentally. Myself I wasn't physically abused. I shouldn't say that because I was strapped and I was slapped and also got beat on for using my own language. I was about seven, eight years old at the time when all this happened to me. Oh there was a lot of strapping, like kids that either stole or lied or talked out of line. Some of them that ran away, came back and they were beat on, their hair taken or shaved off, and I remember they would take their clothes off them and put a wet towel on their backside and they were strapped. A lot of times if they were a bed-wetter they would take the sheet and put it over them and they had to stand in a corner like that. I remember the one time, must have been about Grade Three, I was sitting there in class and one of the guys to the right of me, he said something to me and I used our language and I remember getting slapped off of the chair and before I got up I had my arm pulled. My arm hurt real bad for a long time because of that. I remember that like it was yesterday.

I have a really difficult time, even at my age, to speak my language because I still have this feeling that I'm going to get beat on. You know even though I understand it, I read it, I write it, but to actually get up and speak it, I have a hard time with that. With my family right now, I have a lot of support from my wife. Like we've been together 26 years and I mentioned it to her a few times, the things that I went through as a child. She said, for herself, she was fortunate that she didn't go through what I went through. There was a lot of drinking in our lives when her and I first got together, and when our oldest boy was born we decided that we didn't need to bring our children up in this way. So we've been sober now since 1974, it's been a long time for me.

When I first started my education journey, my son came to me this one day and he asked me, "Dad, what is this?" He showed me some of the language and I couldn't answer him. I felt I should do something about it so I thought, "I'm going to learn the language." I'm even getting to the point where I'm actually using the language by speaking it. I have a good teacher now in Marie. She's kind of taking me out of this little shell I'm in. She uses the language around me all the time and I really feel that's what I need.

My life has been a circle, I left residential school over thirty some years ago and my life has brought me right back there to where I left, and I got educated there again. I picked up where I left off. I did six years there and the thing I had a difficult time with was going back into that building after all those years. I remember the first time I went back there, I think it was in 1994, I was going back to get my Grade Twelve. I had a real difficult time with going into that room because that's where the dormitories were. I could still, in my mind, see all the beatings that went on in there and all the abuse. Then the second year I was there I went into this other room that's another place where a lot of the kids were beat on, where a lot of them had their hair shaved and all the strappings went on, and there was a lot of fights in there. But when I left that building after those years I walked down those stairs on the outside, on the red stairway there and, I looked at the building. It really made me feel good to be able to look at that building. If I didn't go back to school, I don't think I would have gone back into that building again. But I had to go back to make me feel good.

The final thing for myself would be to fully regain the language and to be able to teach. I can read and write the language but I'd like to be able to get a degree in linguistics, that's my goal. I started this, like I say, six years ago but I still feel I haven't completed yet what I started out to do.

What I would really like to leave for my kids is to show them a good clean way of living, a good spiritual way and a good cultural way. What I mean by cultural is to be able to use our adopted ways like the Pow wow and to use our way which is the Sweatlodge, and to be able to go out in the *seme7* world and make a living. I try to be a role model to not only my children but to other children that I'm around, to show them that you're never too old to learn. I feel if they see me work hard at what I'm trying to do then maybe they can pick up on that.

The thing I would like for any child is to leave that alcohol alone, which is very bad for anybody. I would like to see the kids here in our community have something they'd be proud of, like a gymnasium. A place where we can have some pride in who we are and to have sports and to be able to have different functions on our Reserve. Something to keep the kids away from the things I feel are bad for not only them, but other kids, too. I would like to see our school here to be full Secwepemc immersion like what they're doing at Chief Atham at Adams Lake. That is what I envision.

Today, I feel that the children are very fortunate because they don't have to go through what we went through. Our children are not forced into things that are not our ways, like the religion.

Vivian Ignace

My name is Red Willow Sun Woman, my mother and father were members of the Lower Nicola Indian Band in the Merritt area. I was sent to residential school here when I was seven years old, so that would have been 1954.

My family, were highly spiritual people and we had our healers. My mother Minnie and my father Sourelle Moses came from a very loving family. We lived with our grandparents, my mother and my father had their home right next door, our uncles and aunties lived all around us. My grandparents and both of my parents spoke Nlaka'pamux, so I had very little English for the first seven years of my life. My parents and my grandparents Jimmy and Elizabeth Moses were wonderful human beings. Them days we never had social assistance, so everything we had they gathered. They worked very hard and I remember lots of laughter, lots of stories.

We were raised with the willow stick. So grandmother Red Willow looked after us, disciplined us from a very early age, we couldn't run, couldn't hide. That was a wonderful way to raise the family because it taught us to respect one another, to help one another and to work together, play together, cry together. We would rise early and my grandfather or my dad would get up ahead of us and make fire and Granddad would go out and bring in the water. My father would be making a big breakfast for everybody, sometime there would be twenty or thirty people sitting down to one meal. My father and my grandfather, they'd whistle just like the birds, that was a nice way to wake up. I guess it was sort of what I would call heaven on earth. We were close to the earth because we got all our food from the earth and the water was clean and the air was clean and we were loved and appreciated and we were taught that we had some rights. Every child was recognized as an individual.

Sometimes my grandmother would take me and put me up on the back of the saddle, she'd be looking for herbs for medicine. Life was simpler then, people worked, and they loved to work. We didn't have dolls, I used to like playing with whatever I could find with the animals or with the bugs.

My grandparents and parents were respectful of their people. My father, my grandparents and my uncles they would hunt for people. People would come down, bringing something to trade for some fresh meat. If somebody was sick they would help them out, my aunt would go clean and cook for them.

My grandmother was my greatest protector and provider. When I was little over two, maybe going on three, she suddenly died. She couldn't go anywhere that I didn't know about, I was her shadow, I just wanted to be there with her even in death.

My older siblings started to leave home at certain times of the year. It would be a joyous reunion and then they'd be gone again. I never knew where they went. It seemed like each time they left and came back, they'd be different. My brothers became more hyperactive, talked louder, were a little rougher, my older sister she was getting more detached, but I would see change in them. I wondered about that change but no one ever spoke about it. I started to feel fearful because I didn't understand it.

Then it was my turn to go to school. Our parents got us ready gave us a bath packed a little lunch, I remember my dad buying a little bag of chips and a pop for each of us kids and mother packed our clothes in a paper bag. We all got in Dad's truck and we were taken to Merritt and there was a big truck there and a whole bunch of loud kids, happy jumping around. They all crawled up on the back of that truck and my dad helped me up. He handed me my bag and my pop and my chips and he said, "Be a good girl now." When we were all loaded up, I was sitting there and I was so nervous, I was getting cramps. I just didn't know what to expect.

My sisters seemed pretty comfortable and my brothers were pretty excited. I can see that truck now, it must have been a five-ton cattle truck and they picked up kids in Quilchena and then they came over to Kamloops.

When we got into residential school the first place I had to run to was the bathroom. All of us kids made a fast exit, grabbed our stuff and went for it. My sister took me by the hand, walked me down that hall and there was a dark tunnel and there was a light at the other end. I heard these hasty very heavy footsteps coming down the hallway. I didn't even have words to describe what that was and the clinking of these beads and a woman appeared, in a black dress, scared the heck right out of me. I remember backing away and pulling away, my sister was saying, "Don't be scared, that's Sister."

We were ushered into this room and given a locker and a bunch of clothes, marched right into the shower room. Someone came in with a little brush and scrubbed my knees and my elbows and shampooed my hair and put this smelly thing in my hair. I found out later it was for head lice. It went in my eyes and I could taste it, I never ever seen anything like that back home. We got dressed in clothes that were too big, and we all lined up for haircuts. I had my hair cut twice in my life and that was the second time, they took it right up to my ears, boy that was a shock. Then we were shown the dorm and I grabbed my cousins hand and I wouldn't let it go, so they had to put us together because neither one of us would let go. Everywhere we went we all moved like a little troop, twenty or thirty of us going together.

A lot of kids were crying on that first day and days after that. I'd lie in my bed, it seemed like the only place where you could be with your thoughts and by yourself was in your bed after lights out, and cry myself to sleep. Always looking for Mom and Dad, my goodness, my brothers I'm sure they were going through the same kinds of things.

The food wasn't that great, we had porridge everyday, jam sandwiches, we ate a lot of apples, raw rhubarb, stew, milk and drank lots of water. Went through all of seven, eight, nine, ten, with my food allergies raging, raging eczema. They bandaged me up from my ankles to my hips and then from my wrists up to my shoulders and up around my back, bandages, bandages. I'd have to march up and down the stairs, three or four flights of stairs, little straight legs going up, trying to come down bandages falling off. By the time I got to about ten, I remember looking at my wrist and going gee I must be getting better, I can actually get my hand around my wrist where there wasn't a bandage. Gradually it just disappeared.

It took me two years to learn how to print and how to do my alphabets, because we didn't have that at home. Our mother never went to school, father I think went to Grade Four, but he was too busy working to give us the alphabet and our grandparents couldn't speak English. I remember sitting at these tables with little boys and little girls, just like myself with a great big black pencil, trying to do our letters. I finally figured it out, I think by the time I got to Grade Three I was reading. We had Dick and Jane, Spot, stories about upper middle class families. Here we were little Indian kids reading about somebody driving a fancy car and mother wearing hat and coat and gloves and high heels and having a dog named Spot. I thought gee who are these people and who lives like that?

We always prayed, I guess that was kind of a favorite time for me. We'd wake up with a prayer, go to sleep with a prayer, pray before meals, get up and go to church, Sunday of course everyone went, throughout the week you had a choice. When I was about nine or ten, there was some decisions I could make on my own and that was one of them, I was going to church and off I'd go. I'd find time to be by myself, we could get up and have an early morning shower or bath, I would get up every morning and do that. Whenever I could be on my own or to bed early or going to church or wherever, because we were constantly with other children, there didn't seem like there was much of a quiet time.

I didn't make it this far without help and I realize now that even as a child and a baby, a child in residential school that I was learning all my lessons of responsibility and through all of my experiences discovering who I am, who I really am. I have to thank all those people regardless of the quality of care that was given to me, my family, my parents, my community, the Catholic orders and all the teachers. I'd like to thank them for having been the best teachers they could be, regardless of where they were coming from. I always knew as a child that there was more to life than just what I was experiencing in residential school. The sheer magnitude of loneliness and anxiety, frustration, confusion, through all of that internalized abuse it was teaching me inner strength and inner power. What we did to get through some of that hard times, our little group that came from the Merritt area, we all hung together. We took our quality time together, we talked with each other, played with each other.

Playtime was kind of an interesting time. We used to put our coats on then we'd go outside. Right after school, they'd give us a little snack, it was a jam sandwich or it was a little apple or a piece of rhubarb, that was a hard one to take. We'd play until a half-hour before supper, we'd come in wash our hands and line up and go to supper. After all these years, I could still smell the stew pots coming from the kitchen. The boys ate on one side, and the girls on the other and we'd see them as they passed in the dinner hall. If I could see my brother I would wave, I didn't see them much, maybe might pass by them going into school and I would sit listening for their voices in the dining room. Of course there was a wall that separated the two dining rooms, but I would just sit and listen for their laughter. I sure missed them.

When I was about Grade Three they moved me into what was called the intermediate. There was a lot of peer pressure, our little bunches were really defined, those that came from this area or that area. They were always fighting, it seemed to be something to do to corner some little child, someone smaller than them and pinch them or pull their hair or taunt them.

Then I started noticing some children had better clothes and better shoes, they had things that I didn't have, they would have barrettes for their hair and they would have a nice sweater. I got my first sweater when I was about ten. It seemed like sweaters were really expensive and we just got what we absolutely needed.

There were some holidays that we participated in. There was always Hallowe'en for the school, I remember the nuns would tell us goblin stories. And then one of the nuns would run in with a big scary mask and scare the heck out of all of us little kids. We'd go running around screaming and I would just run and scream as loud as I could and they'd chase us around with these masks, that was kind of fun. Then we'd get little bags of candy with an apple and some nuts. And on Valentine's they'd give us extra treats.

Oh I used to like going to the dances because then I'd see my older brothers there. Friday nights we had the movies, there was always an old duster, like a western, but mostly it was something to do with wars. Maybe once a year we'd get a Walt Disney or a family movie. The girls sat on one side of the gym and the boys on the other. It was a lot of fun, everyone would sit there looking at their friends, their cousins and be a lot of talking, laughing and giggling and if you were particularly bad that week they would make you sit with your back to the screen, so you could hear it but not watch it. I had to do that a couple of times.

Once in a while we'd get a visit from one of our relations from home. I remember my auntie coming and calling for one of my cousins and she didn't call me, so I just threw a temper tantrum right there and the supervisor had to go out and get my aunt and bring her down because there was no way to pacify me. She came down, they took us out for the afternoon, Saturday afternoon, we went uptown and had dinner. Visiting time was really a great time when they'd come, after they left I'd sink into a little depression and just cry myself to sleep at night.

One time my parents came to visit, my mother bought me these barrettes, with a rhinestone on it and they were flowers. I can still see the colour, it was little green barrettes. It was so beautiful, I remember talking to God that night after lights out and I was still glowing, so thrilled about this little possession I had these two barrettes. I couldn't have been more than eight and I remember saying, "Oh God if I died and went to heaven, I'd just would be so happy because I have my barrettes." I was so happy.

We slept twenty or thirty in one dorm, when it was really cold in the winter, I'd crawl into bed with my cousin and we'd double up our blankets because it was so cold. In the morning we'd get into trouble, but we did it anyways. I never went anywhere without my cousin Doreen, we were the same age, the same age group, went to the same class, same dorm. That was nice having her there with me.

I never was a very good student, I was always a slow reader, slow in arithmetic, I just couldn't grasp simple algebra, it was just beyond me. Reading, oh my God, that was a nightmare. Now that I think about it I really didn't learn to read until I was in my early thirties. I don't know how I got out of high school. I remember writing government exams in Grade Twelve and getting just a pass. I always went to school reluctantly, I didn't care for it.

I didn't enjoy school, it wasn't fun, it wasn't my thing. I did it because I was sent there and my parents would get mad if I even suggested that I wasn't going back. But, I always said one day I'm running away from there. But, every year in September I'd go back and feelings of gloom and doom would just seem to wash over me and I just couldn't shake it.

When I turned about ten, I guess, Sister Leonita was looking for new recruits for what they called the Kamloops Indian School Dancers. I was recruited. There was a lot of discipline because they started practicing I guess towards the end of September. They would get the words to the songs and we'd have to sing everyday. We'd sing about seven or eight songs and then she'd give us our steps.

It was fun sometimes, most of the time it was just something to do to keep us busy. We got to do concerts and they'd dress us up and they made a fuss about us and give us special meals and take us on trips. We did concerts for the Catholic church, we went down to Vancouver and to Kelowna and Vernon and Prince George and Merritt for different dioceses. If they were fund raising for something they'd bring us dancers in. They'd billet us out, sometimes the billets were great, sometimes the billets were a nightmare. One time I was billeted with this family up in Prince George. I was scared the whole time I was there.

But, you know I have to say that probably through that experience with the Kamloops Indian Residential School Dancers, I learned some assertiveness skills, I learned to smile even when I wasn't happy, I learned to get along and talk with people and that was good. I learned a lot through that Irish nun.

I remember when the church would call us over to Merritt and we'd have to do an Irish program for them there. My parents would come to the concert, and they would always sit close to the front and there we would be doing the Irish jig or singing our songs.

I could hear my father yelling in the crowd, "That's my girl, that's my girl" really loud. People would be laughing and I would get really shy. The shyer I got the louder he'd yell and my sister Val would be doing her number and he'd be yelling, "That's my girl."

When the show was over, we'd get to mingle with our families for a few minutes, so we'd run and change and pack everything up really fast. We'd just be flying because then we could run out and visit our families.

Dad would always have money for us, he'd give us two or three dollars and he'd have pop and chips for us. And then we'd have to get on the bus and say goodbye to our folks and head back to Kamloops. We'd get in sometimes at midnight and we'd be so hungry, it would have been a long, long evening, so they would always march us into the kitchen. Sister Leonita would open the fridge and give us cheese, bananas, oranges, bread, milk, cookies and cakes, that was our reward for a job well done. She would always set it up ahead of time so they would have sandwiches made and really good stuff that the other kids would never get and we'd just eat everything, just eat it all up, then we'd go to bed.

I noticed there were a lot of children that weren't having any fun, I don't know how they coped, but I'm sure they were doing the best that they could. A lot of children were by themselves. We had our little group, so we hung out together and looked after one another.

I wanted to join sports but Sister Leonita wouldn't let me, I was good at track and field. I wanted to play basketball and she said, "You're one of the kids that belongs to the dancers and if you hurt yourself it's going to be hard to train someone else in your place." So, we'd watch the games and not participate. When the nuns weren't looking we'd get a bop on the head or we'd get kicked or our hair pulled, we'd be swore at by the other kids in sports. So, that part of it wasn't good.

At about age thirteen I decided to take a job working at the school. I needed to start working, I figured I was old enough to work. I just did what we'd call house keeping, I was making beds, scrubbing floors, doing laundry and washing dishes. I think I was making like seventy-five dollars a month. We'd work every day except Sundays. I was probably the youngest student to stay the summer, I think there were four. There was always one other person from my family, and maybe two other students.

So, we took care of all the visitors that came in, cleaned their rooms, helped in the kitchen. I remember sitting out in the yard there one sunny afternoon with a couple of priests. This priest reached over and he ran his hand inside my leg and shocked the heck right out of me. I jumped up and ran into the building, into my room and locked the door. After that, because I had been sexually abused as a baby and I wasn't going to put myself at risk, I was really careful.

He was a nice man, but he just seemed to like to sneak a feel up if he could and he did that until I was sixteen. I know he treated us all really well, he always bought us treats, he took us for pizza or hamburger or ice cream in the summer months. I was careful of him, I would lock my doors and every now and then I would hear someone trying to get into my room. I'd always put a chair up behind the door, make sure no one could get in from the other side. I could hear them creeping down the hall and scaring the heck out of me, trying to get in and then creeping away again. But, I needed to work, so I just had to be careful.

When I think about it now, and where I am today, my healing program, and all of the relationships I ever had, my family, the people I went to school with and the caregivers, the priests, the nuns that was all very important for me to do that. I didn't understand it then and it didn't feel good going through it. We got a lot of religion and when I left school I always said that I was never going to go back to that church again.

I guess if I didn't come to this residential school I probably wouldn't have heard about the Creator the way I know him now. I wouldn't have heard about my Christ, I wouldn't have heard about the Holy Mother and that part of my spirituality. For years I was confused about prayer. I remember hearing, just tell God about it, tell God about it, that it'll be taken care of. But I never knew how to do that. I had to come into my spirituality to find myself. I think the Creator, my God, my Christ, my Holy Mother speaks all languages and I do have a great desire to learn my language, Okanagan, to learn Nlaka'pamux. Because that's what keeps us a unique vibrant living people, culture is our strength.

My healing journey has been really something. Through my early twentys I got into drugs and alcohol and when I was in my forties, I lost one parent to alcohol. I think back about some of the things that made me so stubborn and so angry. We received a lot of discipline in the school. There was so many of us they had to keep a close eye on everybody and we had a lot of strict rules. There was a lot of rules. You know we all had to move together, there was a set time for everything, you had so many hours in the day and we had to do so much and there was so many of us and if we got out of line, we'd be given the strap.

I got a couple of good straps across my hands, I'd just cry and they burned. That was for whispering after dark and not ready for bed and wanting to play. The extreme of course was setting us outside the supervisor's door and kneeling all night long and waiting for her. I was scared to get off my knees in case she stepped out and seen me off my knees.

I remember how crippled I was getting off my knees in the morning, I couldn't sleep all night. I hated it if I was in trouble that day because then the nun would be telling everyone, "Oh that Vivian you know she wouldn't listen, she's talking back," or "I told you not to talk to that girl, she was in trouble. I told you not to go with her, no one was to go with her, but you're not listening, you were talking with her." So, she'd use you as an example and just be saying how bad you were and that I committed a capital sin. There was always the fear of capital sin, mortal sin that you would go straight to hell and there was a lot of stories about hell, that was a really scary scary idea.

I always figured if I was bad that I was going to go to hell, I never knew a compassionate God, I knew there was a God, but I was always scared of the devil more than I was of God. Our spirituality the thing that should have been our strength was working against us. You know, they played with us that way, I didn't like that. I didn't have words for it then, but I can see it now. That was a way of control.

If you were hurt or you'd be crying around, they'd just leave you crying by yourself. They didn't want to comfort you, they didn't want to hear about it. Everything was always, "It's your fault just go sit in the corner." No one was allowed around you to comfort you, but I used to always go. I would make it my business and go right over there and I got into trouble a lot for that.

I say I learned to be stubborn. We got a few beatings, I could still feel that knuckle on the back of my neck, on my spine, hurting, but it made me strong. At a very young age I was learning compassion, I didn't have words for it then, I just didn't like the way they treated the kids. I was one of the kids, but I didn't like the way we were treated, I did something about it.

Anonymous

I come from Stwecemc. Before I went through residential school I lived on Dog Creek Mountain in a lumber camp with my mom and my dad and my other siblings, the ones that lived at home. The other boys worked in the mill and they had their own place.

I remember the freedom, I remember the relationship that I had with my mom and my dad. It was still clean, I guess I can look at it in that sense where I never learned any unnecessary behaviours in order to get attention because I got a lot of it.

I'll never forget the day the priest came to the cabin in some blue car I remember. Me and my brothers and sister got picked up from the mountain. I remember getting the little bag that my mom packed for me. I'll always remember what was in there, there was some dried meat and some kind of fruit, it was lunch to take for the road and a pop bottle of tea. A little bottle with a screw cover on there. And I remember Mom standing at the doorway, and I could see her crying and I can remember having this big lump in my throat. My brother was sitting beside me. He kept telling me everything was going to be alright, that they'd look after me. I don't remember too much of the ride into town. But, I'll never forget the day or the moment when we got to the school and there was lots of kids just getting out of cars and out of buses and out of whatever vehicles they were brought into the school. We were all divided into age groups and I had to go to this dormitory, and they had this barber chair and I watched these guys get their hair cut right off, nothing. I remember looking at them and telling them my dad just cut my hair, I just kept getting pushed, pushed me in the chair and they cut my hair off.

And we were herded into the shower room. I remember the first few moments of my life that I ever knew what shame was like. Being pushed into the shower with no clothes, they pushed me into the shower with all the rest of the boys. And then they had us put this powder under our arms and in all the little crevices in our body, in our hair, in our head we had to rub all this stuff in and then we had to get into the shower and we had to use this white soap. I remember how awful that soap was.

Like everything was so foreign, we had to go kneel down to pray before we went to eat and go down and line up downstairs and kneel down and pray again and file into the kitchen and stand around and pray again. Holy smokes that food was really blessed, really had to bless that rotten food so that we could eat without getting sick. I remember some of the stew meat that we had, the meat or whatever it was, was spoiled sometimes.

162

I never got to see my brothers or my sister, I wasn't even allowed to look over the other side of the school for my sister until I was probably in Grade Three. It actually took time to talk to my sister, maybe Grade Two and then she left anyway. My other brothers were gone. After awhile, I remember just me there because my brother came to school in Kamloops. There was a few of them from back home that came here, but I don't understand why I had to go to Williams Lake. There was quite a few of them I remember used to catch that other bus and come down here to Kamloops and we had to go up there.

I think the horror in my lifestyle was in the Mission up in Williams Lake when I was probably six or seven. There was some boys in the dormitory. They took me down to the end of the dorm and they threw me under the beds, they were fighting I never let them hit me. I ended up running and I went to the bathroom and they followed me in there and they beat up on me in the bathroom toilet stall and they locked that stall door and they beat up on me, they assaulted me. I remember feeling the ugliness. I guess at that time I didn't understand what it was, but it hurt and I felt so dirty. I felt like I didn't want to belong anymore, anywhere.

I don't know how but I talked to my sister, I remember crying and talking to my sister and I told her what happened to me. She told me to go talk the principal so I went and talked to him. I told him the names of these boys and what they did to me. I can remember him looking at me and shaking his head and telling me that I'd never be clean again in my life. That I had to go to confession and after I had to go and do penance. I was seven years old, I didn't even understand why, why these boys hurt me and why did I have to go and kneel down and pray and ask God or Jesus Christ or whoever the hell he was at that time in my life to forgive me for what I did and I didn't do a damn thing.

Everything and anything that happened after that day was a piece of cake. Nobody in this world could humiliate me to that level at that time in my life. I learned how to say yes sir, no sir, no ma'am. I learned how to fight and I learned how to hurt other people. There is only one of those boys left alive today that hurt me at that time. But, I can remember even today the effects of what it did to me. Because I learned in order not to get hurt I had to learn how to find a place to hide and the pattern of my life for emotional pain started.

Whenever I was hurt emotionally I went to the study hall, I used the study hall as a place to hide. I was safe there, nobody could hurt me, nobody could touch me. Every time after we got off the bus until supper, I was there, then after supper until eight o'clock or whatever time they would let us stay at the study room that's how long I stayed. Or I sucked up to the teachers and I cleaned the blackboard and swept the floors and did whatever it was I had to do in order to hide.

I had a hell of a good education, it was all through pain. When I was in pain the intensity of my learning level increased. All my energies that I had went into my education. That's probably why all through my life no matter when I was hurt, when I lost my mom, when I lost my dad, through all the relationships in my life when there was a separation, I went back to school and when I went to school I had good marks. So lo and behold I'm going back to school again in September. But there was a pattern that went on there.

In Williams Lake there was always friends, little cliques of people, that I connected with that I called my friends, our little gangs, I guess. We learned to help each other out in a lot of different ways.

And then one year the school in Williams Lake was too full and they brought me to Kamloops here. I don't know how old I was. I must have been at least twelve or thirteen. I was either in grade five or six, maybe grade seven, I'm not sure. I don't remember who brought me here, but I know I went to Williams Lake first then they brought me from the Mission down to here. There was probably ten or twelve of us that got transferred.

I remember going up to the dormitory, I could feel all these eyes on me checking me out. I was just another Chilcotin, they called it 'Chilicootin' because we were from the north they called us Chilicootin.

I remember this supervisor, he's one of our own people. We had our clothes all stamped or name tagged. I can't remember if we had numbers or name tags. In Williams Lake my number was 30, I was number 30. I remember fixing my bed and I looked at all these other kids and their beds. I thought these kids don't even know how to fix a bed, because in Williams Lake we had to fix our bed like in the army. Throw a quarter on there and it would bounce six inches in the air, that's how tight the blankets were, that's how we had to fix our beds. I remember fixing my bed and these guys were laughing at me, I didn't care.

Then the supervisor told me to go into his room, he had to talk to me. It was Fall time and it was dark outside already. I remember going into his little room. He had this bed in there and he had a desk, then he closed the door, that fucking asshole I'll never forget that. He told me he would protect me, he said, "I'm the only protection you're going to have here because you're an outsider." He said, "If you don't listen to what I tell you to do then I'm going to let those guys do whatever they want to do with you." He said, "I'll tell them to beat up on you everyday, I'll tell them to hurt you, if you don't do what I ask you to do." So I asked him. "What do you want me to do?" Started that shit all over again just like the Mission. But this time it was somebody that was suppose to be in a trusting position. Somebody that was suppose to have been looking out for our welfare, this guy abused me. Every time he got drunk I got drug into his room, I hated it here, this guy was one of our own people.

Those things that happened in Williams Lake were different, those were kids that were doing those things, this was an adult. This was supposed to have been somebody that was supposed to prevent these things from happening to us.

So my beginning in Kamloops wasn't very good and because I was an outsider I was always fighting anyway, he couldn't stop that. It didn't matter – after school, sparring sessions behind the gym. I became really, really mean, nobody could make me cry. I always fought two or three people at a time. I remember these boys from Salmon Arm and Kamloops, a few other of the boys here, a bunch of others.

I never told anybody what this guy was doing to me, too ashamed. Because I remember they used to tell me I was the supervisor's ass fuck. I remember always fighting over that, I was beating the shit out of them or getting beat up by three or four of them. But I made some friends here, people that looked out for me and I looked out for them, taught me where to hide when I needed to hide.

There was a guy from Fountain, his name was Cecil. I don't remember his last name but he became my good friend. He was a good soccer player and I remember how many hours he used to have me follow him around and chase him around in the soccer field, trying to teach me how to play soccer but I always had two left feet. I was always tripping around and falling down. And I played basketball, but I was never into sports like a lot of the other kids in the Indian School.

One of the things that I always remember is you never show your emotion. You had to walk around with this, when I think about it, the terms these people used to use 'wooden Indians.' They used to stand outside these tobacco shops and barber shops and stuff with a stone face, just you never let anybody know whether you're happy, sad, mad, glad, or whatever. You just had this look, impeccable wooden Indian look.

I remember that even went home with me. My mom, I remember her asking me, "Where is my happy boy? Where is my laughing son?" I remember telling her, "You kicked him out long time ago when he was just a baby and they took that smile away, they forgot to put it back."

I remember how many years I just hated my mom and my dad for abandoning me at the Indian school and being angry at my siblings for abandoning me at the Indian school where they had their own friends or whatever and their own things they had to do, so they never had time.

I can remember my nephews and nieces coming into the school and then pushing them aside because I didn't have time for them. Because I had my own friends, I had my little cliques of people. I got talked to about that from my niece and my nephew for not standing up for them, for not teaching them how to stand up for themself, not warning them what they were up against. Standing by and watching things happen to them without saying anything or doing anything, watching my own family molest those little ones and not saying anything. The guilt and shame that I lived through for how many years and sitting down with my nephew and my niece and talking to them and telling them when they are ready to deal with the sexual abuse in their life to come and see me. I want to talk with them, to share with them what I knew, something that I knew that happened with them, if they didn't remember or it they remembered, that I wanted to talk to them. I didn't abuse them but I watched them be abused and I let it happen. So those cycles that started in the Indian school just took right off into our own home.

I watched the alcohol and the drugs sweep through our homes. I watched the anger, the resentment, the bitterness, live within the walls of our home. And I watched them filter into the relationships that we each got into, watched them filter into our children and for some of them down to the grandchildren.

The bitterness, the anger, the guilt, the shame, it's really sad to watch the little ones in our home. It could be thirty degrees outside and they'll have clothes right down to their wrists, right down just about to the end of their toes. Every piece of their body is covered in shame because somebody might look at them. Somebody might see something in them, those little ones, so they're not allowed to express in a nice cool way on a hot day. I see all those signs and symptoms of everything that happened to us in the Indian school, in those little ones.

I never wore a t-shirt and shorts until I was thirty-five years old, sad. I was one of those people that had my shirts buttoned right down to the cuff and a t-shirt underneath, long johns and a shirt. Because I was ashamed of who I was, I was ashamed of my body, I was ashamed of what had happened to me.

All the things that came out of all that, how bitter I was. Even to this day there is certain people in my life that I totally despise and some of them are here in Kamloops. I just see them and blood curdles in my veins, and I hear names of people and I can feel the hairs on the back of my neck stand up, ready, wanting to hurt somebody. For the most part in the past ten years of my life I've been pretty mellow. But just to hear certain names in my life I can feel the tension in my whole body build up.

In 1992, I was sober at that time for probably thirteen years. I went out on a drunk in Williams Lake, one of the street people is one of the boys that abused me in the Indian school. I went to the liquor store and I bought a bunch of booze. I drove around all over town until I found this guy, it was early in the morning just after the liquor store opened. I found him, I said, "David, Come." He came to my truck I said, "Get in". He said, "How come?"

I told him, "Just jump in the back, you'll see." And I drove him way down to the creek bottom, down Glendale. There was already about five or six guys down there drinking.

When I got down there I took that half gallon of wine and took a forty pounder of Silent Sam and a twenty-six ounce of Southern Comfort and I walked up along the creek and I told this guy to follow me. We went around the corner from everybody and I sat there and I gave him that jug and I told him, "I want you to drink."

Then he started drinking that wine and I could feel that fear that was coming from him, he knew but he didn't know what was going to happen to him. He was watching how I was drinking. I'd drink lots of this Southern Comfort and I'd wash it down with the vodka, then vice-a-versa and he must have felt the hate in my eyes and I remember looking at him and telling him what he did to me. I told him you and your brother, this is what you did to me, and he was going to run and I told him, "Don't try to run, I can out run you, if I catch up to you I'm going to beat your fucking head right into the ground." I remember him sitting there and he was scared and he started to cry and he started to apologize. I told him you're thirty years too late, I was going to kill him. And then my nephew and my brother came looking for me, they seen the emotional state that I was in. I was so angry that I was crying and I was looking at this guy and I was crying and I just told him how much I hated him. My brother took my keys to my truck and he took this guy back to town.

I remember sitting there and crying and crying and crying, I couldn't quit crying. Drunk probably intensified my cry. It was the first time in my life that I had faced one of my perpetrators. Then I could feel the hatred and the anger and everything at its fullest extent, right there.

That wind never stops, used to hear it in Williams Lake at that old Indian school in the stair well, hiding in the dark corners, sneaking in the kitchen stealing food. Same thing here climbing along those pipes getting burnt knees and burnt hands, climbing on top of them pipes going down to the kitchen. Those people were always looking down the hall to see if anybody was walking and we were always on top of those pipes getting burnt. We had socks and towels wrapped around our hands climbing down and having a hard time to hang onto anything because it was slippery.

I remember just listening to that wind, that howling wind and being so lonesome for home, so lonesome for freedom. At that time I didn't know what it was, I didn't understand what it was but now I know what I was looking for. That freedom of speech to say whatever it is you want and who you want to say it to. To talk about that pain that was inside without being emotionally torn for days on end. I watched my own family and I watched my own people, the ones that came through these schools. I watch the pain that they go through, wanting to tell them this is what you need to talk about. This is the things you need to do in order to get to that place that we visualize and dream about. Happiness, a true sense of happiness, not all this other bullshit happiness, but honestly be happy. I played all those other roles all those years, people coming to me and saying how you doing, well gee it could be the happiest day of my life and I would be just wanting to cry. Never being able to be honest with people and say do you really have time to hear what I want to say?

I can remember going home during the summer holidays when I was a kid and the turmoil that went on every Sunday. Mom telling me to put on my good clothes to go to church. My dad telling me to get on my horse to go up the mountain and go to church in the mountain, go learn about the plants, go listen to the wind, go learn about the animals. I'd pick up a bible and go sit with my mom for two, three hours. My dad always knew I was weak, because I'd go to church. As soon as I got out of church I got on my horse and I was up on the mountain the rest of the day. That's one thing I was glad about my dad never had that residential school experience. I'm grateful for that because I had the luxury of two worlds in my own home. I learned my language from my dad, I learned about the medicine, I learned about the land, some of the old stories. I still have a shiver down my spine when I see these priests with these white collars. When I see them my whole being flashes back to that time. I can remember the first time in my therapy sessions when I heard the expression 'spiritual abuse' I understood it to a 't.'

After I started my healing journey I was fortunate that I went to work in the old Mission. In my early recovery I was able to rejoin some of the spirits that I had left behind in that Indian school. I was able to sit down in that corner where I was abused and cry and get angry and do all those things that I needed to do. If I hadn't done that I would have killed that son of a bitch down at that creek, he would have been dead and I would have been in jail. Then when I came to training for life skills coach I did my training up in this building and I can remember re-connecting with my spirit in this building. I remember doing part of my life chart and when I came to that part where I came to school here and I talked about those things. I remember going to counselling. For years I went to alcohol and drug counsellors and different therapists and my trust level was so low, I didn't trust anybody. I never stayed until I really knew that the people talking and listening to me were really sincere about what they were doing.

There's only been three counsellors and maybe two therapists that I've really trusted. I felt the sincerity of the work that they were doing and I could tell my whole story. I could sift through the different emotions and different feelings and learn to understand something from it. Why did I do this? Why did I react this way? Why did I come to the conclusion that I came to? So now when I tell my stories the pain is still there but it is not as intense as it was when I first started talking about it.

Now I realize I have a lot to offer other people that have gone through these places because the teaching that I was given, the traditional tools that I was given, the life that I live today, looking and working with medicines. All these things are connected to nature and that's where I would like to go with it to be able to assist other people to let them know that they're going to be okay, that nobody is going to hurt them anymore, and that they won't be going through this pain alone anymore. There are other people out here, they don't have to cry alone anymore. They don't have to hate alone anymore, whatever emotion they carry they don't have to be alone anymore.

Loneliness is a killer, it kills everything inside of you, you become absolutely nothing, I've been to that place three times in my life and I don't like it.

I can look in the mirror today and see all those other little people, those others from ten years ago to thirty years behind me, I can see that person and that person is okay now. That little person behind there isn't hiding anymore, I can look in the mirror and see those things today and understand it.

I remember the first day that I walked through these buildings. Going into that dorm I remember I just wanted to stand back and kick holes all over in those walls. I remember sitting outside at lunchtime and daydreaming, going through my mind the things that happened here. Going through a list of names that I remember of people that were here. The thing that I remember the most about this place was being treated as an outsider and never being included in a lot of things that happened here.

The hardest thing I did since I left the Indian school both in Williams Lake and here in Kamloops, was to learn how to forgive myself. I blamed myself, I blamed my mom, I blamed my dad, I blamed everything and that issue of abandonment with my parents, with my siblings and then learning to forgive myself for abandoning my spirit in so many places and leaving parts of my life in a lot of different parts of the country. After being sober for nine or ten years of going back to these places and sitting down and offering tobacco and praying and asking my spirit to come back and be with me. Going into the Sweatlodge and crying and talking about the things that happened in these places, things that happened to me in different areas of my life and going in and talking to the Creator and to the rock spirit and to my grandfathers and grandmothers and asking them to help me to clean my life, to take all the ugliness and the bad medicines and everything that was put onto my life. It is no longer a mistake, it's a lesson so that I can teach somebody else, I can show somebody else that they don't have to hurt like that anymore alone.

Anonymous

I started school in town from Grade One to Grade Seven, so it was day school for me. I was able to go home and come back. A lot of it was good. That was when I stayed with my grandparents. Then I went to Grade Eight, after my grandfather passed away, and my step-dad and my mother took me to the residential school.

The first year there I had two male teachers and they were really good teachers. We had to stay at the school and we had to do a daily routine of getting up early and going to church and praying during the day and during the week and Saturday we went to confession and we had our three meals a day. The sleeping routine - we had to brush our teeth and wash our face and put our nightgowns on, and before we went to bed we had to kneel down beside our bed. Every night and every morning we had to do this. So that part wasn't too bad.

The clothing - it was the residential school clothing. We could wear our own clothing after school. During the week we had to wear tunics with a t-shirt and the brown stockings and the shoes, oxfords. And we had to wear tams. We had a special set for Saturday and we had a special set for Sundays so we could go to church. Those were the only times we used those was when we went to mass. Like it was bright green and we had the tunics and white t-shirts. We had navy blue t-shirts and long stockings. I think we had blue tams and blue sweaters too. Some of them had green, it was mixed according to your size.

We ate three meals a day but it wasn't that good, the things I seen there at meal time. It seems to me the nun was always pulling one child up to the front and making that child kneel down and would spoon-feed the child. I could never understand why they did that. Maybe because the child didn't want to eat what was served. We used to get dry bread and a dry bowl of porridge. Saturday and Sunday we got corn flakes though. Most of the time we had only one helping so a lot of the children were very hungry. You know it wasn't all that good.

The girls that were dancers seemed to get rewards but they had to work hard for them. They had a big mirror up there and you had to dance in front of that. I used to watch some of the girls, my two sisters were dancers. When they used to get them girls up to dance and if they didn't lift their legs up high enough, the nun came along with a stick and hit you in the back of your legs right across your calf. Oh that would hurt. To see the girls kind of buckle when they got hit.

Every first Saturday and Sunday of the month the parents would come over and you could go out for the day. My mom and my step-dad would come over and get me. Sunday they would come over again and pick you up and take you out, like they could take you out shopping. You could go home on Sunday to visit your family and then you'd come back that evening. You had to be in by a certain time.

I seen a lot of things there that I didn't really approve of. I was too young to understand why all of these things were happening.

Friday night was the show and Saturday night was the dance or have I got it wrong here. One night was for show, one night was for dancers and one night was for sports. Saturday was the day when the cadets came over. You had to get ready for the cadets if you were in cadets. You had to shine your shoes and put your uniform on and go in drill practice in the afternoon from one to four. They'd have drill practice at the gym. Sometimes if we were good we'd go and watch a basketball game on a Friday or Saturday night we were able to watch a basketball game or a volleyball game. If you were good, you could go to the movies on Friday or Saturday night. If you were good you could go to the dance, like they had the socialization where the boys and girls could come in and they could dance together, but it was always chaperoned.

I always had to prove to the other girls that I was an Indian. Once the girls got to know that I was okay, then they didn't really harass me or bug me about it anymore. As for the nuns I don't know. They didn't really bother me. I got strapped once and I got my mouth washed out once. I had to kneel out beside the sister's bedroom all night because I was caught pillow-fighting, but that was my own doing. I guess it was probably because I said something I wasn't supposed to say. I got my mouth washed out with soap, it didn't taste very good. I got a strapping because two of the girls were fighting over the bathtub. The sister thought I was involved so she pulled me into the storage room and I got a strap. There was three of us girls that got the strap, on our hands.

The sister used to tell me I was bold, and I don't know why I guess maybe because I had Indian and white, they figured because of that I was bold. I didn't really like the way a lot of the other children were treated. You know it was bad, it was really painful to see them like that.

We had different chores to do like sometimes we would be peeling potatoes. They'd have maybe about four or six girls peeling potatoes. Then we went into the kitchen and we had to serve the sisters, the priests' dining rooms, and the working men's dining rooms. The staff of the kitchen, well they ate in the kitchen. A lot of times I had to work in the kitchen and after we'd start off in the boys' dining room and we'd have to clean up in there and then we'd clean up in the girls', then we'd go clean up in the kitchen.

If you were from Kamloops you hung around with the girls from Kamloops. Or if you knew your relatives from another area and if they liked you, well they kind of hung around you too. The girls from up toward Alkali they hung around together. The ones from the coast they hung around together. There was another girl there the same age as I am and she was the same color of skin as I was and we got close, because we both knew we were a bit different, like we had lighter skin. So we got to hang out quite a bit and we pretty well supported each other when we needed to.

When you went to bed, though, that was the part where you really got lonesome. You could hear a lot of little girls crying. I know my sister used to sleep in the bed next to me and she used to push her bed up close to mine you know and she'd wind up sleeping with me and I'd push her back, in the morning, so she wouldn't get into trouble. Then the thing I didn't really like was when the girls wet the bed. They'd have to take their sheets and wash them out or else, put on their wet panty. That wasn't good, you know, things like that was really not healthy.

On Monday we had to do the laundry and we'd be down in the laundry room. This one great big guy used to work there, he'd stand there and he used to stare at us. We got to the point where us girls we'd never be alone in the laundry room because he was always around. So we'd always make sure there was somebody else with us. When we'd take the boys' clothing to the other side, we'd always make sure there was two of us. And we followed up on the other side of the girls', because it seemed to me he was always kind of lurking around. He really made you feel uneasy. I heard stories about him too, so you always had to be on your guard.

On Thursdays we went to the sewing room where we had to do mending. If there was any ripped sheets we'd have to sew sheets or we'd have to darn socks or we had to mend the shirts or we had to patch pants. We did this on a sewing machine and we had to sew by hand so we learned how to do that.

We had to get up by five o'clock and be ready by six o'clock. We had to have our teeth brushed and our face washed and our hair combed. We had to be dressed and have our bed made, you know, and we had to have our corner all neat and clean. As soon as we were finished, we had to line up by the door and the nun would go and inspect all the beds and everything. When you wet the bed, you had to put your sheets at the foot of your bed. You had to fold up your other blankets and dry your mattress out. So she would go and inspect the beds, then we'd go to mass first. We had to go in single file into the church and we'd be in there until seven o'clock mass started. We were out of there by seven-thirty. We went down and we had breakfast and then at eight o'clock they gave you an hour to do your chores. Then we would go to our classrooms and have school. Every morning we had to read the bible in class and say a prayer before we started the day. Then we went until three o'clock. After school we either went up into the sewing room or we went to do our chores for supper, so that was basically what we had to do Monday to Friday.

We always had to be doing something. Sundays we used to go for long walks. We'd go through the meadows like where George Leonard's trailer court is now. We'd walk along the road, that road right up until we got to the Red Bridge, like there was a road right along the riverbank and we'd just follow that road. Then we would cross onto the Red Bridge and there used to be a corner store right at the end of the bridge. That was where we would go to buy candies, then we would turn around and walk back. You did enjoy it because it got you out of the building. Where the trailer court is now there's a big field there and they had some games down there. I think it was in the early part of March. They had soccer games and the boys played lacrosse down there. They had gymnastics at the school for the boys and boxing.

My cousin drummed and sang and one of the other girls hollered that I could Indian dance. I didn't know how to dance. I just remembered watching this guy down in the States, down in Sumas. My cousin was drumming and singing, so I got up and I started dancing, I was flopping all over. My legs and arms were going all over the place. I just made up the dances and Sister thought it was really good. My cousin and I were laughing and the other girls sitting at the table were really laughing because they knew it was all made up. [Laughter] I'd look at her and she couldn't help it, she just started laughing and she was trying to sing and drum at the same time. It wasn't too long after that my aunt and uncle came in and they started teaching us how to dance because they wanted the Elders to come in so they did. So we learned how to dance.

In June they had a parade in town so they got these boys on the float. They decorated the float up and they had the girls dancing on another float and then they had the Indian dancers. I went to watch that parade and they had all of these kids up there and they were drumming and singing and I think that was the beginning of where it started to open everybody's eyes.

Right from the time I was old enough to start talking, right up until about six or seven, my aunt said we spoke Shuswap. We didn't speak anything else. Then in residential school we weren't allowed to talk our language anymore.

What impact did the residential school have on my adult life? It was total confusion because I was brought up to believe that man and woman were meant to be together. Like we weren't able to have any contact with the boys. It was a sin if you looked at a boy, it was a sin if you touched a boy. Everything was a sin you know. It was strange and it was total confusion about believing in God, you had a very mixed concept of God. Like you were afraid of him and yet you weren't afraid of him. If you sinned, you were going to go to hell and the part that scared me was always the devil and hell, you know, you always heard that, "Oh, you're sinning you're going to go to hell, the devil is going to get you." That's all I heard hey.

One night Sister was getting us all to pray and one girl was there kneeling and she just jumped from her bed next to mine and she let out a scream. And Sister spun around like she just went by her bed and was just about where my bed was. That girl just jumped right across the bed and onto the other bed just as if she was a dog! She jumped back into that dog form and leaped back to her bed again. And boy Sister, she was running around there, throwing holy water on her. Saying prayers for her! Pray for her, the devil, and all of this. It scared us, some of the girls jumped in bed and covered up. She just transformed into something and did everybody get scared. The Sister told us to get down on our knees and pray, get out of them beds! So we were all scrambling out of bed to kneel down. That was scary that night, you know, and the girl she was a real loner. She was very quiet, very shy. To me I think she was very different, you know. I think about it now, she was a very gifted person, she had the gift of transformation. If she wanted to go someplace you know she could probably just change and go. I often thought about her after I left school, wondered how she made out, or if she ever got to where she was supposed to get to in life.

When I left school, I drank quite a bit and had bad relationships. Then I decided I wanted to quit drinking because I knew there was more to life. Finally, when I did quit drinking, it was April 20, 1979, I said, "No more, I'm going to change my life," and I'd been through two relationships already. The kids' dad, well he left me. My second marriage ended in disaster, that's when my kids were in the residential school. When my kids were there, he came and took them out

172

of there so thank God he was smart enough to do that. My kids didn't stay there that long.

I talked to my aunt and she helped me. I talked to people and they got me into Round Lake, that's where my healing started. I was able to go to Sweatlodges and take care of my healing journey and then I got involved in AA and in AA intertribal roundups. I got involved in women's healing circles, mixed healing circles, workshops, any kind of workshop I knew that would benefit me, I went.

I don't force the catholic religion onto my children. I don't force any kind of belief on them. I just told them all I want you to do is believe in the Creator as you understand him. That's basically what I want them to do. I don't want them to be afraid of God the way I was

That's how I take care of myself these days. I do a lot of Sweatlodge healing myself. When somebody wants to Sweatlodge, I go and do it. I learned how to run Sweatlodges when I was at Round Lake. I went out to different Sweatlodge ceremonies and learned from different places and I came back. This man came up to see me so I asked him if he would build me a Sweat Lodge, and he went home and he come back a year later. So we went down and built a sweat lodge. That's how I take care of myself today and that helped keep me on my healing journey, and sharing with other people things that have happened in my life.

I believe the truth will help the people heal. It wasn't their fault, what happened to them. I feel they should practice self-forgiveness, that's the biggest part of their healing. What I really believe in is the truth will set you free. You have to have self-forgiveness in order to be forgiven too for the mistakes that you have done in life. I don't call them wrongs or sins, I call them mistakes, you know, everybody makes mistakes and it's an easier word that can be accepted. Whereas, if it's a sin, then you cringe and you think about all of the shame and it just seems to come and crowd around you. If you say it's a mistake, then that's easier you know it's not so harsh or so demeaning. It doesn't make you feel like you're the baddest person in the world. I believe that they can come to the truth, then it's okay.

I also see encouragement for others to open up to tell their story, so they can heal. I want to see our Native people heal so our children can heal too because we have too many children who are, what you call, products of the residential school. We have to break the cycle and we've got to take that courage and break the cycle. I know I have done that and I know my brothers and sisters are doing that. They're starting to take courage to break the cycle too.

There is hope and my mother has broken the cycle too, so that's the big plus for us. Now she's trying to encourage her children to break the cycle. My children, I know, they want to break the cycle, because they've talked about it already. We want to break that cycle so my grandchildren don't get abused and their grandchildren. You know so my great-grandchildren don't get abused.

We can all be healthy people. I feel it's really important for us to heal now because with the way things are now for our future, we have to get stronger because things are changing for us. You know the races of people are all changing.

Pictured above is a senior boys soccer team. Sports were introduced in later years and were one way of getting away from the day to day monotony and were probably a way of releasing one's anger and frustration.

There were dances held at the school which were heavily supervised. It was one of the few times the boys and girls would have an opportunity to interact.

In talking about the dances a former student said that one of the nuns would circulate amongst the boys and girls; and she would say, "share the wealth" as she pushed the couples apart that she felt were dancing too close.

174

Any kind of sports were a break in the daily routine in the latter half of the residential school years. Pictured left is a girl's basketball team.

In one's healing process there will come an understanding of why a person feels a certain way during a certain time or place.

The bottom photo shows children returning to the Kamloops Indian Residential School.

For many the fall or coming of September is a depressing time, it is an unconscious reminder of returning to school.

Diane Sandy

What I remember is my Dad was a rancher or he looked after cattle on the range, and I remember staying out there in a tent. Just the family, way out there wherever he was working. We had a pot belly stove and stuff like that - just peace and quiet up there. And then we were moved to the Reserve here in Bonaparte and we lived in a log house by the church. We all lived in the one room place. The beds, your eating place, the stove where Mom cooked was all in one big room. I remember we didn't have a floor, it was dirt. And the next time, I don't know when they put a floor in there but after it was dirt it was easy to keep clean. You didn't worry about anything. But you know, that was togetherness. You know, you were all together and not split up by anything. That's closeness.

The first time we went to the residential school, we were all hauled to the school in a red and green truck like a bunch of cattle. There was about three rows of benches in the back and you were all put in there. From Lillooet all the way down and they would stop up at Skeetchestn and pick up the kids from there. That's how they took us to school. It was pretty scary the first year beause most of us did not really know English, we didn't know what we were in for.

Well, we were actually more in a daze of what's happening. What's happening? Why are we here? What do we have to do here? We didn't know. I spoke fluent Indian at the time because Mom always talked to us in Indian so that's all we understood. So when they told us what to do we're wondering what do you mean. Not understanding and they spoke to us in English and if they didn't push us to tell us what to do we wouldn't have known what to do. They told my mom that if they didn't take us to the residential school, if we didn't go to school, the Indian agent would take us away from her. So, you know. That's what she told me if she didn't send us to school then the agent would take us anyways.

So when we got there the boys were put on one side and the girls were all put on the other side. We couldn't understand why they did that, separating the family. Put the boys on one side and the girls on the other. The boys were crying and wondering why they couldn't stay with their sisters and stuff like that. That part of it was sad. I mean we were all crying when we had to leave from here because we didn't know why we were going. Everybody was crying and then we got over there and we saw all the kids there. There was quite a few of them anyway, and they were all hauled in the same way, by truck. Some of them might have went there with their parents help like horse and buggy or something.

The first week in September, that is when they came and took us all and we had to stay there for the whole year, to the end of June. There was, for most of us, there was no coming out for Christmas or anything because we never had the money. At that time nobody traveled that far on horse and buggy because that's quite a ways from here to Kamloops. I guess if a person had a car they may have been able to. But at that time it was mostly horse and buggy to travel.

For us who didn't understand English it was really hard. It was hard because when the nuns kept trying to tell you to say a word and you didn't know what it meant or why you had to say it – it was frustrating not being able to understand what they were trying to say to us. After we started learning some of them were smacked on the head if they didn't speak good you know, like "smack." If they didn't do what they were supposed to do or if they spoke without being spoken to - what were we supposed to say when we didn't understand it? For me I kept quiet most of the time trying to absorb all the newness of the environment we were put into with all the kids. Different kids, some of the language was different. Like the Secwepemc, the different phrases, the different dialects. We didn't understand that and it was sort of confusing. So, I'd say we were pretty confused the first year until we were able to start speaking English.

Mom always talked to us in our language and when we got back we used to speak in English at the time. You start losing the language. "What did you say? What did you mean?" I was turning white I'd say at the time.

The daily routines, you'd wake up in the morning, it was six or seven o'clock in the morning, you would go have your shower, your bath, brush your teeth. When you'd first wake up you kneel down by your bed and pray. And then you'd go and do your wash up and brush your teeth and stuff like that. They had baking soda for toothpaste, it tasted awful. Then you went to mass and then we had breakfast. When you go to eat you have to pray too, before you eat, and then we went to school. It was sort of like more church than school. When we got into the classrooms we prayed, we got in there and right after prayer we had catechism and then we had dinner break and then after dinner, one o'clock we would be back in school again until four.

Dress was a tunic, a maroon colored tunic and you wore, either you got black bloomers or you got white ones, brown socks. Long brown socks that grannies used to wear. That is what you were given. And darn it if they didn't cut our hair. The first week at school it happens they put us through a line up and they poured coal oil over our heads and combed it out and cut our hair short. And that was to prevent lice, something we never heard of. So, most of our hairdos that first year was straight cut and bangs, and some of us had long hair. We all cried seeing all the hair being cut off, put in a big pile there. Very strict, very, very strict. Like if you didn't do anything when they told you to do something you were either made to stand at the door, kneel or get the strap, one or the other. Even if you talked back you were given the strap. I pitied some of the girls though – like one was a very heavy student. She wouldn't do what she was told. She always ended up with the strap in front of all the kids. So that just scared the heck right out of us you know. We knew we had to do what we were told to do or we'd get the same thing. And the ones that wet the beds – oh, that was sad for them because they were made to stand right at the door as we were sent downstairs, with their wet bed sheets over their heads. It was so sad to see them. The nun would come and check their beds and if it was wet they were made to kneel outside the nun's bedroom door and sometimes they were forgotten and ended up you know curled up outside the nun's door all night. Oh yeah, some girls were really cold, you know, with just their night gowns. Some of them were treated pretty rough.

Abuse? I guess it would be abuse, getting strapped, knocked on the head, knuckles smacked by rulers, and the poor girls with their sheets over their heads. When I see those girls today I often think if their self-esteem was still affected or not. If it had been me, it would take a long time to forgive and forget.

We had to learn how to sing and dance like, you know, and then we had to compete with the ones downtown. That was when we got a little older, about twelve or thirteen. We were taken downtown in Kamloops to compete with the other groups down there, the *seme7*. And we had to make our own costumes for these dances. They judged our costumes and then we would dance and we all had different costumes. You would have to do your sewing for this and that is where I learned how to sew. You know I sewed my finger one time and that nun just told me, "Just take it out, just lift the needle". She didn't get excited. I was just screaming because the needle was right through my nail. And she said, "Just take it out." Learned how to darn, our socks wore out after awhile and we had to darn them and then we had to darn the boys' socks, the nuns' socks, the priests' socks, mend the boys shirts and pants. Never ending and then we had to can — tomatoes, crab apples all these things — which I hate to this day. Crab apples...

I was treated not too bad other than the fact that when Sister Mary William was going to smack my hands and I took the ruler and broke it. I was wearing jeans underneath my skirt and we weren't allowed to on a Sunday. And that time one of the boys' supervisors smacked me across the face in church for trying to get a hymn book. I told Father Mulvehill all about that - there was blood all over. The rest of the time it was okay – it was, when you sit and think about it now. It wasn't all that bad, you learned how to speak English, I learned how to sew, I learned how to darn, I learned how to knit, learned how to pray, learned how to get along with the other kids. After awhile, you know, there was little gangs there from Merritt and Chase, sort of like sparring off every now and then. Testing our territorial space, see who was the toughest.

My mom always said, "Don't ever forget your prayers - never forget praying." I did for quite a few years after we left the school because there was too much praying. You know what kind of sin could we get into. We had to confess – I even asked Father Egan one time, "What the hell kind of sin did we do when we were in school - did I have to go to confession?" He would give us these 'Hail Marys' to say, and this is years after when I saw him down at a funeral and I was talking to him about it. Like it just blows my mind when I think about it, sin. God, I do that now and I'm out of school for all those years, for all those prayers I did before you know. What I do now is all forgiven.

After awhile we learned how to cope. Putting up with what we had to. What else could you do? You couldn't run away. Sense of direction for me even if I ran away — where would I be running to? You know it was quite aways from Kamloops to Bonaparte. How would you get back? No money or nothing. Lord knows some of them tried to, they were brought right back, and the embarrassment they had to go through you know when they were sent back to school. That was scary. Either they were - with their pants taken down and given the strap

178

by the Sister Superior in front of all the kids. It would teach us a lesson not to run away. And it wasn't just a little smack – that was hard cause you heard it eh - one slap after another on the butt. This one that was really bad was that Dorothy, her name was Dorothy, she never gave up. She ended up being sent home because they couldn't break her I guess. That's what I would say about that.

Coping – yeah, you learned how to cope. You had to learn how to cope to survive there – you know being away from our parents. Many of us cried at night, late into the night. I mean, why were we sent there? But what could you do – what could you do?

We used to sneak smokes and cigarettes. That was the funniest when we first learned how to. Lord knows where we got those cigarettes. It was Edna Porter, Annie Williams, and Marie Antoine got them. One of us got cigarettes anyways, and we smoked that when the sisters had their sleep. Here we were blowing through this little hole out into the air so it was a mist. I think to this day she knew what we were up to but she would come around and we would all pretend we were sleeping you know. This one nun, she was small but man, she was one tough cookie. And stealing – well, we stole bread. If we got into the pantry we stole bread, carrots, anything you know because half the time we were hungry. We'd get watery mush and for the life of me I can't understand, why. They had dairy cows you know and yet we got watered down milk, and that's what they would put on our mush – I don't like milk in my mush to this day.

Sara Sterling, Diane Sterling and Nancy Pete, and Wilma Basil, we would have to practice our dancing. I said, "I'm not going to be in this for long." Sister Leonita said, " Come on girls this is how it's done." So I started shaking my feet up all over the place - really high – Sister Mary Leonita started clapping her hands. "Now, that's the way I want you girls to dance!" So, I was in charge of teaching those girls how to dance. When I talk about it to Nancy Pete and them they laugh. They says, "You didn't want to dance but you ended up being the one there to show us how to do it!"

We'd have to go down and get the coal for the furnace and once in awhile we'd see the guys there and we would sneak us some snoose. Lord knows why we had to. Trying snoose just to be naughty, I guess, a little bit of rebellion. I remembered cleaning Father Campbell's room - you used to have to clean their rooms. And I used to see all these empty wine bottles and I'd think God, he sure done a lot of mass to end up with all these empty wine bottles. Father Campbell, he was always half corked. So I asked a nun that one time, "Why does he have so many empty wine bottles? Is it just him that drinks it or does he share it when he says mass?" They took me away from that job.

These nuns, I will never forget the time they picked on my sister, Doreen. She just went wild, punched the heck out of them. They were pretty big nuns too, Sister Regalias and a few other nuns there. She got expelled after that because she hit them – punched them. When it ended, they put her in a room upstairs cause she was a senior then. Saw it happen. Locked her up in the room. They just locked her up after she punched the sisters up. They shipped her home after that. She must have been about fifteen or sixteen, somewhere around there.

What I am today, one beautiful person you know. I don't hold anything against them you know because even though they put us through this hardship and stuff like that you overcome that and like I said, life goes on. Because if you hold that inside, it's not good. That's how I looked at life – like life is life. Here I am today - I have kids and grandchildren.

Today, I look after myself through prayers and sweats. I look after my granddaughter. I went through workshops in healing yourself. I think I knew how to heal myself a long time before. I never forget Mom telling us to never forget our prayers. "That'll get you through anything if you remember to pray." Lord knows all through my life I was young all hell bent, outgoing, drinking, and I survived. Life goes on. You say life is how you make it. And this is mine. I think all my men would say the same.

Anonymous

Before I went to the residential school, I was with my parents and my grandparents. The Secwepemc language was my first language, I didn't speak very much English. I came from a loving home. I was taken from them and it seemed very brutal at the time, I couldn't understand it.

My first memories were of me lying in the back of this wagon on a mattress and my mom and dad driving the team heading towards the bus, to a place called Lemonade Flats. That's where the bus would stop and pick up people on the way into Kamloops.

My father was crying and he was saying, "Oh, my baby, you know she's too young to be leaving us." My mother told him, "You have to be stronger than that, you know. You have to look at her life ahead of her, she's not too young. The other girls have started at that age and besides, you know we can't keep her. They'll come and take her away." My father was crying and my mother was being strong. In reality they were the opposite. My mother was frail and tiny and almost sickly. And my father was the macho type, but their emotions seemed to be different at this time. I don't remember my bus ride, I don't remember anything after that. It seems like I fell asleep, I'm not sure what happened and the next time I came to I was in the hospital. Before the children would go to school here, they had to be sent to the hospital to get their tonsils out, that was a government rule.

I remembered being in the hospital, waking up and having a very sore throat. There was blood everywhere and I was crying. The nurse came and cleaned me up and she said she'd bring me a bowl of ice-cream. So right away I stopped crying. Ice cream and treats were really new to me because we lived on traditional foods. Indian ice-cream, I thought maybe that's what they were bringing me, so I just waited there. Pretty soon they came by with a bowl of ice cream and gave it to me. But it was too cold and I really didn't like it. I tasted a bit of it and then I just laid back down and I kept crying, looking for my mother.

My mother and my older sister Lizzy came by and spent some time with me. My sister told me, "Oh, you're going to be going to school. Mom won't be able to go there with you because you're carrying on too much and crying." So when they got me ready to leave my sister and mother couldn't handle me. I was throwing a fit and screaming and I was hanging on the bottom of my mother's pants and I didn't want to leave with anyone. I didn't want them to send me to school.

Eventually my mother and sister were crying too and they said that Father O'Grady would be picking me up. The next thing I remembered I was sitting in this station wagon and it was coming across the red bridge heading over this way. The city looked huge and the lights looked different. Everything looked glittery and I wasn't really used to all the lights, growing up with a coal oil lamp.

When I got to the residential school, it looked huge. I remember thinking, how am I ever going to find my way around here, everything's so big. When Father was talking to me, it seemed to be hollow and echoing. It seemed strange, you could smell the polish of the floors, it seemed so different. Father O'Grady packed me on his shoulders all the way to the recreation center downstairs. The noise down there was like a beehive.

I couldn't understand anyone or anything, maybe it was because of the language barrier. I'm not sure what it was. I wouldn't let Father O'Grady go, so they were going to get my older sister Winnie to take me upstairs to bed, because I still wasn't feeling well from my tonsil operation.

My older sister was twelve years old when she began school and they had her with the senior girls already or the intermediates. I started school in 1948, I was six or seven. So when I got to the school, the older girls were watching a movie at the time. Those days we were taken to the gym for one movie a month and I guess it was movie night.

I couldn't be left with them, so Father O'Grady had to take me to bed. When I got upstairs the lights were out and it was dark tin there. There was a little purple light or something out in the hallway. The dorm door was open and he was telling me "Okay, you say your night prayers and everything will be fine." He asked me, "Do you know how to say your night prayers in your language?" I told him, "Yes, I do." My grandparents taught me. I wanted to kneel on the floor, but the bed seemed really high. When I finally knelt down, I disappeared under the bed, it was so high. He said, "Oh, you can't kneel down there. You can kneel in the middle of your bed." So he picked me back up and put me on the bed and then I said my night prayers. He said, "There, do you feel much better?" I nodded and then he tucked me into bed and told me that my sister was at a movie and that I would see her the following day.

I remember laying there crying and crying. My sister snuck in after lights were out and I made her crawl into bed with me and I told her, "Don't leave me." I remember my arms around her neck. The next morning when I woke up, she was gone and I felt terrible. After that she would sneak in. I don't know how long this went on but eventually I had to get used to being by myself.

Everything was so strange. We were given chores to do. My chore was dusting and the next day I thought I did not have to do it. They told me, "No, you got to do this chore everyday right after breakfast. You go and do those chores." So my chore was dusting the ledges although I could barely reach them. The following month we were given different chores. Whether you knew how to do it or not, you were assigned something to do and you learned eventually.

We didn't have a whole lot of toys to play with, you just had to learn how to get by and provide for your own play things. We put together jam jar rings, you know, the red rubber rings. We would collect those in the garbage bins wherever they were being thrown away. We would string them together like rubber bands. The girls would skip with that in the school yard. We would find rusty old nails and little strips of boards and we would nail those together and make stilts, and the girls became really adept walking on stilts. You would see them walking in the schoolyard and up the hill.

The older girls in our group would bring in the Sears or the Eaton's catalogues, and we would cut out paper dolls from the catalogue figures, little clothes and so on. Shoeboxes became cars, so that would entertain us for a whole weekend, playing paper dolls.

I finally learned some of the girls' names. I started playing with them or talking with them. A couple of the older girls took me under their wing and took care of me. One was a cousin and the other was just a friend, they were from Bonaparte. They would take care of us, looking out for us and making sure the other kids didn't bully us. They would help us with combing our hair or little things that made life just a little bit more bearable. You know it was nice to know that the kids wouldn't beat me up if Jeannette or Edna was there. Then they would tell me a little joke or stories. When their parents visited them, they would bring something and they would share it with us, an apple or a few candies or something.

We were given lockers, they were called presses and they were made out of wood. We were given a press, two or three people to a press. There was coat hangers in there and a little shelf on top for your junk. You could stack your boots and coats in there in the winter.

We kept tin cans and we would cut them into strips, and then we would wrap them up really good with brown paper so you wouldn't get cut from it and then we would wrap our hair in that and curl it. That was later when we were about eight or nine years old. We learned how to do that.

When we were hungry, we used to break open the milkweed and drink that. When I was helping this ethnobotanist, he was saying that the milkweed was poisonous. And I told him "No way it isn't. We used to drink that when we were children. We would get so hungry and thirsty that we would pick the milkweed and we would either chew on it or drink the milk substances inside of it." I told him it wasn't poison because I'm still here and I was one of them that drank the milkweed.

Some of the braver girls would run down into the orchards and steal some apples. It had a big fence around it and it was guarded by dogs, out here where you see the apple trees now, just down in front of the Museum. There seemed to be a lot more fruit in there back then, it was just full of all kinds of fruit. We were never allowed into it. Some of the girls would go down into the kitchen and steal carrots. I remember just the older girls who looked out for us would go and steal food.

One Saturday I remember having a whole turnip to myself, I don't know where I got it. We scrubbed out a doghouse over down on the other side of the playground. We scrubbed it out until it was clean and climbed inside there. I remember peeling the turnip with a butter knife and eating it. That was our Saturday afternoon sitting in there eating, munching away on stolen turnips.

Once this bully got after me, she was a mean girl and she would take whatever she wanted from you. If she saw you with a comb that she wanted, she would take it away from you. If you tried to stop them they would beat you up, throw you down, kick you, sit on you, punch you, whatever. So the girls would be very scared of these bullies. The girls never had very much so these bullies usually ended up with pencils, pens, barrettes and combs, whatever they wanted, they took. A lot of the times we wouldn't fight back, we would just let them have it. We would end up with nothing, eventually you had to belong to a gang and the gang protected you. That was sort of a way of life. You had to belong and if you didn't you were vulnerable and beaten and so on.

The supervisors would be oblivious sitting there knitting or reading or something and let the kids do whatever. There were rules and we were called only by our numbers. Like "Number 232 to 280 go have a shower." And they would just send us out. "Number forty to eighty go to confession."

You got your change of clothes in a bundle once a week. That contained your clean towel, your washcloth, your underwear and maybe a clean blouse or shirt. We had these tunics. The top part was made from unbleached cotton and the bottom part was made from army pants or something, it was brown material. And we had brown sweaters over the top. They were wool and very itchy. I never did figure out why I kept breaking out all the time, wasn't until twenty years later before I realized I was allergic to wool. I remembered being given sweaters full of holes and we used to wear those over our nightgowns.

I remember my older sisters perming my hair, getting ready to send me off to school and she said, "I bet this perm won't stay in your hair very long once you get back." She told me what would happen and I didn't believe her. Some of the kids would come back with lice and they would cut everybody's hair. Everybody had real short hair when they were little. When I started, I had long hair and they chopped it off the first day I was here.

The loneliness carried on all the way through school. This place wouldn't have been such a bad place if my parents would have come to visit me. But they never visited very often because when they did, I would always break down and cry when they left and they just couldn't take it. I think in all the years that I was here they came to visit me maybe two or three times.

We used to go home for two months in the summer and two weeks during Christmas. The kids really looked forward to that. It was just such a happy time and every time we went home my parents were still there, still carrying on, never ever being away. They were always there for us. When we got home there they were, it was like time stood still, they would be there, still waiting.

I remember my grandmother grumbling in our language and she was saying, "It's going to totally change them, they are going to be no good for anything anymore." What they meant was that our culture was totally wiped away and being replaced. We were now unable to care for ourselves because we didn't know what to gather, we didn't know what to do to survive. All of that was taken away from us. And they said that from then on things were ruined. But I never understood that until just recently.

I thought maybe they were turning against me. After a few days of watching and listening I realized they still loved us, but they looked at us a little differently. It wasn't the same, they still cared for us and they still loved us, but it was sort of aloofness I guess because we spoke English they looked at us differently.

We always looked forward to having bannock once we got home and the Indian ice cream and the funny stories about Coyote from my grandparents. I had one grandmother who used to tell some pretty good stories. I remember the shrieks and the hilarious laughter from the older sisters and my cousins as we sat around in my grandmother's porch in the summer time.

I didn't get to attend a lot of classes while I was in school because they found out I had a singing voice. I didn't want to be in singing, I wanted to be in dancing but they said I wasn't a dancer and they put me in singing lessons. They would pull me out of class and we would have practices, three times a day, an hour in the morning, an hour in the afternoon, and an hour at night. They would have choirs, two people singing together or maybe a group of six. We would practice for months and be assigned to the Spring Festival.

I don't remember much about the class except that we had tiny little desks, the boys on one side and the girls on the other. You weren't allowed to look at them, even if it was your own brother. I remember seeing my brother in the back of the class. I went to talk to him and he was really nervous. He said, "Don't come over and talk to me." I asked, "Why, I want to talk to you?" and he was saying, "You are not supposed to." I told him, "Why, you are my brother?" And right away I was taken to the front of the class and I was given the ruler on the palms of my hands.

They asked, "Who were you talking to?" and I told them that I was talking to my brother. And they said, "Yeah, right your brother." They must have known he was my brother, but they made it seem ugly. It was like I was just in there to chase boys or something. That was their attitude. I was very young, I couldn't have been older than eight or nine and these subtle accusations were already out there.

I kept trying to run to my brother whenever I would see him but I always got into trouble. Eventually I just quit. I guess he got strapped or something. He always avoided us and he would just turn away when he would see us. Then you wonder why there are families today who have never gone beyond that. They have grown up around dysfunctional families. To this day I can't put my arms around my children and even my grandchildren. I had a bit of a problem when they were younger. I can do that but after awhile I just don't. It's like an invasion of privacy or something. It's an uncomfortable feeling, that's all I can say.

Parents wouldn't put their arms around you. It wasn't that they didn't love you. They just couldn't. When they were children, all of that was suppressed and it became a way of life. You weren't allowed to speak unless you were spoken to and you only answered what you were asked. That was another suppression.

You weren't allowed to make a noise once the whistle blew. There had to be total silence. Line up according to your number and file to the dining room in total silence. File to the church every morning in total silence. Get up and get dressed in total silence. You weren't allowed to speak until after breakfast when you went to the recreation room or when you were sent to the playground. Otherwise every time in between you had to be quiet and just go about your routine.

When I was about twelve years old, I was home for the summer. I was cleaning out the front room cabinet where the family pictures used to be stored and came across one that I had never noticed before. There was a picture of some children playing at the residential school playground, a little girl that looked like my cousin Edna sitting on a swing, and a big girl that looked like me pushing the swing. It looked all too familiar, Edna used to push me on the swings while singing "I'm so lonesome I could cry." The two girls in the picture were smiling and looking like they were having a fun time. I asked my mother "Why am I bigger than Edna in this picture?" Edna is five years older than me but in this picture, I was the big girl. My mother replied "That's not you, it's Nellie." She was upset and she turned away. My sister Myrtle told me Nellie was an older sister I never knew, she died before I ever got to know her. The subject surrounding my sister's death was too painful for the family, no one ever talked about it before or since.

My sister Nellie died at the age of thirteen here at the residential school. She had hepatitis or yellow jaundice as it used to be called. She was sick for months and was not taken to a doctor. It wasn't until after her death that my parents were notified. When my father came to the school after hearing of the sad news, he beat the principal and punched him down a stairway. All of this was before my time.

I was told many more horrific things that took place here such as the children riding the train while running away from here and what happened to them. Those children who died were from the Lillooet district. Before I came to the school, my mother told me some of the happenings to prevent me from running away, and to avoid being punished.

As much as I want the memories of my educational years to be positive, it just can't be. By telling a small part of those sad years, I hope I can begin to look at my grandchildren's education as something positive with many happy experiences that they can look back on.

A lot of behaviours carried over. To some degree it was good but yet it wasn't. Clean shiny floors and spic and span kitchens came before hugging your children and spending quality time with them, which isn't good. I wished I could have pushed that all aside and spent time with my children, just talking to them, caring for them as they grew up. I had an old house with wooden floors, and I spent hours packing water and scrubbing floors and doing laundry over a wash tub with a wash board.

I would like my children to know their language and culture. I want them to have a good education. I don't think that just because you are a doctor, lawyer or a teacher that you should forget your language and culture. The Secwepemc language is just as important as Spanish, French, Japanese or English.

It is important to know your roots, to know who your people were, that's the way it should be. Not being puppets, living some other way that you weren't meant to be. You should be totally open to your family and friends.

It's just the beginning of taking a hold of who we are. We are First Nations people who had everything intact when we were yanked away from our families and assimilated into another culture. We have to take that same step and totally immerse our children and grandchildren in the language and culture and begin raising them in the traditional way, not totally the way we were brought up. There are a lot of teachings that are better for us.

We have the extended family and we have broken away from that. It could be one of the causes of suicides, not having the closeness that families had. In the past if an uncle or an aunt saw their niece or nephew out there misbehaving, could be downtown, could be right in the home, they could be reprimanded right there and told, that's not correct. An extended family member could move forward and maybe give you bus fare to go home or simple little things, maybe a cup a coffee and spend twenty minutes talking to you.

When a child was born and they were giving a name to the child, they would have a feast. This was my grandmother's time and my mother's time as well. They would say "Okay, this is so and so, we will name him after his great grandmother," and they would give a name. They would say, "When you see this child out in the community doing something, move in and help him." By that comment you know whether you were an aunt or an uncle. Everybody had a hand in raising that child. I think that is missing among our people today.

When I came back to the residential school after spending a summer with my grandparents, I was just so happy that this new nun was there and she was asking me questions about my background. And I told her, "Yes, my grandfather is the Chief." And this other nun had said, "He's one of those savages." I wondered what she was talking about. I didn't understand the term. It wasn't until years later that the conversation came back to me and it haunted me.

Eric Mitchell

We supported each other, my cousins and my brothers and all of us kids, hey. We created a system of support for us to cope. We had little gangs. We were more family groupings, you know, the people that knew each other hung around together.

Later on maybe you got friends and they moved around in their groups, kind of thing, or little gangs, we called them. We did everything together outside of class because we were all different ages. For me what I need to do now to complete that part is to give them a gift and to thank them for that, recognize them for that.

One incident that stood out in my mind was when our dad came to visit us the last time. I remember we had a really good visit. I don't remember what was said but it just felt really good. And then the next morning we woke up and we were told that he died, and they didn't really go into too much detail, just that he was dead. We found out later he was hit by a car at the red bridge. But anyway, it was quite a shock and especially being kids and in a place like that. And I remember I just kind of wandered away from everybody, I didn't want to be with anybody. I had all these emotions going on inside that I never felt before and so I ended up sitting at one of the windows on the stairway, the ones they have between every floor. There was like a little landing and then there was a window. I was sitting there just looking out the window. I don't know what was going through my head or anything, I was just trying to process what I was told, I guess. I just sat there and different people would come by and they would go up and they would say, "Hello," or whatever, and "What are you doing?" you know, "Oh nothing I'm just resting here." I'm just looking at the thing and making excuses, so they wouldn't talk to me, so they'd just keep a going.

It seemed like a long time and eventually my cousin Dougie, he came looking for me. He came to be with me. My dad, that's his uncle, and so it was really good having him there, somebody I know and somebody that knows what I'm talking about when I'm talking about my dad, my feelings or something. So he stayed right with me and we sat for a long time and pretty soon it was getting to a time when it was getting too many people or something and then we went outside, to the track. That track is still there, that circle or oval, it was a track and field track, but now it's like a road, hey. We started walking around and just talking and talking I don't know if they realized we were out there, but nobody came looking for us and then I finally calmed down enough, so we went inside and went to sleep.

I don't remember too much after that until they were burying my dad. The next kind of hard emotional tug was seeing the casket going down. I don't really know what happened, I don't remember that part. For me it was just that moment there, and that time, then nothing until that casket was going down and I guess I realized it, holy cow, where are you going? And I remembered I really had an outpouring of emotions then. Today I have a hard time, maybe not right today. It wasn't so long ago I was worried that the different things I was doing for myself, emotionally healing, that I felt I couldn't cry, I had no more tears, hey, I had no more tears for nobody.

I started realizing if anybody could bring that kind of emotion on, is my two children, my partner there, and my grandkids. They're the only ones that could ever pull that hard again, on my heart. Those are the things people remember and today when I see, especially kids with their mothers and their fathers, mostly their mothers, you know they don't realize how lucky they are that they're there. I didn't have that chance to be with my mother you know, and the way they treat them, it always didn't sit well with me. Then eventually if they were friends of mine or close, then I would tell them that you know. You don't know how lucky you are to have that person there, alive, they're right there. They're not gone and wherever they go, they'll come back, and I'd tell them things like that. And people and their friendships, you know, a lot of people are very shallow in their friendships and stuff. It's times like in that place, that the friendships I made that's a life long thing that will never go away.

In saying that out loud, even now, I realize that Dougie and I have always had an understanding about each other. I just realized today how much he helped me and that we've allowed us to grow apart and it makes me want to go and let him know that. Maybe we'll get to know each other again, you know, better. I don't really know his kids. I know maybe his oldest one or two but I don't know even the names of these kids. I think that needs to be corrected. My grandkids need to know their people up there in Fountain and things like that.

I heard talk last night someone was mentioning that in the ten months we were at school disrupted those traditional gathering times and methods. Especially the ones when all the kids were gone. Then it was just the two people and depending on how old, they were some just totally lost, that part of themselves. For us in the summer time in June and August, when we went back to Lillooet, that's what we did. We were either down the river catching fish or packing salmon up, or being sent out with those birch bark and cedar root baskets tied onto all of us kids. They'd send us up into the mountains and they knew we'd eat lots and everything. We were out there all day and if everyone of us brought back a little bit then that's better than nothing. We were doing that and the men were out hunting. You don't realize that around Lillooet, even though when you drive through it doesn't look like much, but there's lots of game in the mountains. The men would bring back these big bucks and there was a huge effort of gathering food. And my grandpa and my grandma had a big garden and an orchard with apples and peaches and pears and all those things.

My two older sisters, the only time I ever remember seeing them was at the school was when we had to go to the gym to watch them do their dance routines. One of them she was part of that. One year my sister Barb was the "Queen of Hearts" for Valentines. I remember that because she came over and wanted me to dance with her. Holy smokes no, no, no, I was trying to hide away. I had to go dance with her. That was the only time she did that she said because she never was allowed to see me at any other time. So if she had her pick, well then, she wanted to see her brothers. I remember she danced with me and then with Allan and we both were pretty upset. At the same time we did get to touch her and see her and hold her.

My younger sister, I never got to see her at all. If anything we may have had a chance meeting when we'd go eat. We'd all line up there and that was somewhat of a torture too because you can see them right there. The girls were like from me to her but you couldn't talk to them, you couldn't touch them, you know, even if they're your sister or something. I remember Jean York said one day this little guy walked by and he had a little rooster tail and he looked so cute, she said and she couldn't help herself and just went over there and give him a big hug and put him down and he went on his way like nothing happened. It's funny thinking about that, we were so close but yet so far away.

The only time we did get to see our brothers and sisters was when somebody came to visit. They'd tell you that somebody is here to visit and they don't say who it is or anything. Turns out it wasn't just our dad that visited. Sometimes I think I remember our grandpa visited at least once, and then I don't remember this time but Leonard Marchand said he used to come and visit us.

This one time he sent us a big box of *stuann*, you know dried salmon just fresh off from the river. Holy we got that and we were looking around and tried to hide it. Reach in there and get some and call our brothers or cousins over and hey look, got a whole bunch here, don't let nobody know. You know they'll take it from us and we were just so afraid that we just had to hide it.

Pretty soon the word spread that we had this *stuann* and of course everybody likes *stuann*, hey. Then they were after us, give me some, give me some, nope, nope, nope. Well they bothered us so much. They said, "Well there is a lot there you know," and so we put some of it away for us. Then we said, "If you guys want it so bad for each strip is a nickel." And they paid, we would cut five strips each and they'd have to give us twenty-five cents. You want it that bad you got to give us a quarter. I don't know how in the heck we came up with that idea. We made sure we had some for our own selves to eat, for me and my brother Allan and our three cousins from Lillooet.

I was afraid of the unknown and being there, but when I think of those people (the nuns and priests) I feel more angry to them than fear. When I try to think of how I felt, then. At the same time in finding ways to survive there, you had to be really careful, you know really cautious. The one thing we knew was to never be caught alone, especially in the hallways or where others can't see you because something will happen. This one brother who was there, I don't remember his name, he was just like a short little guy and he had big big feet and big hands and if you were alone and walking by and he happened to be walking by, just when he'd get passed you, he'd either hit you, slug you, or kick you, just to hurt you, just knee you. So I remember he did that to me he booted me in the butt. We all knew about him and one day, some of the older guys, there was about six or seven of them. I don't know what time of year it was or whatever, but for some reason there was nobody around and they went in there and tuned him up. After that he was a little easier to get along with, and it's no wonder he never got them into trouble. He could have easily told on them. But, that was his way I guess, that's the only way he knew or understood anything. That's one reason we traveled in bunches.

This one time we were in the soccer field with Brother Murphy and another Brother. Brother Murphy was the soccer teacher and coach and he really knew the game well. We were doing something and I forget exactly what I did, I think it was I kept getting the ball away from that Brother and he started getting mad and we were just little guys. But we were pretty quick, I guess, and we had a good teacher. We kept getting that ball away from him. I don't know if we were teasing him, but gee he was getting mad, hey. We knew when we can get them mad then they're out of control, so we'd poke at him, tease him and then pretty soon he got mad and started coming after me, so I kicked the ball away and I started running. He's got long legs and I couldn't keep a running, so I started ducking around and circling just going like a rabbit and he couldn't get a hold of me. I was getting tired and he was still just a ramming down behind me and I thought of something. I stopped really quick and I got down on all fours and I tripped him. Oh he went down and I run away a little ways and I stopped because I needed a breath. And when he stood up I thought here we go again, but then he realized Brother Murphy was there and he was mad, red right up to his eye balls. But when he got up he looked around and he saw everybody looking at him and he quit, hey, calmed down. After that incident it seemed like they were more careful not to let themselves get that way again, so that was in our favor.

They seemed to treat us a little different. I don't know what it was, maybe it was because they realized we egged them on and got them out of control we had that kind of power over them a little bit. I don't know what it was exactly. So when you ask me if I was afraid of them, maybe I was a little bit at the beginning but the more I caught on to what was going on there, the more I used that to my advantage, hey. And I use to get into trouble a lot.

These John Wayne movies, of course, they're cowboys and Indians, you know. That was the attraction there, lots of shooting and lots of action and lots of this and that and then I remember watching it and then all of a sudden it clicked. All of a sudden at that moment all the things my grandpa use to talk about started making sense. I started realizing what he was saying. It really gave me I guess the word you would use is empowerment.

My grandpa use to tell us stories of priests of how they didn't like him because he would question what they are doing. He would tell them what they were doing was not right. When he said the first thing he did, when he was Chief, the very first time, he told his people to take down the cemetery fence and move it to include all the people. There were people that died because of alcohol or something the priest deemed to be sinful and they wouldn't allow them to be buried in our own graveyards. So now when you go to Fountain you'll see the old gate it's way in the middle of the graveyard and the new fence is way back. Stories like that empowered me and helped me to watch and hear and listen to the kind of mind games they were trying to pull us into.

Elvis came around, he made all the movies, so we pretty much watched every one of them. I don't remember what other kind of movies, but I always liked the ones with horses. But after that time you know we wouldn't cheer so hardy for old John Wayne, he was no hero to us.

I like to credit my grandpa for helping us to manage to be there and to have something to hold onto, to help us make changes after we got out of there. After

I left there I went back home, stayed with my uncle and auntie. That didn't work out too well so I moved to another home where they had a ranch with horses and cows, that's where I stayed for four years before I was on my own.

There's a lot of change in people going on right now, if you're willing to look at it. For myself, it was the birth of my daughter that forced me to look at myself. I tell her now that her and I grew up together, emotionally. Because in her needs she forced me to look deeper and deeper and that was hard, hey. I tell people during that time sixteen to twenty-three years old, anger, that's who I was, I lived it, I breathed it, I expressed it, everything that was who I was. In order to change, I had to let that all go. That's pretty scary so it took a lot of trial and error and my daughter had to take the triumphs with the mistakes all in one. It definitely was worth it because we've come to terms with a lot of it. My daughter, she lives not too far from us and we get to see our grandkids all the time. She tells us that our son who is ten years younger than her has a better set of parents than she had. Everybody, I think goes through that, but if you have a lot of emotional problems it's even worse and the kids they're the ones that ultimately feel it the most.

When I was between sixteen and twenty-three there was seven years when I look back at what I call the dark time in my life. Where I was introduced to alcohol and lot of anger, confusion and just crazy, crazy times. It wasn't really until we had our daughter when I seriously started taking a look at who I was and to look at changing.

I remember one time sitting in the bar and it was only early afternoon, and one of my uncles walked by. He was already pretty drunk and this guy I was sitting with said to me, "Look at that. You keep doing what you're doing, you'll be just like your uncle." Well that made me feel angry. No way, I'm not going to be like him, my uncle worked hard every day, but he drank it all up every weekend. Just like that for years and years and years.

So that was kind of a beginning. Why did I get so angry? Why did my friend even say that and here he is doing the same thing, yet out of his mouth came these words that really hit me. To this day that same uncle, I left alcohol quite a while ago he just up and said enough and he quit drinking and now he's got a good life and good home. An inspiration to me, because that was his life, work and drink and that's it. Today he brags to his brothers and his peers, "If I want a tractor I'll go get it, if I want a TV. I'll go get it, if I want a dish I'll go get it." I have money, that's what he was telling them. Not much but he gets that pension every month and he can make loans on his own name, and he feels good. He did that all on his own, he didn't go to no program or whatever. I'm sure he heard a lot and listened and watched, that's the way he does things. Once he made up his mind that was it, he just walked away from it.

My uncle talks about learning things from the Elders, watching them what they do and then thinking about it and trying it himself and making lots of mistakes along the way but he figures things out. He looked around and seen what was going on and realizing things for himself and then one day he just up and quit.

Christina Casimir

I am Christina Casimir and I'll share my story with you. My parents are Tommy and Sadie Casimir. I am a daughter in a family of fourteen. Mom and Dad were together until I was four years old when my mom left to go on her own journey. She took me with her so I lost contact with my sisters and brother. Because of this traumatic experience I forgot I had a brother and sisters.

My mom brought me back to Kamloops at age six to go to the residential school. That is when I met my brother, James, my sister Amy, and my sister Babs. Mom told my brother James to get me ready for the Indian school by telling me what the procedure was. My brother at age twelve with his good humour decided to have a little fun. He said, "The first person you're going to meet when you get to the residential school, make sure and be careful of. This person will be coming up from the basement, she is dressed in black and has a little white rim around her head." He said, "She is the devil." Mom brought me to the Indian school a couple of days later. I know it was hard on her to let me go to the Indian school, but she felt that it was necessary. We were walking into the Intermediates recreation room. Suddenly from the laundry area this nun emerged. She was dressed in black and white and her beads were jangling. I started to scream and scream. I hid behind mom's skirt and kept saying, "The devil, the devil." Mom said, "This is a nun and she's gonna be looking after you." I was so scared that my mom was leaving me with the devil and I didn't know what the devil was. I felt the devil was bad. I turned around. Here comes another woman dressed in black with a white rim. I got just as scared of her. Mom said to the nun, "I don't know what happened, my daughter is quite upset. Is it okay if I stay for a while?" Mom stayed for a few hours visiting people and comforting me. Then she had to leave, I cried. She left with the promise that she'd be back. So the routine began. Each year I had to go back to the school. I got very upset. I usually lost things as an excuse to try and not go back to school.

The first year I was at school, I was sent home for four or five months. I was unable to adjust to the Indian school. The nuns asked my mom to take me home for awhile. I was so happy that I could stay home. I would do almost anything just to be with Mom.

Mom brought me into a Sweathouse at age eight to help guide and protect me. She must have known she was going to leave this world early. I believe in spirituality. When I was nine years old, my mom died. It was very difficult in a lot of ways. I felt the difficulty had to do with the Indian school. In other ways it was a godsend that I was away from all the things that hurt me.

What kept me going in the Indian school after my mom died, I joined a dance troop. We were permitted to learn Irish dancing and other European dances. I thoroughly enjoyed dancing and that was my main escape from the rigorous routine and from the lack of affection and love.

I grew up in the Indian school, I spent ten years of my life there. I had a great number of good years there. I was considered one of the privileged kids, I was a dancer. We were allowed to get soup after our practices and occasionally after we performed a concert. We danced in town at the Yale Cariboo Music festival and at the bull sale. Out of town we danced at the Pacific National Exhibition in Vancouver, Vanderhoof, Kelowna, Penticton, Summerland, Prince George. We practiced often. We practiced every day morning, noon and night, from September to April and then we learned new dances from April to June. We went home for the month of July and came back for the month of August and practiced for the Pacific National Exhibition performance. This is what I did for approximately eight, nine years of the time that I was in the residential school along with approximately forty-two other dancers.

Sister Leonita was the nun who taught us how to dance, she was an exceptional woman. She not only taught us how to dance, she taught us how to sing. She knew how to put a concert together. We were the best in the province. The dancers carried on fund raising and made it to Mexico. They were honoured to go to Mexico to dance, to do the Mexican dances. So that was the pinnacle of our dancing life. I couldn't go because I went home to baby sit. In order to be a part of this exceptional dance group we had to practice every day. I missed a lot of dancing and the nun was quite strict about practice.

We weren't honoured that we were Native children doing Native dancing, we were honoured to do European dances. There aren't too many people that can be classified as ambassadors for the Canadian Government visiting any country. The president of Mexico honoured the dance group while they were in his country and he provided safety and security for them. Our dance troop was classified as amateur. Mexican people are very strict, for example only professional people could dance on this one stage in Mexico. Our dance troop was privileged to dance on this floating stage. The Mexicans were so honoured when the dancers did the Bull dance, the Spanish dances and the Italian tarantella dance, the Del dance. The most profound one was the Mexican Hat dance with the youngest in the group. The Mexican people threw roses to them. When the kids came back and told the story, I was so happy. I was so thrilled and envied that experience.

Sister Leonita would lift her black dress to the ankles. She used thick black leotards or stockings and she would teach us dance steps. If it got complicated where she couldn't teach us these dance steps, she would get older girls in our group to take over. We each had our age group when we started off. Our first dance was the four-hand reel, then we did the Mexican Hat dance and the eight-hand reel. Each year, we came back in the summertime to the residential school. It was quite hilarious sometimes. That was I think the fun part of it, where the nun looked very goofy at the time, she would dance for us.

There was nothing the matter with disciplining us to be excellent, to be the top, to compete even with white kids. We were just as good if not better than the white kids. They gave us a vehicle that opened doors and those doors have not ever been closed for me.

We performed, at different functions in town to raise money and people would donate to see us perform. We mainly performed concerts throughout BC, the nuns and priests got paid for us. We never saw the money. It paid for our gas, our trips to different locations and back. I know some of the girls feel we were entitled to some of the money. I feel we are entitled to the trophies that we won. We always won first and second, very seldom did we ever arrive at third place.

The most painful experience I've ever had besides losing Mom was to lose my pretty little niece. She was born to my sister. The priest told me the day before I couldn't go to the hospital to see the baby. So the next day I was busy in the recreation room. Father Kerr came and said, "Christine I want to talk to you." So he told me. He said, "The little girl you wanted to go see in the hospital." I said, "Yes, is there something the matter with my sister? Does she need me to help baby sit?" He said, "No she (my niece) passed away." Something in me just tore apart. Even though he apologized profusely and brought me over to see my sister and helped me try to cope with it. I couldn't forgive him or the Indian school. That's what affected me in my later life. Learning how to deal with grief and learning how to deal with people dying.

In grade six the residential school teachers tested us with the provincial government tests. There were six of us. The teachers took us out of the classroom and we were placed in the study hall along with the high school kids that were taken out of their class for the same reason. After the testing was all over the teacher Joe Michel asked us to come out of the classroom, each of us individually. I thought "Oh my God I'm going to be punished, oh my God I flunked, oh gee something happened." When it was my turn to go in I realized most of the kids who came back in were not upset. There was not any crying and they didn't have any furrowed eyebrows. I thought it must not be that bad. I went out and talked to Joe Michel. He told me, "You know, the tests found that you're a pretty smart girl. There were six of you in my class that went and were tested. You are part of the exceptional kids. I want you to try harder in my class. I want you to do more, I want you to be more involved because you are quite a smart little girl. I am going to keep my eye on all of you to make sure you try harder." So I did try hard that year and probably the year after. But, I got more involved in writing poetry, theatre, and drama. I was on the debate team.

High Mass was great because I could sing, and the boys went to High Mass. We got our rewards by seeing them. Of course, the boys were very interested in the girls too. Why not, we were all young and very attractive. The boys looked great in their uniforms. They wore navy blue dress pants or gray dress pants and pure white shirt with a navy blue or red tie. The girls wore uniforms. I got in trouble describing the girl's uniforms in a note to a boy. When I was in junior high I said the ties looked like balloons. The shoes we wore looked like logging boots. The socks I called them something similar to what my dad wore. The bloomers we wore, even my mom would not wear and the uniforms looked like sacks. The haircut was atrocious. It was like someone put a bowl on our head and cut. Absolutely no style or skill. It seemed like they intended on trying to make us look unattractive. That was how I felt about those uniforms.

I left the Indian school because I felt I wasn't being listened to and this happened February 16th, 1965. I didn't just walk away from the Indian school, it is known as 'running away.' I left on a Friday evening when the kids were going to a movie at the gym. I walked away with no extra clothes on my back. I wanted to go home, I wanted to spend time with my dad. I was really scared because I was put into the residential school for ten years and then forced to integrate into white society without any form of preparation.

When I left the Indian school the way I did my dad was quite hurt and he didn't know what to do with me. Then of course, he went to the extreme and he said, "Okay, if you don't like the Indian school, I will send you to the reform school." So fortunately he did not do that. Dad said, "The place for a young girl is to be in school, she needs her education." It was not that I didn't enjoy school, it was that I was frightened of the change to integration. I was very frightened at the time and no one would listen. I went to St. Ann's Academy. I loved the theatre there. I enjoyed some of the non-Native friendships I made. However, some of the white kids called us orphans and that stigma bothered me. I told them I am not an orphan. They said, "All the kids that go to the residential school are orphans." That hurt and I tried to tell somebody and no one would listen. So I ran away like I said on February 16th, 1965. I started my own life, I was bussed to the public school. I didn't do very well because the transition was terrible. So the school let me slide by and I was to repeat Grade nine and ten at the time. I went from a kid that was a 'B' student to a kid who was going to flunk which was quite a transition for sure.

At least I got to stay home with Dad. Then I went and stayed with my boyfriend, David up in Skeetchestn with a family who adopted me. They are the late Chief, Charlie Draney and his widowed wife May. May adopted me since I was seventeen years old to the present. She helped me learn how to be a wife, a woman and a person in the community. Also, how to contribute in a positive way. The great thing about it is May and Charlie fully accepted me.

Which brings me to 1980 and the disciplining of children. My life with my kids was still changing. I was either very strict with them or I was very lenient. One day I got so mad at my kids for not getting their chores done. I did not beat the heck out of them. I just got mean, grabbed my son, then grabbed my daughter and made them go to the kitchen sink to do dishes. When I saw what I did I started to cry. I got so upset about what I did to my own precious children. So I said that was it. I called a counselor. One of the exercises he gave me which I hold true to today. He said, "I want you to go home, let your house get messy, let your house get dusty, let your kids get dirty, do those things." I went home and I tried that exercise and believe me it was tough. It is not tough today, I haven't gone to the extreme. But I let the dishes go in the sink and just spend time with the kids. I would let my kids go and play football even though I wanted my daughter in ballet. I would let my son climb the mountain and come back. It became easier. It was very tough in the residential school, because we had to be clean, we had to be perfect.

Looking back into the past the nuns would de-lice us when we didn't even have lice. They put coal oil in our hair to get rid of nits that we didn't have. The oil or chemicals damaged my naturally curly hair. So that was forty-six years ago and it has been a gradual change. The only thing that I had to get rid of was my angry voice, such as hollering and yelling and chastising my kids. I learned this at the Indian school. That is where I was disciplined and that is where I learned how to discipline my kids. They didn't have to be okay, they had to be perfect. When we went out in public, we had to be perfect. When we went to a family gathering they had to be perfect. I had to learn that nobody is perfect.

That a man could be a friend, that my kids could be my friends. They didn't have to be perfect. They can be excellent but they don't have to be perfect. So that took many years of looking into myself which was a healing journey.

When my son died I decided to quit drinking entirely. That was my commitment to my kids and to my grandchildren in honour of my son David Shawn. I continue healing and I will continue growing for the rest of my life. One does not stop growing. The old tapes may go away, may change from what you were taught when you were a kid, when you were a young person. It takes quite a while. What I saw in the residential school, for example I saw emotional abuse. I saw kids that were very lonesome for home. I saw kids that were left out. I was part of the privileged few in the Indian school. Those that were in sports and dancing were given privileges. The other kids were left out and they felt it. They let us know it, too. Some of them did continue to let us know when we grew up to be adults. I know the control the nuns and the priests used on us was public embarrassment and humiliation. For years I tried to avoid getting publicly embarrassed. It was so painful as a young kid, as a teenager, as a young adult.

One belief I had was that I would keep my own kids no matter what. I would bring them up a lot better than I was brought up. I would bring them up with my culture as much as I could and I did. When I was a young girl, Mom told me I was special and Dad he treated me special. I try to pass that onto my kids and I know that I am not perfect. I know they do not expect me to be. I do not drink and I do not smoke. It does not make me feel better than anybody else. It just makes me a person continuing to heal. I first started learning how to speak my own language as an adult. It was in the residential school building located in the dormitory where I slept as a young girl.

My son can't understand why it is so important to have an opinion about something? Well, at the residential school we were taught how to be conservative. That we could not have an opinion. The nuns, priests and the teachers taught us this. One of the priests my mom knew said, "You know, you were never oppressed." But we were oppressed in the sense that we could not do our Indian dances. We were not allowed to speak our own language. We could not go and live in an extended family at home as we wished.

I still come home. I have my quiet time and I pray as well. I do not begrudge the Catholic church for teaching me how to pray. I have asthma so I am unable to smudge. I still pray to the Creator, I still honour the Creator in nature. I go to church with my sisters who need me to go to church with them on occasion or my friends. I still love High Mass, and singing. I'll continue healing for the rest my life. I'll continue growing and learning. Who knows what my future will bring? But I know I'm moving in a direction where my community will be healthier, and my family will be healthier. I want to make this a better place for my grandchildren and my great grandchildren. I hope I have not left anything out. I want to thank my great grandparents and my grandparents, and my parents. Kukstsetsemc. Also, my Indian name is Red Eagle Moon Woman. I'm proud of the name. Once more, *kukstsetsemc Secwepemc te qelmuc. Kukstsetsemc kukpi7.*

Appendix

ACKNOWLEDGEMENTS

By Lori Pilon, Special Projects Manager

On behalf of the project team I am pleased to acknowledge and thank the following people who contributed to *Behind Closed Doors*.

Our deepest respect and appreciation goes to the storytellers for coming forward to share their stories notwithstanding the pain in remembering. Thank you for the honesty, wisdom, humour and hope that you have given us.

Sincere gratitude to the project team. To Leona McKay for helping to get the project started. To coordinator Agness Jack for sharing her experiences, for her concern over the well being of team members, and for bringing the various pieces of the project together. To interviewers Cherlyn Billy, Kathleen Reynolds and our reluctant warrior Chuck Jensen, for their sensitivity and compassion; and to our transcriber Jenna John whom because of her expertise helped in many aspects of the project. To Bryan Rattray and Renee Spence for tirelessly editing the stories. To Pam Jules and Yvonne Fortier for transcribing and to Roberta Sorioul for arranging meetings and providing support services to the project team. Thank you all for your hard work.

Thanks you to the Advisory Team that helped develop the proposal, shared their stories, and provided direction, encouragement, and on-going support. Annette Anthony, Marie Baptiste, Carol Blank, Russell Casimir, Cynthia Davis, Ken Favrholdt, Lilly Gottfriedson, Marianne Ignace, Walter Isadore, Agness Jack, Chuck Jensen, Diane Jules, Eddy Jules, John Jules, Mona Jules, Richard Jules, Vicki Manuel, Charlotte Manuel, Colleen McLean, Leona McKay, Jan Michel, Bella Morris, Tassie Nelson, Cloudy Peters, Robert Simon, Lori Schnieder, Renee Spence.

Special thanks to our traditional helpers Rod and Jackie Bandura, Felix Delorme, Patrick Adrienne, Terry Deneault, Diane Sandy and Lorraine Billy for sharing their circles and sweats, for their advice, and for their prayers.

Special thanks also to Cynthia Davis and the Sexual Assault Counselling Centre for providing trauma training and counselling services; and thank you to Cynthia for professional advice, editing, and weekly chats.

Thank you to Robert Matthew and Marianne Ignace for providing training; and to Robert Matthew, Wayne Christian, Ron Ignace, Cherlyn Billy, and Cynthia Davis for writing articles to further understanding of the impacts of residential schools.

Thanks to Chief Atahm School for use of computer equipment, to Secwepemc Cultural Education Society language department and Simon Fraser University program for use of audio and video equipment, and to Peerless Printers.

Thank you to the Secwepemc Museum and Archives, Royal British Columbia Museum, Kamloops Museum, Joan Arnouse, Les Williams and North Thompson Indian Band for photographs.

And a very special thank you to the Aboriginal Healing Foundation for funding this project.

The Long Trail Home

By Robert Matthew

Long before the Europeans arrived in this country, the Aboriginal Peoples had their own spiritual beliefs. The people believed that everything in nature had a purpose and a meaning.

Storytelling was used to teach the many lessons of life. The mythical transformer, Coyote, was the central figure in many of the stories. Each Coyote story explained some aspect of nature, or how some portion of the world had been created. Each story had a moral, instructing the Secwepemc how to live in harmony with nature and with one another.

Traditionally, Elders and parents recognized a child's potential and helped shape the child towards adulthood. Growing up was a natural learning process. The children were taught skills to help their families survive. Over time they learned to be a productive member of their community.

However, in the early 1800s, the Aborignal way of life was weakened by epidemics, and by the influx of newcomers during the gold rush. By 1862 the diseases had reduced the Secwepemc to a minority in their own land.

The Catholic missionaries arrived in Kamloops in 1842. At first they only wanted to convert the people to Christianity. The missionaries learned the language and translated the new religious teachings in Secwepemc language. During this time the Federal Government developed the assimilation policy which stated that all First Nations had to give up all aspects of their life and adopt the culture of the white society.

The missionaries and the Federal Government decided to establish residential schools where the children would be forced to live for long periods of time without seeing their parents. Discipline was very strict. Any practicing of traditional beliefs or using ones' Aboriginal language was quickly punished.

The goal of the school was to make Aboriginal Peoples laborers and semi-skilled tradesmen. A high quality academic education was deemed unnecessary. Restricted to an elementary education for eighty years denied Aboriginal people from realizing their potential. It wasn't until 1952 that the school produced high school graduates.

The missionaries had complete control over the children in their care. The absolute power often led to physical and sexual abuses. Today former students have found the strength to bring out the truth and to begin their healing process.

Historically, Coyote has had to face many dangers and challenges. Often he was injured or even killed but he always came back to life. In the same way, the Aboriginal people have had their traditional ways tested. For over 100 years the people have been oppressed, but today, like the Coyote they have returned to life.

Like in traditional times, the people are using storytelling to educate and to heal. The real strength of the survivors of the residential schools can be found in their stories.

Language and Culture

By Ron Ignace

Presently, Canada prides itself on its tolerance towards other cultures and so Canada should; we must cajole and encourage her in this attitude.

Canada has a rich and diverse Aboriginal cultural heritage. Presently, there are fifty-two Aboriginal languages from eleven different language groups. These languages are thousands of years old; relatively speaking the English language is an infant in relation to the Aboriginal languages in Canada.

These languages have been developed, maintained and enhanced by thousands of generations of Elders down through the ages. Our languages carry with them stories of this land called Canada.

Stories of its geography, geology, flora and fauna, its peoples, history and wildlife. In short, these languages contain within them vast amounts of intellectual knowledge representing a great reservoir of cultural heritage.

Despite this fact and despite Canada's claim and pride in being a multi-cultural society our languages have been driven to the brink of extinction by Canada, through the residential school system.

At one time there were sixty languages but eight are now extinct, a couple of these languages are touted as having a chance to survive, the remainder may become extinct in the next twenty years.

Presently, this is rationalized by arguing that if we are to succeed in the 'real world' what use or function do our languages have? It can be shown that our languages have great healing powers. In our language there are stories of who we are as Aboriginal Peoples, our history and cultural and spiritual beliefs, as well as stories about the lands in which we have lived for thousands of years.

The roots of what one needs in order to be 'Canadians', can be traced back to the residential school era. This type of thinking forgets the role of orality in the formation of the Canadian society. We are reminded by John Rolston Saul, that "Native people have been engaged in the ultimate aggression of a testual [Canadian] society." (1997) He points out that an obvious component of the Indian community is its orality "which remains as one of the three pillars on which the [Canadian] society was originally constructed. If much of the Aboriginal culture has been taken into the larger complex [Canadian] culture, then the oral must have come with it." [JRS, 1997, p. 210]

Regardless of our languages being such an integral part of the Canadian fabric, Canada has undermined and deliberately allowed Aboriginal languages to flounder. This rich linguistic heritage is threatened with extinction while Canada spends millions upon millions on preserving 'heritage buildings' while the amount of money spent on preserving our languages is a drop in the bucket by comparison. It has been said that the loss of this great linguistic heritage will rival the great global environmental catastrophic. A truly great loss. Finally, the process of healing from the aftermath of the residential school era can only be complete if language is an integral part of the healing circle.

TRAUMA AND THE HEALING PROCESS

By Cynthia Davis, KSACC

It has been an honour for our Centre to be able to offer support to survivors of the residential school experience as they began recovering memories and telling the stories that have too long been untold. We believe and respect these stories given to us in this important book, healing journeys will continue until the survivors feel the time is right to share the next "layer of memories" with us.

Survivors of people-made catastrophes are believed to suffer longer and more intensely than survivors of natural catastrophes. Herman (1992) noted, the knowledge of horrible events periodically intrudes into public awareness, but is rarely retained long. Whether those horrible events occur during war, in residential schools, in concentration camps, in communities, or in homes, it is difficult for survivors to recall what sometimes feel like unspeakable or incomprehensible secrets. Traumatic events are also often difficult to describe verbally, because they more often are remembered by the survivor in vivid sensations and images rather than words.

An experience is defined as "traumatic" if: (1) it is sudden, unexpected and not normal; (2) it exceeds the person's ability to meet its demands; and (3) it disrupts the person's important psychological needs. These psychological needs were considered by McCann and Pearlman (1990) to be:

1. **Safety** - the need to feel safe and reasonably free from harm.
2. **Trust** - the need to believe in others' promises and to depend on others for help.
3. **Esteem** - the need to be valued by others, to have one's worth confirmed, and to value others.
4. **Independence** - the need to control one's own behaviour and rewards.
5. **Power** - the need to influence and direct others and self.
6. **Intimacy** - the need to feel connected to others individually and to also belong to a larger community.

Because most residential schools were run by churches and the government, many Canadians have difficulty understanding the severe trauma experienced by the children who were confined in them. However, for any of us, being removed for years from our family, community, language, customs and spiritual beliefs (especially during childhood) would be "traumatizing." Witnessing or experiencing abuse, sleep deprivation, serious hunger, neglect or degradation would each compound the severity of that trauma.

Daily (1988) described the impact of residential school trauma on communities in the following manner:
Separation of the children unnaturally and geographically from parents had a drastic impact. The structure, cohesion and quality of family life suffered. Old production skills tied to the land were lost. Parenting skills diminished as succeeding generations became more Institutionalized and experienced little nurturing. Low self-esteem and self-concept problems arose as children were taught their own culture was inferior and uncivilized, even "savage." (P110)

Some of the variables that increased the severity of the trauma experienced by children attending residential schools were that:

- The child was forcibly taken from his/her family or community.
- The child was not able to positively interact with his/her family at times between six and sixteen years of age.
- The child was not allowed to sleep through the night (or was regularly awakened to be abused.)
- The child did not encounter "kind" adults for most of the years.
- The child was not given sufficient amounts of food to eat.
- The child was humiliated in front of others.
- The child did not have friends or siblings available for comfort and support.
- The child was severely punished for using his/her language or speaking positively about his/her family or culture.
- The child's physical appearance was immediately altered (e.g. hair chopped off).
- The child was not allowed to keep a sense of "inner dignity."

Almost all human beings have common reactions to people-created trauma. These reactions include fear, anxiety, depression, decreased self-esteem, anger, survivor guilt, sleep disturbances, emotional numbness, and memory loss.

If traumatized human beings receive adequate psychological and economic assistance and community validation, support and protection as soon as possible after trauma, the effects are less severe and of shorter duration than if assistance is delayed, unavailable or blaming. Long-term trauma survivors often suffer more from sleep problems, headaches, stomach pain, substance abuse problems, anxiety and depression than survivors of a single traumatic situation.

The healing process from long-term trauma often occurs over many years. Herman (1992) states that the four major stages of recovery from trauma are:
1. **A healing relationship with someone**
2. **The establishment of safety**
3. **Remembrance and mourning**
4. **Reconnection with life and others**

To offer support to survivors of long-term trauma in their healing journeys is an important role and an honour. We must name and understand serious abuses so that they will no longer be repeated. At the same time, there are influential forces that work hard to silence those speaking truthfully about past (and present) shameful conditions in this world. This book and these survivors' stories help us to remember the truth and to heal.

References

Herman, J.L. (1992). Trauma and Recovery: The Aftermath of Violence from Domestic Abuse to Political Terror. New York: Basic.
Martens, T., Daily, B. (1988) The Spirit Weeps. Edmonton: Nechi Institute.
McCann, I.L., Pearlman, L.A. (1990). Psychological Trauma and the Adult Survivor. New York: Brunner/Mazel.

Trauma

By Wayne Christian

What is it? Where does it come from? How does trauma get transferred to our children and grandchildren? How do we deal with trauma. Trauma is when a person is rendered powerless and great danger is involved. The person experienced, witnessed or has been confronted with an event that involves actual or threatened death or serious physical or psychological injury to oneself or others and the person experiences intense fear, helplessness or horror. Post Traumatic Stress Disorder or PTSD is when you have experienced trauma and you re-experience the trauma in the form of dreams, flashbacks and intensive memories. You also show avoidance behavior – a numbing of emotions and you experience hyper-arousal as evidenced by insomnia, agitation, irritability and outbursts of rage. PTSD occurs within six months after a traumatic event and can be one year, twenty years or forty years after the event. If we understand that traumatic events are ones where people are rendered powerless and their lives are threatened, then we would understand that since contact with the white race, our people have experienced trauma under the laws of Canada. The residential schools are our holocaust. The government forcibly confined and rendered our people powerless by their laws and policies of cultural genocide. We are speaking of 150 years of trauma and horror where our children were systematically brainwashed to not resist the government's legislation of assimilation and genocide.

The last residential school closed in the 1980's and the public schools have been open to First Nations' children since the 1960's. As individuals, families, leaders and communities our lives are reenactments not only of our own buried traumatic experiences, but also our family's history. The intergenerational transmission of trauma is well documented that parents who were abused are more likely to abuse their own children. Parents who did not learn how to parent will not be able to teach their children to parent, mothers who were rejected by their mothers tend to reject their own babies. Statistics show us that 1/3 of parents who were abused as children continue the pattern, 1/3 of the parents do not continue and 1/3 remain vulnerable to the affects of stress and are more likely to become abusive under such stress.

What happens is that the traumatic effect is passed on to each successive generation unattached to a verbalized memory experience that could help the next generation make sense of the feelings and place them in proper context. The intent initially is not malicious but protective. How many times have you said or heard people say, "my children will not experience what I experienced as a child." If we do not take responsibility for the emotions attached to the trauma and we do not talk about it, then we act it out.

By the time the traumatic effect has reached the third or even worse the fourth generation the affect is passed on automatically without any cognitive framework that would help the child make sense of what he or she feels. These feelings are passed on through non-verbal intricacies of basic attachment behavior between parents and children. Today, statistics show us that we are repeating history, as 40% of children in care of the provincial system are Aboriginal. These children display behaviors and feelings from many generations who attended residential school in Canada. These children or grandchildren of residential school survivors are continuing the cycle. There is a healing process that individuals who experience traumatic events need to understand for their own and others' healing journey and safety.

Stage 1 - Understand the trauma by remembering and reconstructing the trauma.
Stage 2 - Experience the emotions associated with the trauma in a safe and therapeutic environment. Feel the feelings.
Stage 3 - Empower yourself, finding a meaning in the trauma, develop a survivor rather than a victim mentality.
Stage 4 - Be human, recognize your behaviors and emotional triggers and the ability to truly experience your life with all the natural stresses and joys.

Remember: healing takes time, there is no quick fix and every person who experiences trauma, needs their own path of healing. Healing is a lifelong process. To begin the healing process, individuals need to feel and be safe. There needs to be an established safe environment and a sense of security for individuals.

When is the healing process not advisable?

It is important to understand the healing process needs to be controlled by the individual who experienced the trauma. Healing or talking circles or any process that advocates self-disclosure or "tell me your story" without trained professionals are not advisable as they re-traumatize individuals by a process of forced memory recall. If you were severely or repeatedly traumatized or are coping with a great deal of stress, it is advisable to learn methods of stress reduction before dealing with the trauma.

If you have one or more of the following reactions to dealing with your trauma understand it is normal and you need a trained professional's assistance:

- Hyperventilation, uncontrollable shaking or irregular heartbeat.
- Feeling that you are losing touch with reality, even temporarily for instance, having hallucinations or extreme flashbacks of the event.
- Feeling disconnected, "spaced out", unreal, or if you might be losing control
- Extreme nausea, diarrhea, or other physical problems.
- Self mutilation or the desire to self mutilate.
- Self destructive behavior such as alcohol or drug abuse, self induced vomiting or overspending.
- Suicidal or homicidal thoughts.
- Memory problems.

How do you know the trauma has been healed?

The process of healing from trauma, does not mean you will never again remember the event or never again experience any symptoms. The healing process means you regain or increase your ability to love and care for another, including yourself, and to work and participate in some activities you find meaningful. The more progress in your healing, the more flexible you will become. There are six areas to help you assess if you made progress in your healing from the trauma.

1. You have a clearer, more rational picture of the trauma than when you began the healing process.
2. You spent time grieving, raging, or experiencing other feelings associated with the trauma with professional assistance.
3. You developed skills and attitudes that help you take control of your life, as much as is possible and practical.
4. You started to forgive yourself for the behavior during the traumatic event about which you felt irrational or rational guilt or shame.
5. You mastered effective stress-reduction skills so you can function better in your day to day life.
6. You developed a sense of joy in living and a connection with a spiritual being whether it is God, Buddha, or the Creator.

The First Nation communities need to follow a similar healing process:

1. To build an understanding of how trauma has and continues to impact the people in the communities.
2. To talk about the feelings in a safe environment. Talk it out before people act it out. Talk to your children about the trauma of residential schools.
3. To find a collective meaning and purpose of the trauma. Develop a survivor rather than a victim mentality. Stop the lateral violence with each other.
4. To learn to be a collective community, understand and not react to behaviors and attitudes that originate in residential school trauma.

The leadership of First Nation communities need to foster and support community development:

1. Focus on making safety, first and foremost.
2. Invest in families and prevent intergenerational trauma from being transmitted further.
3. Create trauma debriefing skills for all community members and staff and council.
4. Truly treat children in our communities as our most valuable resource, focus financial and human resources on preventing child abuse.

The residential school system was a systematic government process meant to de-humanize our people by stripping our language, culture and spiritual beliefs. It was the foundation of the colonial government policy of cultural genocide and psychological warfare in order to take our lands and resources.

The residential school has been our holocaust. We endured all types of abuse, shame, ridicule and physical violence from the system and have survived. It is time we truly take our place in the circle of the world, as Protectors of the land, water, winged ones, plants and four leggeds.

AGMV Marquis

MEMBER OF THE SCABRINI GROUP

Quebec, Canada
2001